Acknowledgments

This book is dedicated to all of you who provided inspiration for it, who read it, who gave me comments and suggestions, and who told me it was OK to write a book. You know who you are. It's also dedicated to all of you who want to write a book but haven't done so because of the voices inside and outside your heads saying that you aren't novelists, or poets, or even writers. Ignore those voices, every last one of them, or better yet, give them names and have them sell cars to one another.

One

For months afterward, they joked about Val's death.

It started with wisecracks among Vishnu and his friends, aimed at the parade of geezers. Within two days of Val's passing, the parade was sidling past Vishnu's shop in the early hours of old men, with the casual innocence of raccoons in nylon tavern jackets. They glanced into the driveway where Val's carcass lay, pretending to other business while scheming about the rights to her vital organs. A month after Val kicked the bucket, Pastor Bob told Vishnu that enough was enough. "It's time to dispose of her properly before the fall rains come, or open hostilities break out."

Members of the neighborhood at large were pulled in. Evan the Evangelical Gardener buttonholed Nelda Lindholm, the old lady who lived two doors down from Vishnu, as she watered her sidewalk bed of pansies one morning. "Looking good," said Evan. "By the way, Val died two weeks ago."

"Who?" Nelda peered at him through her bifocals, trying to figure out whether the blurry figure was Vishnu or one of his friends.

"It's a strange world," continued Evan. "Up and down. Val dying, only thirty years old. But then, if it wasn't for Val's death, White Fang would never have met her soul mate. So beautiful it could make you cry."

"Yes, yes," replied the old woman, racking her brain for the identity of either Val or White Fang, wondering how she could have overlooked a death or a romance in the neighborhood, and calculating the market value of this news in the local biddy coalition.

"And now White Fang just sits and pines all day. Her lover drowned himself, you know," Evan said, shaking his head. He looked around as though to catch eavesdroppers, then leaned closer to Nelda. "They say it was Val's death drove him to it," he whispered.

"No!" Nelda covered her mouth in horror and delight.

Evan nodded slowly. "Left White Fang all alone. Unrequited love is all the more desolate when you weigh nine thousand pounds. At least there's no children. None that we know of, anyway."

Two

Vishnu Tensleep, wind in his dark hair and dawn sun reflecting off his shades, grinned like a monkey. He bore down on the pedals and his bike surged forward in response.

Elsewhere, according to the Seattle Times, the world was busy. Lance Armstrong was on his way to victory in the 2000 Tour de France, spawning trenchant debates between medical equipment designers and the International Cycling Union about the athletic benefits of radiation treatment. Aging supply-side economists and tomato sauce barons threw their hats in the air as Russia, with the financial backing of Pizza Hut, launched a manned spacecraft. Brigitte Bardot made a request to Pope John Paul II for a papal denouncement of bullfighting, leaving Catholic rodeo organizers with a crisis of faith.

Elsewhere the world was busy, but Vishnu was letting it all slide. It was a beautiful Thursday morning in Seattle and he had the whole Burke-Gilman trail virtually to himself. Fifty miles to the east, the Cascade Mountains cradled the half-risen midsummer sun. It just doesn't get, thought Vishnu, any better than this.

Sure, he had his trials and tribulations. A case of the doldrums with his girlfriend. Increasingly frequent visits from his late father first thing in the morning, squinting from the mirror with puffy eyes and crows' feet back at Vishnu's thirty-nine-year-old mug. And, now and then, a sense that a few things in life might have slipped past Vishnu Tensleep, bicycle wizard and sole proprietor of Vishnu Tensleep Cycle Works (Est. 1984, Repairs and Good Karma For All Makes and Models, Closed Tue & Wed). In a few hours, Vishnu would take on those trials and tribulations, and maybe include Lance, Pizza Hut, and the Catholic Church, but right now they all felt as distant as the mountains reflected in the still water of Lake Washington. Right now, Vishnu's soul was filled with the pleasure of motorless flight.

"This thing's a little tricky." That's what the guy who'd sold Vishnu the recumbent bicycle told him. Vishnu's business didn't include new bike sales, and he rarely took in used ones to sell, but he couldn't pass this one up. Looking more like a chaise lounge on two tiny wheels, the recumbent put the rider in a reclining position with his feet out in front, low to the ground. "It's hard to get the hang of the steering, leaning back like that, and I feel like my butt is going to drag on the ground. I think it handles funky, but it's a gas to ride, once you get used to it. If nothing else, people stop to let you cross the street because it's so weird looking."

And it was a gas, moving twenty miles an hour, a foot and a half above the pavement. Vishnu wove the bike back and forth quickly to test the handling. Nothing funky about it, he thought. Snappy, perhaps. Spicy. People needed to get off their butts and ride their bikes a little more.

The warm morning air rushing past his face was an exquisite massage. He felt strong, alive, invincible. He shifted up one gear and dug in harder yet on the pedals, relishing the feeling of the blood pumping in his veins and the exertion of his lungs. The Road Warrior rides again. Who said thirty-nine was old? Bring 'em on. Vishnu sent the challenge to all the people who'd ever said that. Me and Mel Gibson will take 'em.

"Left, dude!" The adolescent tenor came from over Vishnu's left shoulder. He barely reacted before a pair of punk kids, maybe eighteen years old, blew past him. One sported a lemon-yellow shoulder bag of the type favored by bike messengers. The other wore tattered jeans accented with a big metal wallet chain and calf-height leather boots.

"Thanks, dude," called Hole In His Pants, and continued a monologue to his friend. "Anyways, I got into this, like, this club, and this, like, chick, was like, Dude, and I was like…" And the two were out of earshot.

A surge of adrenaline, fueled by wounded pride, slammed into Vishnu's nervous system. Punk kids. The gauntlet was thrown. Vishnu shifted into top gear and mashed on the pedals. With great effort he matched the pace of the two riders, but the recumbent was not a racing model, and the best Vishnu could do was to trail about a hundred feet behind.

Vishnu doggedly tailed them in this manner for about three minutes. Tricks of the air allowed Vishnu to hear fragments of their, like, conversation. He couldn't make out what they were saying, but it was painfully apparent to him that, while his lungs were just about to flop out of his mouth like a pair of inverted tube socks, the youngsters were chatting away as though they were sitting on a park bench.

Rounding a turn, Vishnu saw them whip around the left side of two moms wheeling strollers side-by-side. Reckless damn kids, thought Vishnu. To pass the women safely on the pavement, he would have to brake, and he was loath to lose any ground on the Young Turks. Instead, he hollered, "On your right," and cut from the asphalt to the adjacent gravel jogger's path, about fifty feet behind the two women.

Later on, Vishnu would describe the wreck to his friends as an event rich in detail, long in the telling. In fact, of course, it was a quick affair of a few discrete thoughts, emotions, and images. A blackberry patch that had somehow rotated to front and center. An unusual tilt to the horizon. Disappointment that the feet were so very, very far away, and seemingly indifferent to being between the body and the ground. The familiar surprise of how hard it is to alter the orbit of Planet Earth with the impact of a single human butt. Gravel, lots of gravel. Bouncing and sliding. Quiet.

Blunt obscenities rose in Vishnu's mind, matching the siren of pain rising in pitch and intensity, centered in his left buttock, and raising the alarm in the rest of his body. The flavor of tinfoil permeated his mouth. His peripheral vision was gone. He lay motionless on his back, tangled in the bike, head pointed up the trail, looking at the serenely blue morning sky. He tried unsuccessfully to suck in some air, wondering on some reptilian level whether he was going to puke, pass out, or maybe just die. A few seconds later, he managed to draw a ragged breath, and it became obvious that nothing so dramatic was going to happen. He moved his arms and legs experimentally.

"Sir? Are you OK?" A woman's head came into his view, upside-down, peering in alarm at him past the sun visor of his helmet. He tilted his head and saw the wheels of a stroller.

"Uh, yeah, uh, I think so," stammered Vishnu. The woman bent a little closer and inspected him like a mother bird examining one of her fledglings, lying on the ground after its first and unsuccessful trip from the nest. Vishnu forced a chuckle, which made his ears ring, and disentangled his legs from the bike. "Heh heh. I'm OK. I'm perfectly fine. I'll just get up here," he said, smiling crookedly, struggling to his feet, and trying to sound like a normal part of his early morning routine was to slam himself into compacted gravel on a bicycle, a few times if necessary, just to limber up a bit. In point of fact, Vishnu wasn't at all sure he was perfectly fine. His ass was on fire, various scrapes and cuts were announcing themselves, and damage reports were arriving on the bridge from several other decks. But he had just fallen off a weird bicycle in the presence of two attractive women, each of them at least ten years his junior. Thirty-nine wasn't so old that such things didn't matter to him.

The second woman had joined them. Both women looked at Vishnu, unconvinced by his attempted bravado. One of the strollers held an infant, fast asleep. The other contained a girl of about three years old, who stared wide-eyed at Vishnu.

"That a silly bike, Mommy," said the little girl.

"Yeah, it is," agreed Vishnu wholeheartedly.

"Do you want me to call an ambulance, sir?" asked the woman with the infant.

"Oh, no, it's nothing. Heh heh heh." Vishnu forced another chuckle, which enhanced the ringing in his ears. "I'm fine, really." Go away, he pleaded inwardly. Please go away, so I can crawl under a bush like a dog that's been hit by a car. Allow me that dignity.

"If you're sure…" said the woman with the little girl.

"Absolutely. Totally fine. Fit as a fiddle." Vishnu gave them his most confident smile.

"Well, OK," conceded the woman with the infant. The women turned and began to walk away with their strollers. The mother of the little girl looked over her shoulder. "Take care, sir."

"I will," promised Vishnu.

The little girl piped up. "Did he falled off his bike, Mommy?"

"Yes, honey, he did."

"Is he gonna die?"

"No, honey, I don't think so. I think he'll be OK."

Vishnu clambered onto the 'bent, wincing as his butt settled onto the seat, and pedaled slowly in the opposite direction. Safely out of sight of the women, he pulled very carefully off the pavement onto a grassy spot next to a bench. He dismounted, leaned his bike on the bench, and lay down on the grass on his back, arms flopped out at his sides.

Flamed by two punks half his age, one of them wearing jeans and boots. Taking the most painful fall he'd had in years. And on flat, dry, straight ground, all by himself. No, worse. In the presence of two women who were probably in kindergarten when he started college, and who called him 'Sir' and treated him like an old coot who'd fallen with his walker on the sidewalk. Which, given the road conditions, wasn't an unwarranted perspective.

He looked over at the bike, which stood in the grass next to him like an innocently grazing horse who'd just thrown his rider. "I suppose you think this is funny," said Vishnu. The bike did not bother to respond.

Feeling dissipated, dispirited, and disparaged, Vishnu mounted up and began to pedal back home. Hell with it, he grumped to himself. I don't really need the rest of the ride anyway. I've got work to do.

It was still a beautiful summer morning, but to Vishnu it was tinged with the incipient decay of early autumn.

Three

Vishnu arrived home to his abode in the south Ballard neighborhood about seven-thirty. Across the street, the water of the Lake Washington Ship Canal flowed peacefully on its way to Puget Sound. Entering the side door of his shop, he parked the bike by his workbench and went through the door that separated the shop from his apartment. Peeling off his t-shirt and flinging the sweaty garment into his laundry bin, he noticed that the light on his phone message machine was blinking. He shuffled over and hit the PLAY button, flipping off his shoes as he went.

"Hi honey!" said a rapid-fire feminine voice. "I got back really late last night so I thought I might catch you this morning but you've probably gone out for a ride. What a beautiful day, huh? Anyway, I know we haven't seen much of each other in the last week, but I've been invited to teach the massage sessions at the Holistic Smudging Yoga Retreat up on Lopez Island this weekend. I don't have to leave until later this afternoon, so maybe we could have lunch? I'll come by around noon. Oh, I picked up the flyers for the band's performance next Monday, and I'll bring them by today. They look pretty good, although the color of paper you chose is a bit loud, and I still think the band's name is a distraction. 'Aguirre and the Wrath of God' sounds angry, like a band that would play at Odin's Tavern, not the kind of clubs we talked about you trying to book. I really think that if you changed it to something a little nicer it wou-". BEEEEEEEEP.

Vishnu sighed, grateful that he'd resisted the salesman's pitch to buy the model with infinite message time. The voice was that of Heather, Vishnu's off-again / on-again girlfriend of the past year and a half, who had just returned from a week-long gig as the in-house masseuse at a Past-Life Facilitation conference in northern California, and whose massage therapy business had a fervently loyal following among the moneyed Seattle New Age chic. Her recent absence had made his heart grow somewhat fonder, although he had no illusions that this would last in her presence.

Vishnu showered, ate a quick breakfast, and placed himself at the service of the greater Ballard metropolitan area. As he worked, he pondered things. He knew Heather's comment contained a deeper comment about the band itself, and of many parts of Vishnu's life. The way he looked at it, Aguirre was just a not-for-profit bit of musical fun, generated by the P-funk electric bass of Vishnu, the inspired saxophonic wailings of formerly itinerant beat poet and currently employed short-order cook Skippy Sullivan, and the steaming drumwork of fourth-generation Ballard Scandahoovian Hans Erickson. In its more accessible moments, Aguirre sounded just like any other competent garage-based jazz trio. In other moments, saved mostly for practice sessions but occasionally leaking out in public, the spirit of Klaus Kinski descended, and the overall effect was raw gobbets of Jaco Pastorius, Rashad Roland Kirk, and Buddy Rich on a mixture of speed and acid. A person either liked it or didn't, and these occasions could be flat-out disturbing to normal sensibilities, although the misfits in the neighborhood loved them. One of the good things about Vishnu's neighborhood (for him at least) was that it had an abnormally large population of the abnormal, who welcomed unusual sounds emanating in the afterhours from live-in bicycle shops.

Aguirre was scheduled to play a gig the following Monday night at one of the avant-garde art studios that had begun to populate the lower end of Ballard Avenue. This was great with Heather, and it led straight into a schism between her and Vishnu.

Heather's problem, as Vishnu saw it, was that she only appreciated the accessible Aguirre, and wanted to ferret out the madness in favor of a more marketable product. The band is talented, she had opined, so why not do more with it, by which she meant promote it to a wider net of toney venues, and in the course of things rein in the playlist to sounds that were identifiable as music to the greater populace. Of course, this was just the tip of a much bigger iceberg, against which the hull of their relationship was scraping with increasing regularity.

Vishnu mulled these issues between the morning's phone calls and customers until precisely noon, when a familiar blue Toyota pulled up to the curb outside. Out stepped a tall, slender, slightly bony woman, her long dark-blonde hair pulled back into a single braid. Her narrow face was smiling yet earnest, with blue eyes preceded by John Lennon wire-rims.

"Hi honey," Heather chirped, walking into the shop and putting her organic hemp carry-bag on the shop counter. She was clad in her trademark combination of organic cotton blouse and long organic cotton skirt. Vishnu couldn't smell it yet over the WD-40, but he knew there would be a whiff of patchouli when she got closer.

Vishnu smiled and looked up at her from the wheel he was truing. "Hey, sweetie. Just give me a second to get this last flat spot." He tweaked a spoke here and there, held his gaze on the stand's calipers as he spun the wheel, then lifted it out and flexed it gently until the residual stresses resolved with a chorus of pings. He spun it again, sighting down the side of the rim. Good-O, he thought, replacing it in the stand. If only other residual stresses resolved so easily.

He stood up, wiped his hands on a rag, and walked around the counter to her. She gave him a quick peck and hugged him gingerly. "Don't get anything on my blouse, honey." She followed that with a bright smile. "How was your week?"

"Good, really good. Lots of work. I reviewed the books and I made enough last quarter to put in two extra mortgage payments." Vishnu smiled and nodded as he said this, a smile and nod with a coded message: "I dare you to take up the tune of how I should move my business into a swankier area, and while I'm at it leave my home on the canal and move into your little bungalow in location-location-location Wallingford."

Heather, of course, didn't need a secret decoder ring. Her spoken response was a simple, "Wow, that's great," delivered with just enough hesitation and distance to convey, "And I suppose you think I'm going to move into an ersatz apartment in the back of a bike shop down in the butt end of Ballard?"

Vishnu said nothing, and his silence said, "Well, if you'd manage to cut through your shroud of organic fibers, you might be able to see that there's a hell of a lot more to life than bourgeois materialism!"

Heather's silence, hands on its hips, snapped, "Listen, if you'd pull *your* head out of wherever you seem to have it permanently stuck, you might stand a chance of getting over your mulish attachment to this little post-adolescent fantasy you've got going here!"

The two silences stuck their tongues out at one another, and each retreated into its respective subconscious. Having covered all this ground before, and not sure what else to do, the corporeal Vishnu and Heather trudged on with the conversation.

"Here are the flyers," Heather said, pulling a hot pink sheet of paper from a folder in her bag. "What do you think?" Heather's expression clearly asked for an enthusiastic response.

"They look good! I mean, the band's name is spelled right, and you can actually see our faces in the photo, and everything. And this, uh, floral-motif border. That's new, isn't it? What a great idea!"

"You don't like it."

"No, no. It's great, really great, honey. I just wouldn't have thought of intertwined roses."

"I was trying to find something that offsets the name. Just a little."

"Heather, we've been over this. It's the band's name. It fits. I like it. The rest of the guys like it. If people don't dig it, that's too damn bad." Vishnu blew out his breath in exasperation. "Heather, we're just a garage band. It's just for fun! We're doing it because we like it, not because it's supposed to fit into some market niche. What the hell is the problem?"

Heather shook her head, looking to the side. "The problem is…" She groped for words that would convey her feelings. "The problem isn't just the band, Vishnu. It's more than that. It's…all of it." She folded her arms over her chest. "It's your attachment to this place. It's your approach to your work. It's—"

"Just what the hell is wrong with the way I approach my work? Look here, Heather! I'm paying my mortgage off double time, and I'm doing it without getting overextended into selling crap that I need to be in a chi-chi neighborhood to sell. My business is fine right here! You tell me the neighborhood is funky like it's a bad thing, but I hear something different when you're talking it up to your Wallingford friends!" To which Heather could say nothing. Being human, and therefore a bit schizophrenic, there was room in her psyche for looking down her nose at south Ballard while simultaneously digging the bohemian cachet of life on the canal. Vishnu pushed his advantage recklessly. "You think that just because you have your nice little house in Wallingford, with your nice little garden, and your nice little—"

"Basement," Heather finished for him. "With room to store some of the crap you can't fit in your little monastic cell, and a nice little washer and dryer that I notice aren't too chi-chi for you to use every week." It was Vishnu's turn to have nothing to say. Being human, and therefore a bit schizophrenic, there was room in his psyche for thinking Heather's neck of the woods was snooty while simultaneously appreciating the luxury of having actual walls on all of the rooms. And a basement with full laundry facilities that didn't need to be fed quarters was completely without fault.

At this point Heather could have gone for the full-court press. Instead, she smiled sadly, looking around the shop. "I'm tired of this, Vishnu," she said. "Tired, and a little scared. I feel like I'm getting old, and I'm wondering where we're going." She picked up a pencil sitting on the counter and fiddled with it absently. "I'm going to be thirty-nine next month. You're thirty-nine. I'm not interested in moving in here, and you're not interested in moving out, and…" She placed the pencil back on the counter. "And I'm not interested in just going along like this forever. I want more. I want to settle down, and if that's not in your plan, then…"

Vishnu was looking at the counter, feeling the weight of the words, suddenly aware that their relationship, which he had thought was steaming along, might in fact be sinking by the stern.

Heather broke the silence. "Look, I've got to catch the boat to Lopez. I'll be back Sunday morning. We can talk more then."

"What about lunch?" Vishnu looked at her, not wanting to end on this note. "Heather, how about we go get a salad, and take a walk for a couple of hours?"

"No, I better get going before the ferries jam up. And you've got lots of repairs to do, like you said."

Vishnu sighed. "Look. Heather. I'm sorry. We disagree about the band name, and a lot of things. But it's nothing we can't work out. Come on – let's go get lunch."

Heather hesitated a moment, then shook her head with another wistful smile. "I don't think so. And I'm sorry too. I'm sorry I imposed my taste on your posters." She took a turn at sighing. "I'm just going to go, honey. A drive would do me good. Give me some time alone to think. You have a good weekend, and I'll see you Sunday. I'll come over about lunch time on Sunday." She gave him a quick kiss on the cheek, pulled the folder containing the posters out of her bag, laid them on the counter, and walked out the door.

Vishnu was tempted to call her back, but he said nothing. She got into her little car, gave him a little wave, and was gone.

"Shit," muttered Vishnu, looking out the shop door and across the street at the canal. A crow landed just outside the door, looked at him, cawed twice, and flew off. If there was a message there, Vishnu missed it.

Four

Not particularly cheered by Heather's visit, Vishnu decided to close up shop and make a warehouse run. It could wait, but he needed to get out of the shop for awhile and clear his head.

Hanging up his tools and cleaning the bench off, he went into his office to get his parts-order list. As he pulled the clipboard from his desk, it snagged the corner of an old manila envelope, flipping it to the floor. Old photographs fanned out like a historical poker hand. Bending to pick them up, Vishnu's eyes were captured by a dog-eared Polaroid he'd not looked at in years. Five smiling young men in greasy t-shirts, a twenty-year-old Vishnu smack in the center. One of the other lads had his arm around Vishnu's shoulder, holding in his upraised hand a large open-end wrench.

The University of Washington student union bike shop crew, spring of 1981. A love nest of eccentric philosopher gearheads. Vishnu had wandered in answering an ad as a way to make a few extra shekels between classes, and immediately knew he was home. It was a place where the conversation ranged freely from the idiocy of the ruling class, to ribald tales of the past Saturday night, to the potential parallels between Hindu cosmology and the workings of the Sturmey-Archer internal three-speed hub. It was a place of shared secrets and dreams. All that, plus minimum wage and a discount on parts.

In addition to finding a den of kindred spirits, Vishnu had also found in the bike shop his niche in the American socioeconomic machine, a niche that combined a hearty meat-and-potatoes mix of practicality, physical fitness, and good old red-blooded American male gearheadedness. Of course, meat and potatoes are pretty bland without seasoning, and the seasoning provided by any bike shop of that era was a spicy foreign sauce made from a stock of specialized tools, with hints of minimalist elegance, and chock-full of heroes with hard-to-spell names like Merckx. Heroes whose images were plastered on the shop walls, captured in moments of sublime mythic physical agony, sweat streaming down their tortured faces, lungs bursting as they crossed the finish line, flanked by dusky, beautiful European women screaming adulation and the desire to have their babies. In America, thin, wiry, aerobically fit men are routinely ignored in favor of beefcake. In Europe, a bike racer is a god. It's a hard myth to resist if you're a sensitive, thin, wiry, aerobically fit young man from West Seattle with dark curly hair and a tentative goatee. Resistance never even occurred to Vishnu.

Vishnu looked up from the photo, recalling the young men who'd blown him off out on the morning's ride. He also recalled how, as the Vishnu in the photo, he had taken a young man's casual pleasure in doing the same to older men. It was a bittersweet fact that, in exchange for having all of the great moments of the last nineteen years, he was now sometimes compelled to move to the right and let the younger Vishnus pass him by. He could be graceful about it, or not, but the fact was that he was thirty-nine. In pretty good shape for thirty-nine, but twenty no longer. Did this matter so much? Vishnu wanted to say no, but he couldn't quite say it truthfully. He felt a pang for Heather, not a pang of wanting to be with her until the bitter end, but a pang of empathy for her concern that her life, too, was passing her by.

On an impulse, Vishnu rummaged around for a thumbtack and stuck the photo on the wall behind his desk. He then tossed the envelope with the rest of the photos in a drawer, and closed it. Time for Vishnu the Elder to go pick up supplies.

He grabbed the clipboard, went outside, rolled the shop door shut, hopped in his 1970 Plymouth Valiant, and turned the key. The slant-6 fired right up, just like always. He revved the engine, attentive to a rattling sound from the engine compartment he'd not noticed previously.

Another quart of oil, he thought, as he moved his foot to the brake, shifted into reverse, and gave it some gas.

A monumental metallic crunching, a tremendous shudder, a clank like a sledgehammer hitting a cast iron frypan, and the engine stalled. This wasn't good.

Like a man sticking his finger in the paint next to a 'Wet Paint' sign, Vishnu turned the key in the ignition. The starter motor strained, but the engine didn't budge. This really wasn't good.

Vishnu jumped out and stuck his head underneath the car. A piece of metal protruded from a jagged hole in the side of the oil pan. Oil seeped from around the wound. Vishnu wasn't much of a car mechanic, but he knew enough to know this was bad.

He ran to the shop, yanked the door open, grabbed a plastic dishpan, and shoved it under the engine.

"Val," he said. "Speak to me."

Silence.

"Was it something I said?"

Nothing.

"Is this it, then?"

The car creaked a little.

So this is how it happens, Vishnu thought. After 283,000 miles of clean living, you start out on a Thursday afternoon errand and drop dead in the driveway.

Vishnu reached under the car and pulled on the metal shard that was sticking out of the oil pan. It wiggled slightly, still attached, and the flow of oil into the pan increased.

Shit, thought Vishnu. Gotta buy a car.

Five

Vishnu sat on the old wooden bench against the front wall of his shop, sipping a cup of tea and trying unsuccessfully to enjoy the early evening. His mind kept returning to a single thought. Shit. Gotta buy a car.

Val lay in state twenty feet away. He hadn't realized how attached he was to that old Plymouth. Val was his first car, purchased from a friend of his granddad's in 1980. In the intervening 175,000 miles, Val and Vishnu had covered much of what lay between Galveston, Cabo San Lucas, Prince Rupert, and Saskatoon, and Vishnu had learned and grown to love her strengths, foibles, and irritating habits.

Emotional muck aside, Vishnu loved the Valiant as a machine. It was aptly named. The slant-6 engine was an archetype of an engineering and manufacturing ethic, lost since the Nixon administration, which held that the metal products of American heavy industry should last longer than an untreated two-by-four left in the Tacoma tideflats. The slant-6 had about twenty moving parts, all of them about the size and shape of a pint can. Each of these parts was held on by four half-inch bolts that couldn't be broken by an orangutan. There was also about a foot of space surrounding the engine, so that a person (or an orangutan) could stick a wrench, his head, and a flashlight into the engine compartment without getting them all tangled up. And to top it off, each part cost about twenty bucks.

It was the stubborn low-budget reliability of the Valiant that had led to a strange and wonderful part of Vishnu's life. Valiants were so cheap and lasted so long that many of them outlasted the Chrysler

Corporation's interest in manufacturing replacement parts. Even the junkyards had been picked over for the choice oddments.

It had begun innocently enough, about five years previous. He'd been loading his week's groceries into Val in the Ballard Market parking lot and had struck up a conversation with an old guy who'd pulled in next to him driving a '71 Valiant Gold Duster. The topic of parts procurement came around, and within ten minutes Vishnu had traded a trunk lid spring for a right-rear-window crank. They traded phone numbers, and the old man, whose name was Gus Anderson, told a few of his buddies about it at the Sons of Norway that night.

Within a month Vishnu was an underground legend among the lutefisk set. One old guy or another would call him up and invite him over, ostensibly to swap some parts or talk about how to make them from scratch, but often the real motive was the chance to offer Vishnu an unfiltered Lucky Strike (which Vishnu would gracefully refuse) and a schnort or two of homemade elderberry brandy (which Vishnu would gracefully accept), and digress into the enchanted land of automotive memories. Vishnu would tell about getting lost on the two-rut track east of Shiprock, New Mexico, ending up forty miles off course at Chaco Canyon just as the moon rose, sleeping in Val's back seat while a pack of coyotes sang to him and took turns pissing on the tires all night.

The old guy would counter with tales of a '44 Buick and a time when for less than a buck he would get a six-pack of beer, throw some chicken-salad sandwiches into the back seat, drive off down to the beach at Golden Gardens, and have a nice time with the missus without having to deal with hippies, weirdoes, racial minorities (i.e., anybody but other Norwegians), drug dealers, or other manifestations of how the country had gone down the frickin' john since Eisenhower turned over the reins to that punk kid from Massachusetts, and that Texas jerk-off had made such a mess of things that even Nixon couldn't straighten it out. Sometimes on these outings, you could park that old Buick in the bushes near the railroad tracks and get a little nookie without worrying that anyone was going to come along and bother you. Nowadays, the kids did it right on the beach in front of God and everybody.

If the conversation went this direction, Vishnu would nod in concurrence with the sentiment that if you were going to have sex at the beach, the least you could do was have the common decency to stay in your car.

Naturally, some of Vishnu's visits led to invitations to return, and he had struck up a dozen friendships of various intensities, which in return got him a steady stream of telephone calls for dinner, bowling, TV watching, and fishing.

The fishing was a little world in itself. Quite a number of the old men retained dilapidated skiffs, powered by cranky prehistoric outboard motors, which they transported on rattletrap trailers with malfunctioning brake lights. These guys thought nothing of setting out into the frigid waters of Puget Sound in the pre-dawn hours, any time of year, in any weather, equipped with some fishing tackle, some herring for bait, some herring for eating, a thermos of coffee strong enough to float a rock, and a six-pack of Pabst for afternoon, which meant anytime past ten in the morning. Fishing seasons were regarded as inapplicable to people who put their lives on the line in the Big War. The concept of fishing licenses was utterly ignored. Lifejackets were a communist proposal of chickenshits like Nader, who wanted to put soft rubber pads on every sharp corner and suck all the fun out of life. "What kind of tightfart crap is that?" they'd bitch, delighted to find a fresh ear into which they could vent their grievances. "I learned to swim by fallin' out of my grampa's boat, right off Brackett's Landing, and it didn't do me no harm! And the water was colder in them days, lemme tell ya! Deeper, too!"

And it didn't stop there. Since the day Vishnu had met Gus, he'd attended five funerals and had been contacted by three lawyers (themselves of the Eisenhower vintage), who informed Vishnu that he was in their clients' wills. The money didn't amount to much, but it was the rest of the inheritance that added up. Vishnu's little apartment in the back of his shop had begun to look like the inner sanctum in a VFW hall, and even so he'd had to rent a storage locker to keep it all. He couldn't bear to throw any of it out. He felt like the unofficial custodian of archaeological evidence from a vanishing culture. Vishnu had frequently told the survivors that they should take what they wanted from the trove, but few of them took him up on it (although for the past three years on Midsummer's Eve they'd all held a vigil in the storage locker, telling sagas extolling the virtues of their fallen comrades and getting swacked on schnapps, aquavit, and homemade rotgut with the flavor and impact of paint thinner). And of the few treasures that had been claimed by the living, all of them had recycled back to Vishnu through subsequent wills anyway, so there didn't seem to be any way out of it.

Vishnu shifted into a more comfortable position on the bench and took a sip of tea. He didn't have to wonder what Heather was going to say about Val's demise. Heather had never liked the Valiant, which she refused to personify as Val. More accurately, Heather didn't really mind the Valiant, although she didn't appreciate its mildew smell during the Seattle rainy season of October through June, or the way the springs in the front seat poked her in the butt through the ancient plastic upholstery. What rankled Heather was Vishnu's fondness for the old car, a fondness she characterized as an unwholesome enmeshment. Why, she wondered aloud on a regular basis, did he spend an ever-increasing amount of time futzing around to keep a dumb old car running, when he had the money to buy a better one, and could instead devote that time to his work, or to their relationship? Heather related to cars the way she related to bath towels. She liked them well enough, and every now and then she got a new one without moping around because the old one was gone.

And if, in Heather's mind, Vishnu's attachment to the Valiant was a cake, the icing was Vishnu's involvement with "all those narrow-minded Ballard fogies and their silly shenanigans." Most of them had looked askance when she told them she was a massage therapist, and one had actually given her a knowing wink, which brought him closer than he'd known to a swift kick in his milky-white shins. And if all that wasn't enough, there was the perfectly good money thrown down a hole each month for a storage locker crammed to the ceiling with beer steins, cuckoo clocks, ships in bottles, antique skis, rusty tools, license plates to cars that no longer existed, and a thousand other dead men's trinkets that nobody else seemed to want, and Heather claimed you didn't need to be Einstein to figure out why.

Vishnu was drawn from his meditations on cars and women by the staccato sound of a motorcycle slowing as it came around the corner. A '60s-vintage BSA Gold Star pulled into the driveway. The cheerful English accent of the old one-banger engine echoed off the shop wall for a few seconds and expired in a cough of blue smoke. A hulking figure dismounted, removed a black skullcap helmet from shoulder-length Oslo-blond hair, and flipped up his mirror shades to reveal piercing blue eyes. Even in a neighborhood chock-full of people who could play B-grade movie Vikings, Hans Erickson stood out. Indeed, the band's name was spawned by Skippy, who dubbed Hans 'Aguirre' because of his resemblance to a cult-film conquistador after a particularly berserk assault on the drums.

Hans glanced at Val, noting the oil-filled pan and the hood left ajar, then grinned at Vishnu. "Vishnu baby! What's in the cup?"

"Tea. But I think it's time for a cold one."

"Now you're talking," agreed Hans, settling down on the bench.

Vishnu disappeared into the shop and emerged a few moments later with a pair of freshly-popped Schmidts. He handed one to Hans, and held his up for a toast.

Hans thunked his can into Vishnu's. "Stomachs and skulls."

"Beaks and feet," responded Vishnu. They both took a pull.

"So." Hans crossed his legs and took another swig. "Que pasa?"

"It's not been the smoothest day. I started it by crashing my bike and bruising my ass pretty good. Then I had my impending middle age rubbed in my face, had a fight with Heather, and Val's engine blew." Vishnu leaned his head against the bricks and stared at the sky, holding the cold can on his forehead.

Hans nodded gravely. His passion leaned towards bikes of the motored variety, and for work he drove an unassuming old Ford Econoline van. Still, he loved his motorcycles (all three of them), and knew how Vishnu felt about his old Plymouth. He gestured towards Val. "I noticed she looked a bit under the weather. You gonna have Evan drop another engine in her?"

Vishnu gave a wry smile. "It's tempting, just to keep the dynasty going. But nah. I think it's time to put her out to pasture."

Hans nodded again. "Any idea what you're looking for?"

Vishnu shrugged. "Basic transportation. I've got to get something quick. I've got a business to run." He sagged further down against the wall.

"So what's this about your butt?" Hans asked, trying to keep the conversation moving.

Vishnu related the tale of his morning's ride. "And I'm not sure what hurt worse." He managed a smile. "Landing on my butt, being blown off by a couple of kids half my age, getting the A.A.R.P. treatment from those women, or having that little girl ask if I was going to die." He sipped his beer and chuckled. "It's really not that bad I guess. I was just having a youthful fantasy this morning, and the world kicked my ass. Literally." He looked at Hans. "We're not young anymore."

Hans rolled his eyes. "Speak for yourself, man. I'm only thirty-six. You're thirty-nine." Vishnu sighed, and Hans kicked him gently in the butt. "Give it a rest, man! You're not old, so don't act pathetic. Next thing I know you'll be answering e-mail ads for dick-enlarging pills! If you were whining about middle age to Heather, I hope she really kicked your ass. She's probably more worried than you are. Is this what you were fighting about?"

"Kind of. Not really. Actually, yes. I don't know. Wait a minute." Vishnu walked into the shop and came back out with the folder of flyers Heather had left.

Hans held one out at arm's length and inspected it. "What's this stuff around the edges? Flowers?"

"Roses. You know, like the Grateful Dead. Retro. But modern. Like a blend." Vishnu fell silent.

"That's a nice touch," said Hans. "But hey, you can read the name and address. Hell, man, it's just a flyer. If Heather's nice enough to take care of the printing, I don't give a shit if she puts teddy bears on them. I can't believe you got into it with her over a floral border."

Vishnu put the flyer back in the folder. "That was just the fuse." He looked out at a tug passing on the canal. "The bomb is really everything else. The way I run my business, the fact that I'm buying this building and she wants me to move in with her. She wants to tidy up the band, and-"

"Hold it right there!" Hans held up his palm. "That's where I draw the line! You can move in with her, tart up your business, and wear flannel Ward Cleaver pajamas if you want, but the band shall remain untidy as long as *I'm* the drummer!" He held his grim demeanor for a few moments more, then collapsed into laughter. "You guys really crack me up, no shit!" He slurped some more beer down. "Especially," he said, "since I notice with a sense of irony that *you* aren't copping to any desire to grunge Heather up a bit. Eh? Maybe a leather miniskirt and one of those matching lace-up bra jobs? Hmmm? How about it? Heather in leather? And a pile of red meat on the side? Now we're talking! The two of you sharing a big greasy plate of steak fajitas in some grubby Tex-Mex joint, Z.Z. Top blaring Pan Am Highway Blues in the background. Never crossed your mind to try and change *her* image, I'll bet?"

Vishnu gave no answer.

Hans studied his friend. "Has it ever occurred to you, old buddy, that maybe you and Heather are on different paths? Right now it sounds like each of you is trying to see who can be the bigger asshole, in order to make the other one flinch." Hans leaned against the wall. "It's not pretty."

"I know," agreed Vishnu. "That's how it was today. And it wasn't pretty."

"You know, ever since I've known you, you've lived near this canal. Remember your senior year of college, when you lived just up the hill? The day you graduated, we sat on the porch and drank beer all night, and planned our lives. You remember that?"

Vishnu nodded.

"You said this was it. That you'd come from the far-flung land of West Seattle and found Paradise, that you'd never move from the neighborhood. You told me that you didn't know how it was going to work out, or what you were going to do, but that your dream was to have a place on Canal Street. You remember that?"

Vishnu nodded again, smiling at the memory.

"You remember what I said my dream was?"

"Not really."

"I do. I said my dream was to get as far away from Ballard as possible. Travel to Singapore on a tramp steamer, ride a motorcycle from Vladivostok to Lisbon, and wind up in a little beach hut off the coast of Brazil with some coffee-skinned babe who was going to support me with her trust fund while I read Goethe and played the congas." Hans paused. "Which one of us lived out his dream?"

"You're playing the drums, anyway, and riding motorcycles."

"And living ten blocks from my mom's house, and hanging fucking drywall for a living." Hans slapped the brick wall. "Look around, man. This is yours! Your business. Your home. You did it! Do you have any idea how much I admire that?" He waved his hand in a sweeping gesture. "And when you look at all this, this shop, the canal, this neighborhood, you see the Left Bank of Paris. Accordion music wafting through the doorways on romantic moonlit nights. Men in berets toting mesh bags of veggies and baguettes home on old bicycles that you've fixed. And because you see it that way, it *is* all that." Hans dropped his hand. "But Heather's not into it. She never has been. Heather looks at the same scene you see, and she sees a bunch of crummy rundown boatyards, a cement plant, a passel of weirdoes pushing shopping carts around in the streets, and an industrial waterway that gets blasted with a sewage overflow every time it rains too hard." He shrugged. "And neither of you is wrong, man. It's just a matter of perspective. You guys see things differently, that's all. You don't have to see everything the same way, but if you can't work it out and both be happy, then…"

Vishnu drained his can, crumpled it, then leaned forward and lobbed it towards a trash barrel next to the door. The can bounced off the doorjamb and clattered back into the parking lot.

"Well, I can see I'm helping you clarify the easy part," said Hans. He finished his own beer, wadded up the can, and sank it cleanly into the trash barrel. "If your attitude was better, you've have made your shot, too. Now, how about we go back to the hard issue. What kind of a ride are you going to get?"

"I dunno."

"Oh, for Christ's sake!" Hans stood up abruptly, closed his eyes, and put his fingers to his temples. "Wait!" he commanded. "Wait! It's becoming clearer! Yes! I can see it now! Vishnu Tensleep, you are at a crossroads! This is a defining moment! The vehicle you select will have great meaning!" Hans opened his eyes a bit and peered at Vishnu, fingers still at his temples. "How much can you spend, my son?"

"Probably about five grand. Maybe I should just get another Valiant. It certainly wouldn't cost me that much, and if I get one that's close to the same year, I can strip Val for parts. I really don't care what I drive."

Hans shook his head vigorously as if to get water out of his ears, palms held up in front of him. "No, no, no, NO! That's the old, responsible, Oh-my-God-I'm-getting-old-and-my-penis-is-shrinking Vishnu! That won't do! You need something different!"

"Like what?"

Hans thought for a moment. "How about a Japanese pickup? You can get a nice one for five thousand. With a canopy, so you can haul merchandise in winter, maybe do a little car camping. And a nice sound system. And four-wheel drive."

"Four-wheel drive? I don't need four-wheel drive."

Hans rolled his eyes in exasperation. “Jeez, man. Get a clue! You live in Seattle! Great-grandmothers have four-wheel drive. Babies are issued four-wheel drive strollers at the hospital. Not having it is like asking what espresso is. Trust me. I know what I’m talking about. I do car consultations all the time for the finer lowlife of Ballard.”

Vishnu was smiling in spite of himself. “OK. You’re right. I’ll look for something with a bit more zip. It wouldn’t be hard,” he added. “Val had a lot of things, but zip wasn’t among them.”

“Now you’re talking! And forget what I said about Heather. My marriage-counseling license was revoked last month. I keep forgetting.”

“No problem. You might be right. We’re both taking the weekend to try to clear our heads a bit.”

“Good idea.” Hans went to his bike and extracted a staple gun from a leather saddlebag. He took one of the flyers over to a nearby telephone pole and tacked it up. “Aguirre and the Wrath of God,” he said, shaking his head slowly. “And they look like such nice boys. Who would have guessed?”

A ‘69 Mustang rumbled down Canal Street. Hans watched it go by with an appreciative look. “Now there’s a car for you. Sweet! A real babe magnet!”

“Exactly what I need, a babe magnet,” Vishnu said, but he also gazed after the Mustang. The sound and look of it reminded him of summer evenings long ago, and something else that eluded him.

“Well, you think about it,” said Hans, dropping the staple gun and the rest of the flyers into his saddlebag. “I’m off to plaster the phone poles of the city with our freshly-scrubbed faces. Band practice tomorrow night?”

“If tomorrow’s Friday, it’s practice night. A little fine-tuning, and we’ll blow ‘em away come Monday.”

“Right on.” Hans kicked his old bike to life, producing a satisfying growl. He flipped his shades back down, fastened his helmet, and revved the engine. “Ich bin Aguirre!” he snarled, twisting the throttle again for emphasis, then popped the clutch and swerved the old BSA deftly out of the driveway and up the street. Above the engine's roar, a maniacal cry bounced off the building walls: *"Ich bin der Zorn Gottes!"*

Vishnu went back inside, came out with another beer, and settled back onto the bench to contemplate the fading sunset, his mood beginning to deteriorate with Hans' departure. Shit. Gotta buy a car. He had an image of car dealers, especially used car dealers, as slick-talking sleazeballs. On the other hand, the only option Vishnu could see was buying a car through the want ads, and the image that came to mind was spending days and days looking at cars that the owners were dying to get rid of because the tranny was about to drop out, so that they could skip the state within fifteen minutes of taking his money. At least with a dealer, Vishnu thought, I can call the Better Business Bureau.

He briefly considered commissioning Hans or Skippy to do the dirty work. Just give them $5,000 and tell one of them to spend it as he saw fit, with a 10% fee upon delivery. He imagined himself hunkered over the handlebars of an old Triumph, slithering home from a warehouse run through a February sleetstorm, merchandise piled like a haystack in a sidecar. Or if Skippy had his way, it would be the rolling thunder of a '59 Caddy Coupe DeVille with fins to rival Namu the Killer Whale. He concluded that it was a task best done for oneself. No sense in ruining friendships or dragging innocent people into the fray.

Vishnu walked back inside and readied himself for bed. As he walked by his office, the old bike shop photo he'd tacked up on the wall earlier in the day caught his gaze, and another memory came home. Colleen McCarthy, who he'd had a crush on all through eleventh grade, who asked him to call her on the last day of school, who spent a number of idyllic days with him that summer, who went with him to the senior prom that fall, and who then immediately dumped him for Brad Davis. Brad Davis, two-hundred-and-twenty-five pounds of buffalo-meat offensive lineman, with a personality like a pile of compost and a brain to match. And a '68 Mustang hardtop, much like the one that rolled past only minutes before. Vishnu's eyes were on the photo, but in his mind he was standing in the high school parking lot with his beloved Cinelli, the first really good bicycle he'd owned, watching Colleen laughing as she got into Brad's Mustang, watching Brad wink at him as he shut Colleen's door and silently mouth the word 'Loser.'

Vishnu scratched the back of his head, and looked around his place. Loser? He didn't usually feel like a loser, but the sting of the memory was remarkably fresh. Was Heather right? Was he living in the past, refusing to grow up?

Six

Vishnu pedaled after Heather through a section of Gasworks Park he wasn't sure he'd been to before. It was hard for him to stay with her, because the paths crisscrossed and interlaced. Now he was right beside her; now behind her; now by a subtle shift of landscape he was beside her but on a parallel path, separated by a low brick wall; now he was behind her again.

"Come on!" she called over her shoulder. "There's too much to be late for, and it's not here!"

And he strained to catch her, but there was something wrong with his tires, or maybe the pedals, and then she was off on a different path and he wasn't sure how to get onto it from where he was.

Heather pulled onto a broad grassy lawn at the foot of the hill, crowded with some kind of festival. Vishnu thought he saw where she had left her bike, but when he got there he found no trace of her. Instead, a group of jesters and clowns appeared behind him, dressed in motley and singing a song he knew by heart, although he couldn't say where he'd learned it. They absorbed him into their game, and he was swept along with them, dancing and singing, but still trying to find Heather, wanting her to join him in the revelry.

Finally, Vishnu spotted her standing alone on a red blanket, arms akimbo. He waved to her and called her to join him, but she just looked away unsmiling. At her feet was a small wicker basket; Vishnu remembered it contained a picnic they were supposed to share.

The clowns obscured his view for a moment, and when Vishnu looked again Heather was gone. He felt sad and wanted to go find her, but at the same time he didn't want to leave the dance.

A dark-eyed woman clasped Vishnu's hand. "Don't look down!" she called to him, and laughed as she spun him in a circle. Around they went, faster and faster, as the clowns sang their song.

Vishnu's eyes popped open and he stared through the dim light for a minute at the crack in the wall beside his bed, heart beating hard. He untangled the sheet from his legs, and lay on his back, sweat cooling on his exposed torso. "Jesus," he muttered.

He rose from his bed, shuffled into his tiny meditation alcove, and sat in front of a large print of a seventh-century stone Buddha, trying for twenty minutes to quiet his mind without much success. What a weird dream. The symbolism was pretty obvious, at least the part about the paths, but the last part was puzzling. He'd really been having fun, dancing and singing. He could still remember snatches of the melody, and tried unsuccessfully to remember where he'd heard it. And, he admitted to himself with a twinge of guilt, the woman with the dark eyes was more haunting than the song. Had he met her somewhere?

Vishnu ate breakfast and puttered in his shop for the next hour, mulling the day's task of buying a car, trying to arrive at the proper strategy. The first issue was appearance. He knew that many adult Americans look suspiciously at other adults who ride bicycles during business hours on weekdays. He decided it would be better to take the bus.

The second issue was timing. In sales, timing was everything, Vishnu told himself out of no particular experience. He decided that 9:45 a.m. was an arrival time that would convey an all-business attitude, that Vishnu was not to be trifled with.

The third issue was the opening gambit. Vishnu settled on what he though a clever ruse: he would state that he wanted to buy a 1970 Valiant. This was sure to take any salesman off his guard, and thus give Vishnu some relative advantage in the ensuing transaction. The chance that anyone would actually have a 1970 Valiant on hand was so small as to defy calculation. On the exceedingly slim chance that the salesman had such a car on hand, Vishnu would have the option of buying it or rejecting it as not up to his high standards and thus putting the salesman in his place.

It was a complicated, manipulative plan, a notable departure from Vishnu's usual straightforward approach to things, and borne out of attachment to Val, excitement over getting a new set of wheels, and anxiety about dealing with people who Vishnu cast as modern-day pirates.

The part of Vishnu that resided in his meditation hall knew it was a strategy doomed to failure, and counseled the rest of Vishnu against it. "Old buddy," said the voice, "it is precisely this anxiety, attachment, and excitement that is making you confused and guilty. Confused, guilty people tend to do wiggy things, and such people with money in their pockets are the bread and butter of places like used car lots and funeral homes. All you're trying to do is get some basic transportation for a reasonable price. Take a deep breath and just be yourself."

The meditative part of Vishnu gave the rest of Vishnu this advice, but the rest of Vishnu was already anxious, attached, excited, confused, guilty, a little wiggy, and wearing pants with money in the pockets. So it was that at quarter after nine Vishnu was riding a northbound bus to the used-car-sales-wasteland of Aurora Avenue North. He rehearsed his opening lines, fingered his checkbook, gazed with lust at a T-top Corvette roaring past, and felt all the while like a man whose wife is lying face-down in the driveway while he's off looking for a twenty dollar hooker. At least he was heading for the right neighborhood.

Seven

Vishnu stepped off the bus at the first used car lot he reached. The bus groaned away in a trail of diesel fumes. Tony's Tigers, proclaimed in black italic script, framed on either side with double checkered flags, and ringed with electric lights twinkling feebly in the Friday morning sun. Taking a deep breath, Vishnu strode purposefully past a large pile of petrified dog turds and onto the lot.

The salesman was peering out the window of the single-wide trailer that served as the office, waiting for Vishnu like a cheerful Moray eel. He stepped out onto the porch, togged out in an off-white linen jacket, peach-colored button-down shirt, tan chinos, and Italian loafers with little tassels. He smiled at Vishnu, then looked up beatifically at the blue sky.

Avoiding eye contact and whistling an aimless tune, Vishnu strolled in a roundabout path to the area containing the older cars that lack street appeal, heading towards a row of small pickups and anonymous sedans along the back fence. The salesman moved toward Vishnu with a slight gimp. "Hayadoin! I'm Tony. Lookin' for anything in particular?" He thrust out a tanned and manicured hand, ornamented with a diamond pinky ring.

"I'm Vishnu," said Vishnu. "Actually, yes. I'm looking for a 1970 Plymouth Valiant, four-door, slant-6, low miles if possible, dark green." He gave a tight smile, trying to imitate Clint Eastwood.

Tony brayed a short laugh. "Yeah, Vince, what a car! My old man had one of them. A four-door with a six. My brother Vito drove it into the East River, but that's another story. Hey! You look like a Mazda RX-

7 man to me. How 'bout that red one? Low miles, one owner. Priced to sell!"

"Actually, the name's Vishnu," said Vishnu, wondering if he had actually ogled the RX-7. "I really am looking for a '70 Valiant with a slant-6. I can negotiate on color."

Tony nodded, looking as though Vishnu was making perfect sense. "Yeah, the color might be tricky," he said. He ran a thick finger along his chin, still nodding.

"The color isn't really that important," continued Vishnu, shifting from one foot to the other. "Actually, it doesn't even need to be a '70. Anything in the early '70s Valiant line with a slant-6 would be good. That's what I really want."

"Plymouth made plenty of good cars in the early '70s, they sure did." Tony smiled at Vishnu, then gazed past his head at an indeterminate point in the sky, as though shipments of old Plymouths arrived by helicopter from that direction at ten every Friday morning. "You couldn't beat a slant-6."

Vishnu started again. "Look, here's the deal. I've got an old Valiant I've had forever, but the engine blew, and all I really want is something to replace it. I don't even want to get another car. I mean, I love my old car. It's just that mine won't run anymore, and…"

Tony allowed himself the faintest of smiles. The Patron Saint of Fools and Numbnuts was on holiday once again, leaving Tony in charge. A distorted buzz came from a loudspeaker on the side of the trailer. "Hold on," said Tony, patting Vishnu on the shoulder. "Gotta get the phone. Don't move." He trotted away from Vishnu; the gimp was gone from his stride.

Tony had a brief conversation and emerged from the office, looking like a little boy who has just found a big bag of candy on the sidewalk. This was one of the ten or twelve demeanors he practiced in front of the mirror each day before taking a dump and going out onto the lot. "Vince!" he yelled. "You ain't gonna believe your luck! 1970 you said! Ain't many people who got the taste for real Mopar class. That call was from my brother Vito, who has just had the outrageous fortune of acquiring a very, very unusual piece of vintage Detroit steel."

Vishnu's spirits lifted. "Is it a Valiant? Even a Dart would do."

"You just wait, my friend," Tony said, in a tone indicating Christmas was coming early.

And even as Tony was speaking, there was a change in the sonic background. Mixed into the usual grind and rush, there was a growing bottom-end sound like a big Kenworth log truck winding out, and a top-end whine akin to an industrial sandblaster. These tones converged into a single roaring snarl. The snarl burst around the corner, accompanied by a candy-apple-red machine, dappled in places with primer gray. It slewed across the gravel, leaving a wake of testosterone like rank phosphorescence, and hooked to a stop in front of Vishnu and Tony.

Vishnu stared. A Plymouth 'Cuda. One of the topmost spires erected on the American Church of Automotive Penile Excess. The throbbing of the motor massaged the soles of Vishnu's feet and tickled his stomach. To Vishnu, the sound was the automotive equivalent of the Stones at Altamont. It was Mick Jagger belting out Gimme Shelter after a twenty-five-year restricted diet of the Bee Gees and Neil Sedaka.

Vishnu's mind swooped back to the past. The year was 1975, and he was fourteen, a tough age for most boys. He was sitting in the back seat of a '70 Plymouth 'Cuda, elbows resting on the tops of the front seats, hanging forward over the gearshift and hanging on every word passed between his eighteen-year-old cousin Bobby and Bobby's friend Lance, a grown man of twenty.

It was a balmy Friday summer evening in West Seattle, and the 'Cuda was rumbling along at a stately seven miles per hour, a cipher in the procession known as the Alki Drive Cruise. "The way you squeeze mah lemon..." Robert Plant moaned from the big speakers behind Vishnu's head. Vishnu was sucking down a chocolate malt. Bobby and Lance held brown bottles of Rainier clamped between their upper thighs. The condensation from the chilled glass left wet marks on the crotches of their cutoff Levi's.

Teenagers promenaded along the sidewalks, dashed in and out of the lines of traffic, hung from the windows of cars. The sound was a mix of voices, finely-tuned exhaust systems, the occasional tooting horn, and a panoply of rock-and-roll blaring from hundreds of slowly moving cars. The open windows of the 'Cuda admitted an intoxicating infusion of salt air, car engines, girls' perfume, and the smoke from tobacco and other inflammable herbs.

"There's Cheryl," said Lance. "Hey, Cheryl!" he yelled. "Check it out!" Lance slipped the 'Cuda into neutral and revved the engine. The custom headers gave off a sound like a small jet flying low.

Cheryl, a foxy brunette just out of Sealth High, let go of the steering wheel of a Pontiac GTO approaching in the opposite direction. She leaned halfway out of the driver's window. "Lance, baby! Romeo!" Her girlfriends squealed, and one of them took the steering wheel as she held both arms out to Lance like Juliet, her ample balcony barely constrained in a baby-blue tube top. She caught sight of Vishnu gawking at her through the open rear window, and blew him a kiss. "Come on with me, schoolboy!" She winked at Vishnu and cupped the straining fabric with her hands. "I'll teach you something they don't tell you about in Health Class!" And then she pulled herself back through the window, and with a gale of teenage girls' laughter was gone from Vishnu's life forever.

Vishnu's mind swam back to the present moment. Undoubtedly, the car on the gravel in front of him wasn't Lance's old car, but Vishnu could taste the chocolate malt in his mouth, and see Cheryl beckoning to him, her cherry-red lips and the cleft of her ripe bosom promising Paradise to a fourteen-year-old boy.

The car's engine shut down, and a carbon copy of Tony, slightly older and clad in mechanic's overalls, hopped out. "Hiya Vince. Name's Vito. Gladta meetcha!"

Tony clapped Vishnu on the shoulder. "Vince, buddy, you said you wanted a piece of Detroit steel? Well, check your johnson, cause this baby'll knock it in the dirt!"

"The name's Vishnu," said Vishnu absently, already moving around the car. This one was even more extreme than Lance's, a real shark mouth, complete with an air scoop sticking up out of a hole in the hood, chrome headers running along under the doors, and ridiculously large rear tires. It was a car straight out of a Big Daddy Roth cartoon, the back jacked up so far that Vishnu could practically see the driveshaft when he stood behind it. "What year is it?" he asked.

"1970," replied Tony. "The top. They didn't get any badder than this."

Vishnu tried to look skeptical. "I don't suppose it's a slant-6?"

"Slant-6?" Tony barked a laugh. "Shit no! This is a V-8, my friend. It originally came with a 340, but the motor underneath this hood is a 440 with a six-pack!"

"A six-pack, huh?" asked Vishnu, trying to sound like he thought that sure was something.

In fact, both Tony and Vito knew instinctively, before the conversation even started, that Vishnu wouldn't know a six-pack from a Big Gulp. From their perspective, the point of the conversation was not to tutor Vishnu in finer mechanical points, but rather to make him feel that Vito and Tony were his pals, his confidantes. A bit of motorhead chat, structured so Vishnu would think they thought Vishnu knew a lot about cars, and thus was a real he-man. Early in life, Tony and Vito had learned how to hunt in tandem like a pair of wolfhounds.

Vito, playing the role of mechanical specialist, came to Vishnu's assistance. "A six-pack, Vince! You remember, the triple two-barrel carb system that came on the better 440s. Oh, man, they were a bitch, weren't they?" He smiled and nodded at Vishnu.

Vishnu nodded back. "Oh, yeah, the six-barrel carb."

Tony the automotive genealogist patted the hood. "Now Vito tells me, after his careful examination, that while this is a '70, the 440 in this particular vehicle is a 1971 model. Ain't that right, Vito?"

Vito nodded at Vishnu, who nodded back.

"Consequently," continued Tony, "as you would expect, that lowers the value of the car as a collector's item, 'cause it ain't a purebred."

Tony looked at Vito, who looked at Vishnu and nodded. Vishnu nodded back.

"But," said Tony, tapping the hood twice with a blunt forefinger and fixing a knowing gaze on Vishnu, "it's got all the beef." He paused to allow Vishnu a chance to comment.

"I'm sure it's got beef, if it's got a six-pack," offered Vishnu. He looked at Vito, who nodded and smiled. Vishnu nodded back.

"Three-hundred-and-ninety brake-horsepower at forty-six-hundred revolutions per minute, my friend." Tony rolled the syllables slowly and deliciously off his tongue. "Now, when I look at you, I see a man who is not distracted by shiny packaging. I see a man who appreciates substance. And that's what this baby offers. Substance. Right, Vito?"

"Sonofabitch'll lay rubber in every gear!" proclaimed Vito, looking at Vishnu. Vishnu nodded back without prompting. Vito beamed him a smile. Guy trains like a fuckin' poodle, he thought. Wish I had me a tennis ball.

Vishnu looked closer at the 'Cuda. It wasn't an auto-show car, carried by trailer and lovingly displayed with the hood up. This car had rust spots, dents, and a crack in the windshield. It had clearly been used hard, on the streets, for a lot of Friday and Saturday nights. This car was big-hair heavy metal bands, hearing damage, too much eye makeup, junior-high-school drinking, personal relationships with the local fuzz, and teenage virginity lost in a K-Mart parking lot. It exuded an ambience of illegal and immoral activities, of neighborhood sleep disturbed in the wee hours, of reckless driving under the influence.

Vito broke Vishnu's trance by thrusting a grimy key into his hand. "Why dontcha take it for a spin?"

"Don't you want some, uh, ID or something?"

"Nah! We trust you," answered Tony and Vito in unison.

Vishnu opened the door, slid into the greasy black leather bucket seat, and creaked the door shut. He looked in vain for a seat belt. He stuck the key in the ignition and turned it. A deafening rumble and the smell of exhaust filled the cockpit. He rolled down the window and looked up at Tony and Vito, whose smiling visages were vibrating. He depressed the clutch, grabbed the big steel gearshift (pistol-grip Hurst four-on-the-floor), and shoved it into first gear. With a jaunty wave to Tony and Vito, he gave it some gas and careened out of the parking lot, narrowly missing Tony's feet.

The brothers grinned at each other. "What a fugazi!" cackled Tony. "He couldn't even pronounce his own fuckin' name. Kept saying Vishoo or somethin'. And didya see his eyes buggin' out? I'll lay you a fifth of Johnny Red he buys it. Did Jimmy work up some legit-lookin' papers?"

"They look good enough. Don't fuckin' matter. The little putz who usta drive it won't be callin' the cops. I figured we'd be into the deal for a paint job and shippin', but now Vince is gonna save us the trouble."

"Sucks to be Vince," said Tony, pulling a half-smoked cigar from inside his jacket. "This ride ain't exactly nondescrip'."

Eight

Vishnu drove south on Aurora, winding it out in third gear up the hill past the zoo. On one shoulder sat a cartoon angel, advocating reason and prudence. On the other shoulder sat a cartoon devil, doing what comes naturally.

Angel: How could you, as a manifest cycling fanatic, own a car like this?

Devil: Oh baby, this car is so hot!

A: The 440 V-8 probably has a shorter life span than a slant-6. And you know this engine was driven too hard, and without proper maintenance.

D: Oh *baby*, this car is so *hot!*

A: This car must burn huge amounts of gas.

D: Don't worry, Vishnu. Just think of it as spending the inheritance of the children you don't have.

A: It doesn't have the storage space of the Valiant. It's not adequate for transporting merchandise to the shop.

D: Rent a truck. Buy a trailer. Drag it home on a tarp. Who gives a shit? Oh baby baby baby.

A: Besides, what would your clients say if this car was parked in front of the shop?

D: Fuck 'em if they can't take a joke.

A: Heather won't like it.

D: Fuck *her* if she can't take a joke.

And so on, followed by a period of the angel trying to make a deal with the devil, who as ever was happy to oblige.

A: Assuming he got a reasonable deal on it, I suppose he could always sell it if it wasn't working out.

D: Of course he could.

A: He really doesn't drive all that much, so overall he wouldn't burn that much more gas.

D: Of course he wouldn't.

A: There's always a market in Ballard for cars like this.

D: Of course there is.

A: The trunk is only a little less spacious than the Valiant. Coupled with the back seat, it might be big enough.

D: Of course it is.

A: He doesn't normally transport things larger than the door opening or the trunk anyway.

D: Of course he doesn't.

And so on.

Vishnu had a subconscious understanding of why modern action films capture the public's fancy, in spite of incontrovertible evidence that tough guys with shaved heads do not routinely entertain the public with high-speed chases ending in bloody shoot-outs and exploding cars. The reason for the attraction to such movies is simple: most people subconsciously hold out hope that there is an alternative universe that contains something more pungent and edgy than a turkey sub sandwich and a diet root beer for lunch, followed by getting a memo from that dickweed in purchasing. Even if these people do not actually intend to participate in that alternative universe, the possibility, however far-fetched, is impossible to put aside. Like discussions about sending people to live on Mars. Nobody actually intends to go live on Mars personally, but sending people in a rocket to live on Mars is an interesting concept. And, like being a collateral victim of a bloody shoot-out perpetrated by shaved-head goons, it's an entertaining fantasy to impose on that dickweed in purchasing.

Vishnu's visceral attraction for the 'Cuda fell into this realm. The rational mind poses the question: Why have a car with a huge engine capable of reaching speeds well in excess of a hundred mph when you can't legally drive faster than seventy? Like many important questions in life, there are multiple correct answers. The rational mind's answer is obvious: No reason. What a silly thing to do. But another answer, orthogonal to left-brain logic, is: If you have to ask, you obviously wouldn't understand the answer. You don't even understand the question. Vishnu's rational mind prattled on with all of the reasons that it made less than zero sense to buy the 'Cuda, while his emotional mind bathed luxuriously in soft-core fantasies of cruising Market Street on a warm summer Friday night in a vehicle that said, "I'm the guy your mother warned you about."

Without having any real intent to do so, Vishnu wound up in the driveway of his shop, next to Val. He turned off the engine and just sat there, his hands cupping the fake leather wrap on the steering wheel. He noticed for the first time that there was a gaping hole where a radio had been forcibly extracted, leaving electrical entrails dangling. I could fix that, he thought. Who needs a radio?

He got out and circled the car slowly. Buying such a car would be a departure from his current lifestyle and, perhaps, his ethics. But what were his ethics, anyway, at least as applied to this car? Vishnu thought about it. At the point of a knife, he might be able to blather a few sentences about the global benefits of saving the world, and how his religion of bicycling fit into that. So far, so good. Maybe a paragraph about not accepting the bullshit TV culture of modern America, developed and perpetrated by and for the corporate fat cats. Fair enough. He might even follow that with a short spiel about trying to forge a brave new society in which people's artistic spirits were allowed to be integrated with their basic physical lives and livelihoods to achieve a higher unity, with a pitch about how combining his music studio with his shop did that for him, while also reducing his global footprint, thus looping back to Ethic Number One. Voila!

Vishnu imagined the ethical mugger weighing this offering, while continuing to hold him at knifepoint. He wasn't sure that he would be spared. He gazed at the bright red of the 'Cuda's door, reflected in the custom header that lay underneath like a chrome python. Maybe driving this car wasn't that much less ethical or artistic or globally sensitive than burning a quart of oil every two weeks in the Valiant. What the fuck, he thought. What do I have to lose, beside a gimcrack social persona and the conditional support of a bunch of uptight, clove-cigarette-smoking vegetarians? And with that thought he got up, pulled a scrap of cardboard from his recycle bin, and wrote in large block letters GONE FISHIN. He wedged the cardboard into the door frame of his shop, leaped into the 'Cuda and headed back up to Tony's Tigers. It was a brave new world, and it wasn't even noon yet.

Nine

As Vishnu pulled into the lot, Tony was cheerfully haggling about an old Triumph Spitfire with a short, balding man in a tight polo shirt and white slacks. A tall, gaunt woman stood nearby, staring into space. Tony and the man nodded about some kind of agreement, and the man guided the woman to the passenger seat, talking emphatically about the car's features and the good deal he'd struck. The woman sat down, her face a mixture of boredom and disdain. Clearly, he would pay later for this, at a time and price of her choosing. The man revved the engine a few times, engulfing the woman's head in a cloud of blue exhaust, gave Tony an idiotic smile and a thumbs-up, and zooped out of the lot.

Tony turned to Vishnu. "Vince! "Is that car a mother or what?"

Vishnu was determined to at least put up a good fight on the price. "For an older car it runs pretty good."

Tony laughed. "Yeah, pretty good. I think you took the paint off Boyd's Gun Shop the way you was windin' it up the hill. Whadya do, drive it to Tacoma?"

"I wanted to make sure I got a chance to make sure it was in sound shape. I intended to be back a little sooner."

Tony laughed again, the easy laugh of a fisherman who has three gaffs and a steel cable on a big halibut, and is joking with his friends about how hard it will be to get it on the dock scale. "Yeah, well, that's OK. I'm glad you got to drive it to your satisfaction. I knew you wouldn't steal it. I know people. You ain't the type."

Vishnu had the uneasy feeling that Tony did know people, that Tony knew Vishnu in ways that Vishnu did not know himself, and that this wasn't in Vishnu's favor. Vishnu figured the best thing to do was to get the transaction over with as soon as possible. He had a growing concern that if he talked long enough with Tony he could end up as an indentured servant, selling cars in exchange for a bed in a closet of the office. “So...what’s the typical price for a car like this?”

“Well, that’s kinda hard to say with a specialty machine like this. All the modifications. You lookin’ at financing?”

Vishnu shook his head. “No, I’m going to cash it out. I figure always pay cash. That's what my dad always said.” Which was a lie; his dad had never said any such thing.

“That’s a great policy,” Tony replied. “Your old man was a smart cookie. Cash is always the best way ta go.” Especially for me, he thought. If Sonny ever comes after his car, I don’t want to have to try to get paid out of your estate. “So I’m prepared to offer you a very sweet deal on your new car here. Are you thinkin’ of a trade-in?” You’re going to say no, aren’t you, you confused little numbnuts.

Vishnu looked suddenly wistful. “Uh...I think...you know, I think I’m going to keep the Valiant for now. You know, maybe see if I can get it running again.”

Tony smiled. A man who was not a car mechanic but wouldn’t take a cash offer on a thirty-year-old hulk with a blown engine was clearly not thinking straight, which was a vulnerable place to be when standing on the lot of Tony’s Tigers. “Well, that’s fine, Vince,” said Tony. “Totally understandable. So, accounting for that, and with tax, title, dealer prep, floor mats, undercoating, and tabs, I could let you drive the ’Cuda off the lot right now for…” Tony made some counting motions with his fingers, “let’s say, $7,500.”

Vishnu bit his lip. “I can’t go there,” he said in a flat voice. He looked balefully at the ’Cuda gleaming in the noon sun. “I can’t do more than $7,000.”

The Triumph with the happy couple putted in from Aurora. Tony looked off to the lot entrance. “Be right with ya!” he yelled. Turning back to Vishnu, he said, “Look Vince, I’ll tell you what. I try never to let personal feelings get into my business. I must be gettin' soft. But I gotta say, you remind me of my kid brother."

"Vito?"

Tony shook his head. "Nah, not Vito. Ricky." The one, thought Tony, who never figured out why he didn't like apple juice because we'd pee in his glass in the kitchen before we'd hand it to him. "Look, Vince," Tony went on, "I can let you have the 'Cuda for seven grand, but not a cent less. Because I like you, Vince." Because I'm going to clear two grand on the deal and save myself the trouble of shipping this ride to L.A. before some meth freak decides to pull a self-repo, and in the process somebody has to get popped.

"Sold!" said Vishnu, his rush of elation tempered by the knowledge that he'd be eating a lot of beans and rice for the next three months.

Thirty minutes later, with no firm destination in mind, Vishnu launched the 'Cuda downhill onto the Eighty-fifth Street northbound on-ramp like a jet fighter off the deck of an aircraft carrier. "Holy shit!" he yelled through the dull roar, the throbbing 440 (with six-pack) adjusting his spine through the greasy leather bucket seat. "What hath God wrought?"

Ten

A pair of legs dangled from a human torso, draped over the front fender of an aging white dump truck. The truck sat in the yard of Engel's Excavating and Rockworks, surrounded by assorted machinery. The side of the truck's bed bore the words EVANGELICAL GARDENER, underscored by a Christian fish symbol. All but the first four letters were rendered in chipped, fading black paint, half-lost to decrepitude; EVAN stood out in fresh electric fuschia. Underneath the left-hand window, truck-driver script spelled out White Fang.

Vishnu parked behind a front-end loader and walked over to the truck. A cheap radio propped against the windshield blared a drop-forged guitar line. The foot at the end of the dangling right leg banged the fender almost in time with the music. A voice from the engine compartment wailed along tunelessly, almost in time with the radio and the banging foot. "I, am, *Iron Man!* Na-na na-na na-na-na, *Na-Na-Na!* I, have, *Got You Now!* Tighten this bolt, and then I'll—*Ow! Sweet Jesus Mary and Joe Bob Briggs!*" The last words accompanied the thump of flesh on sheet metal and a wrench clattering to the ground. The legs kicked in unison, the torso lost friction on the fender, and the whole unit slid feet first to the ground, pulling the upper half of Evan from the engine compartment.

"Doctor White Fang, I presume?" said Vishnu.

Evan spun around. He grinned at Vishnu, shaking his bruised right hand in the air. "Eight years after picking this beast up at auction, I still find it amusing that people could think that I would be White Fang, and an enormous white dump truck would be named Evan. And they're always disappointed to learn I'm not the Evangelical Gardener. I mean, do I look like a gardener?" Evan produced a length of dripping hydraulic hose from a pocket in his coveralls and waved it around to emphasize his point.

"Never," chuckled Vishnu. "You're the manic mechanic."

"Oh, yeah? Well, that makes you the czar of cycling."

"The high priest of hydraulics!"

"The poobah of pedal power!"

"The...uh..."

"Got you!" Evan waggled the hose at Vishnu in triumph. "Now, to what do I owe the honor of a workday visit from the infamous Vishnu Tensleep?"

"I've got something to show you." Vishnu led Evan around the loader.

Evan's eyebrows stood on end. "Is this thing yours?"

"As of this afternoon. You like her?"

Evan looked at Vishnu, at the 'Cuda, back at Vishnu. "Are you kidding me? Can I pop the hood?"

"Sure," said Vishnu.

Evan lifted the hood, with the expression of a little boy opening a birthday present. "Oh, man. Is this a 440? With a six-pack!" He looked back at Vishnu. "You don't see these things every day! Jesus, Vishnu, is this really yours?" and he broke off into an excited giggle. "Hell, man, this thing is probably more powerful than the Fang. You could take a wheel off and run a ski lift with this engine!"

Vishnu stood up and tossed the keys to Evan. "Let's go for a spin. You drive." Evan looked like he might levitate with sheer delight.

They hopped in the car. Evan started the engine, slowly pushed the gas pedal down until the engine howled, held it for about ten seconds, took it slowly back down to idle, and shut it off. A dog barked wildly from somewhere nearby.

"Don't you want to drive it?" asked Vishnu.

Evan, who had been sitting with his eyes shut during the racket, opened them slowly and looked at Vishnu. "No. Just hearing it was enough." He slapped the dashboard. "This is outrageous! My old friend Vishnu subverted to the dark side! I'm so happy for you! What brought this on?"

"Val's engine died."

"Oh. Sorry" Evan's face fell, then brightened. "Hey! You want me to put another one in? I've got a Cummins turbo diesel in the back! We could cut a hole in the firewall, weld in some new motor mounts, stiffen her suspension, and for a driveline I could—"

"That's OK," interjected Vishnu. "No, this car's kind of fun.

"After all those years you'll let her go so easily?"

Vishnu shrugged. "Heather never liked Val anyway."

Evan burst out laughing. "Oh, she'll like this one better! Oh, yeah! This car is exactly what she had in mind."

Vishnu shrugged again.

"You didn't buy it just to piss her off, did you? There'd be much cheaper ways. What'd this baby set you back, anyway? You must have sunk some bucks into it."

"Seven grand."

Evan stared at Vishnu. "No. Come on, what'd it cost?'

"Seven grand. I worked the salesman down from seventy-five."

"You're shitting me! What, did you get it down at the docks from a Russian ship-and-chop racket?"

"I'm telling the truth. I got it over at a used car lot on Aurora. Is it worth a lot more?"

"More than seven grand, that's for sure. Let's go inside and check it on the web."

Vishnu and Evan went into the office. Evan sat at the computer, and a few mouse clicks later a page of 'Cuda photos came into view.

"Let's see," said Evan. "In the 1970 category, we have at the top of the order a fully restored 426 Hemi, color Plum Crazy. Sweet! Only asking $79,000." Evan scrolled down the page. "Here's another Hemi, $89,000, that's a bit high, here's a mint condition 440 AAR for $62,000. Well, these are the show cars. Let's find the garbage wagons." He clicked to the next page, and then the one after that. "This is more like it. A 440 with a 4-speed, $36,500. You've got a 440. Is your engine a 1970?"

"No," said Vishnu. "The guy I bought it from said it's a '71. Does that make a difference?"

"Not for your purposes. Let's see," said Evan, turning back to the computer. "Here's another Hemi, forget it. Here's a 383 for $19,000, a 340 with a slapstick tranny for $16,000. Ah! Here we go!" A picture of a battered hulk came into view. Evan read from the screen. "1970 'Cuda. Raced as stock car. Numbers don't match. Needs work. $7,000. Texas." He looked at Vishnu. "For starters, raced as stock car translates to frame bent in high-speed wreck, numbers don't match means who knows what the engine is, and needs work means we'd have to drive the Fang down to Texas to get it. Let's go back outside and give your baby the once-over."

They walked out to the 'Cuda, and Evan spent a couple of minutes poking into the nooks and crannies. "This car's not in too bad of shape," he pronounced as he dropped the hood. "Not as clean as most of those ones on the web, but I bet you could get twelve grand, maybe more. Provided the cops don't pick you up first."

"It's legal!" protested Vishnu. "Look, I've got the papers right here." He started for the glove box.

"Relax!" Evan laughed. "I'm just pulling your leg. Whatever. Sounds like you got a deal. But with the money you saved, you'd better buy another car if you want Heather to drive with you, and you don't want to scare your upstanding citizen customers. I guess you could always park it down the street, so they'd think it wasn't yours."

"You really think it's a problem?"

"For Heather?" Evan smirked. "Twenty bucks says she won't even get in it. For the customers, I'm just joking. Mostly. But you have to admit, it's a different image than Val gave off. I mean, Val was a limp-dick vehicle. Pardon the gender confusion, but you know what I mean.

Perfectly functional, but no balls. And an emasculated car parked out front of a bike shop is a great subliminal message."

"You think people think that much about it?"

"Oh, come on, Vishnu. You make judgements about people based on what they drive. Everyone does it. A Mazda Miata says the driver thinks he's sporty. A mini-van says you've got kids. Val told everyone that Vishnu's manhood lies elsewhere. And this car," Evan patted the hood lovingly, "this baby says 'Black Sabbath Headbanger. Especially if *you* get out of it wearing your standard jeans and greasy t-shirt. Now, if you cleaned this baby up and sank about twenty grand into it, and you yourself put on about thirty pounds of fat, got a respectable haircut and wore a polo shirt and khakis, this car would would say, 'I'm a rich middle-age poser with a muscle-car nostalgia-toy'. People might be amused, but they wouldn't be nervous. Kind of like the Seattle lawyers that dress up in their biker leather and park their showroom Harley Fat Boys outside the Buckaroo and drink $4 pints of designer micro-brew. You can piss on their Doc Martens in the bathroom and nobody is going to get hurt. But this car is different. I mean, look at it. Cracked windshield, dents, big fat tires. If this car was a bike outside a tavern it'd be a stripped down hog, and you'd expect the rider to be a semi-literate 280-pound longshoreman who'd knock your teeth out with a pool cue for asking him what time it is. Don't get me wrong – I *love* this car! White Fang wants to have its babies. But this car says 'I gon knock yer teeth out, ya lil pissant muthfugger!'"

"You think it's that bad?"

Evan studied the car, then laughed. "Maybe not quite that bad. You know how I am when I get going. But it *is* a badass car, you must admit. It's not the car you'd want your daughter to go to the prom in."

Vishnu looked at his new car. He didn't want people to be scared of him, least of all his customers. He couldn't have mothers afraid to drop off their kids' bikes, just because of his car. But. And there was the problem. But. The 'Cuda scratched an itch he didn't know he had, or had at least tried to ignore, or placate with bicycles. Most men want a fast car, and Vishnu was no exception. And now he had one. And the 'Cuda wasn't just any fast car, it was one of the monster cars of his youth. And then there were the memories of Colleen McCarthy. And Cheryl's baby-blue tube top.

Vishnu thought further. Maybe he did want to stir things up with Heather. Something needed stirring there, anyway. But this felt deeper. This was about his dreams. Was a flaming red 'Cuda what he had been pedaling towards the night before? He had no clear idea.

"Well," Vishnu said finally, "I think I'll keep it for awhile, and just see what happens."

"That's my man!" Evan clapped him on the shoulder. "That's the old Vishnu. And if you need a chauffeur, you know my number. I'd drive this baby for you any day! I got no image problem with it. I want to breed a herd of pups with it and White Fang. Can't you see it? Hot, red, low-slung dump trucks with jacked-up back ends, 800 cubic-inch supercharged nitrous-oxide-breathing engines! God damn, I could move some rocks with those! Hey, don't worry about the image thing. Nobody will really care. Besides Heather, that is. Why don't you go show it to one of your old Plymouth crowd?"

"You think so? I'm not sure they'd dig it."

"Are you kidding? They'll flip! Before they got old, those guys all used to drive flathead Fords without any emissions control crap to cut the power. Trust me."

"OK," agreed Vishnu. He wasn't heading anywhere in particular anyway. And there was one of his elderly friends who he felt pretty sure would be warm to the 'Cuda.

Eleven

Edith Arneson bustled her bulk out of the kitchen and across the living room to find out what in the blue heavens was making such a racket in the front yard. It sounded like a garbage truck was parking on the lawn. She pressed her Coke-bottle glasses up to the wide-angle peephole that she'd had Arnie install in the front door. You couldn't be too careful these days. Between the distortion of the fisheye lens in the door and the fact that she was about a quarter blind with cataracts, she had to do a lot of free interpretation of her visual stimuli. But her hearing was pretty good, and between that and what passed with her for vision, there was no doubt that there was a big, red, loud car parked in the driveway, blocking in Arnie's Valiant.

"Arnie!" she yelled over her shoulder. Whoever it was in the car had shut it off but still hadn't gotten out, as far as she could tell.

"Arnie!" She trundled over to the basement door and yelled down to where he was monkeying with some fishing gear.

"Arnie! There's a strange car in the driveway. You expecting someone?"

"What?" Arnie turned up his hearing aids. He was about as deaf as Edith was blind. "Edith! You want somethin'?"

"There's a strange car in the driveway!"

"Well, who the heck is it?"

"I don't know! Just a minute!" Edith walked back to the front door as fast as her seventy-nine-year-old legs would move her and squinched her face up to it. "Arnie! There's a man coming up the driveway! Some long-haired man! And it's one of those hippie cars, like that awful boyfriend of Lisa's drove. Arnie! Come quickly!" A note of alarm was rising in her voice. "Arnie, he's coming up onto the porch!"

By this time, Arnie was pounding up the stairs like a man of sixty, not the eighty-one years proclaimed on his driver's license. His knobby right fist clenched a miniature wooden baseball bat he used to brain salmon. Just the previous night, the news had featured a story about young men who rob old people in their houses in broad daylight. Between that and the mention of a no-good eighteen-year-old who'd taken out his youngest daughter (about thirty years before), Arnie was in no mood to fool around. Hell if he'd come through the South Pacific in Dubya-Dubya-Two, my friend, just to be terrorized by some young punk. No sirree.

"Arnie, he's at the door!"

"Outa the away, Edith!"

The doorbell rang.

"Arnie, I'm scared!"

"Back away, Edith. I'll handle this!"

Arnie put his eye up to the peephole. The face of Vishnu Tensleep smiled cheerfully back at him, a little pudgy from the wide-angle lens.

"Oh, for gosh sakes, Edith, it's Vishnu!" Arnie flipped the deadbolt and opened the door.

"Hi Arnie." Vishnu spoke up to accommodate Arnie's hearing. He looked past Arnie to Edith. She stood in the middle of the room, an inscrutable expression on her face, the hem of her apron gathered up in her hands. "Edith." He glanced down at the fishwhacker in Arnie's right hand, and looked back at Edith. "Am I interrupting something?"

"Heck, no," hollered Arnie. "C'mon in! Edith, would ya heat the coffee up?"

Edith found her voice and let go of her apron. "Lord have mercy, Vishnu, you gave me a fright!" she laughed in a relieved tone and moved towards the kitchen.

"A fright?" Vishnu asked.

"All I heard was that car in the driveway," she called from the kitchen, sounding like the old Edith. "I couldn't see it was you. Is that car yours? It looks like something those hoodlums drive."

"I was down in the basement," Arnie picked up the tale. "Course, I can't hear nothin', especially when I'm down there. All I heard was Edith yellin' about strange men comin' up on the porch." He chuckled, looked at the fishwhacker in his hand, and set in the stand with the fireplace pokers as though he normally kept it there.

"Well," said Vishnu, "as far as strange men go, Edith, you weren't that far off base."

Edith's laugh rang from the kitchen. "Oh, Vishnu, you're a dear boy. Between that car and my eyesight…" Edith was clattering cups and saucers. She was of the era that reheated old coffee in the percolator until you could clean carburetor jets with it, but she served it in dainty cups with saucers. If there were guests involved, a little plate of cookies came with.

"You want some fish?" Arnie asked. "Sockeye. Fresh from the chimney this morning."

"I'd never turn down your fish, Arnie," replied Vishnu. Arnie broke out in a proud grin. A number of the denizens of old-school Ballard smoked their own fish, using secret methods and brine recipes handed down through the generations. Techniques were debated like baseball statistics when the old guys got together to drain a few schooners. Arnie's preferred fish-smoking apparatus was a metal shoe rack installed in the living room fireplace.

Vishnu and Arnie went into the kitchen with Edith, who handed Vishnu a cup of coffee. Arnie began stuffing a plastic bag full of dark-orange salmon strips.

"As a matter of fact, Arnie," said Vishnu, "I came over because I just bought this car today. C'mon out and tell me what you think." Vishnu and Arnie walked out onto the front porch, followed by Edith. "It's a 1970 Plymouth 'Cuda, with a 440 V-8. Actually, the engine is a '71. It's a little beat up, but it runs good. What do you think?"

Edith peered dubiously at the car, unable to disengage it from memories of her daughter's particularly unappealing boyfriend. "It's a nice color," she managed.

Arnie's stubbly jaws worked a bit, several thoughts rising in his mind. The color was loud, and the neighbors wouldn't like it much if he parked a car like that on the street. And it was a two-door; they were a pain if you had to get in and out of the back seat. Not that he did that a lot anymore, but you never knew, you know? And Vishnu was right about it being beat up, in contrast to his well-maintained but bland green 1971 Valiant Duster. Arnie thought all this, but mostly he thought it looked like a hell of a car. Arnie was a little jealous.

"Do you have time for a ride, Arnie?" asked Vishnu.

Arnie and Vishnu both glanced at Edith.

"You could come, too, Edith," added Vishnu.

"Oh, heavens, Vishnu," Edith made a flapping motion with her hands. "I've got some sewing to do, and Myrtle Ricci wanted me to call her with some recipes. You boys just go on without me. Go have some dinner or something." She gave Vishnu a smile that would have sweetened sugar.

"If you're sure, then…" Arnie let the sentence hang.

"Absolutely," said Edith. In point of fact, she didn't really want Arnie to go out in that car, in full view of God and everybody, but she could see no graceful way out of the situation.

"I'll go get my jacket, then." Arnie hustled inside, as though to get on the road before further consideration could take place.

"I'll have him back before dark, Edith," promised Vishnu, handing her his cup and saucer.

"That's fine, dear. You two just go have a good time."

Arnie and Vishnu hopped in the 'Cuda, rumbled slowly backwards out of the driveway, and took off down the street with a jerk and a little squeal of rubber. Edith stood on the front porch, watching. Her hands were unconsciously twisting the hem of her apron again, and she thought, but couldn't be sure, that Ida Helmdorfer was peering past the white pleated curtains from the kitchen window across the street.

Edith sighed. Men. God love them, but they never seem to outgrow wanting to make fools of themselves in public. She walked back into the kitchen and dialed Myrtle Ricci's phone number, but not to talk about coffee cake.

Meanwhile, Vishnu and Arnie meandered east from Ballard, and ended up cruising south along the winding tree-lined lanes of Lake Washington Boulevard. Between the noise of the engine, the warm wind rushing by the open windows, and Arnie's hearing deficit, there wasn't much chance for conversation.

A few heads turned at each intersection where they stopped, with expressions ranging from disdain to nods of open approval. Vishnu had mixed feelings about this. He was used to travelling incognito, either on a bike or in Val, who just wasn't a head-turning machine, and he was unused to public disapproval. On the other hand, it was a gas to finally get his hands on the controls of a car from his adolescent myths, and to get smiles from total strangers.

Vishnu was also a bit uncomfortable with the scene he had precipitated at Edith and Arnie's house. Having a car that a few people didn't like was one thing, but Vishnu didn't want to be the instigator of heart attacks in his geriatric friends, just because he stopped by to watch Lawrence Welk videos. With this thought, Vishnu glanced over at Arnie. Arnie, far from looking distressed, was eased back in the passenger seat, a faint smile on his grizzled mouth. His right elbow resting out the window, his right leg crossed across his left, he appeared lost in some private world of reflection. If he was harboring ill will, he was covering it well.

Reaching the south end of the lake in Renton, Vishnu pulled into a gas station. "Let me pay for this, Vishnu. I gotta take a leak anyways." Arnie headed off before Vishnu could dicker with him, and disappeared into the attached mini-mart. A few minutes later, as Vishnu hung the nozzle back on the pump, Arnie yelled to him from behind. "Whaddaya think?"

Vishnu turned around to confront an eighty-one-year-old coot with a bridgework-laced grin and a pair of mirror-lens aviator sunglasses with the tag still on them.

"Are they me?" asked Arnie proudly.

"I don't know, man," said Vishnu. "We better get you back in the car before the movie star agents get here."

They climbed into the 'Cuda, and Arnie turned to Vishnu. "I've never had a pair of mirror sunglasses before," he said, as though confessing to a minor crime.

Vishnu smiled back at him, his face reflected crazily in Arnie's new shades. "Careful, buddy. It's a slippery slope. Next stop is leather pants!"

Arnie let out a cackle, which ended in a cough, and slapped the dashboard. "Let's hit the road, boy! It's Friday afternoon, and I hear me some fish and beers callin' our names!"

"Aye aye, captain. Fish and beers to north'ard!"

Ninety minutes later, Arnie and Vishnu were leaning back from a weatherbeaten wood table on the waterfront deck of a fish joint in Edmonds, looking out at the evening sun on Puget Sound. A mound of batter-dipped cod strips and french fries sat between them. Arnie cradled a half-empty schooner in his left hand, and held a piece of fish in his right. He was still wearing his new shades, reveling in what he thought was a rebel appearance. They were alone except for a few gulls that wheeled overhead in the onshore breeze, crying for food.

"So, Arnie. Were you guys actually scared when I drove up today?"

"Oh, you know Edith." Arnie waved his fish strip dismissively. A piece flew off the end and sailed over the railing, causing a commotion among the gulls. "She can't see worth a damn, and fills in the gaps with her imagination."

"Yeah." Vishnu sipped his Coke. "But you were standing there with a fish club, Arnie, and you don't even wear glasses. Except for the occasional gnarly shades."

"Ja, well, don't worry about it Vishnu. Edith was yellin' about hippie cars and strangers on the porch, and I was thinkin' about a cop show on TV. You get a little loopy sometimes when you're my age."

"It's funny. I bought that car totally on impulse. I was intending to get another Valiant, or something like it. Basic transportation, you know? Then this car drives up, and I was, like, fourteen or fifteen again, riding with my cousin Bobby and his friend Lance. Lance had a car just like that. They'd take me along cruising Alki with them, and I thought I was in on the coolest time in the world. In the coolest car on the planet. Man, Bobby's parents hated that car, and so did mine! Maybe that's part of what was so cool about it. I guess it really flipped the old folks out." Vishnu paused. "No offence, Arnie."

Arnie tipped his head back to polish off his beer, thunked the empty glass down on the table, belched, and gave a satisfied sigh. "Lemme tell you somethin', my young friend." He picked up a piece of fish and pointed at Vishnu. "When I was your age – how old are you, anyways?"

"Thirty-nine."

"Huh. Ja, well, I was a bit younger, then. Anyways, after the war, me and my buddies all rode bikes. Motorcycles. Big loud ones. Didya ever hear about the hillclimbs they had around here?"

"A little. From my uncle. Not much."

"Well, let me tell you, they were the big thing among a lotta vets. There was a club called the Queen City Motorcycle Club, usta sponsor hillclimbs and other dirt track stuff. I usta ride with 'em a bit. Right after I got outa the Navy, in '45, I bought me a '36 Harley. Had a big V-twin engine they called a knucklehead, sixty-one cubic inches. I don't know what the hell it was in centimeters, but lemme tell you, Vishnu, it was a big heavy bike. Had a muffler like a tin can and a molded leather seat. I bolted a guard over the muffler and a pad on top of the rear fender so that someone could sit on it if they weren't too particular. Thing'd about shake your jimmies off, and it was loud as hell. The neighbors hated it, especially when me and the boys usta come back to my place after midnight from hoisting a few. And when I'd bring Edith home on it, her folks'd just about—"

"Edith?" Vishnu goggled at Arnie. "Edith rode on a motorcycle? You're pulling my leg!"

Arnie grinned at Vishnu. "Edith," he said slowly, "married me because of that bike."

Arnie's revelation was interrupted by the waitress, a woman of about fifty. "Another beer, hon?" She smiled at Arnie.

"Does a Norsky have a square head? Hell, yes, gimme another!"

"And for you?" She looked at Vishnu.

"Another Coke, thanks. I'm the designated driver."

"You got it." The waitress walked back inside.

"What do you mean, Edith married you because of that bike?"

Arnie settled further into his chair, and clasped his hands behind his head. "Hell, boy, I met her at a hillclimb. I'm not sure her folks ever knew, but her and her friends usta go out in a group, drink a few beers, and cheer on the guys. I remember the first time I laid eyes on Edith. What a looker! She was wearin' a plaid skirt and a blue sweater. She was a blonde, and her hair was all curled. I was full of it in those days, and I rode my bike right up to her, told her to yell for me 'cause I was the next one to go. She said show her why and maybe she'd think about it." Arnie gazed at the water, remembering.

"So what happened?"

"Well, I took off like a bat outa hell and started up the slope. Had that old Harley wound to the nuts. Hit a bump in the middle of the hill goin' too fast, and flew off. Rolled most of the way back to the bottom of the hill. I was covered in dirt, and I'd banged my knee pretty good on the handlebars." Arnie paused again.

"And?"

"Well, I figured Edith would either think it was funny or give me the wave, so I picked my bike up, rode over to her, and asked her what she thought." Arnie nodded as though that was the end of the story, and looked back out over the water.

"Oh, for God's sake, Arnie, what did she say?"

Arnie grinned at Vishnu. "She told me it was the most entertaining thing she'd seen all day. That's exactly what she said. I'll never forget it."

"So that's why she married you?"

"Oh, no, that's another piece. That's just how we met." Arnie rubbed his chin. "We'd been goin' out for about a year or so. I was workin' at Foss Shipyards. Just bought the house, the same one we live in now. Edith was still livin' with her folks, and workin' as a secretary at Seattle Shingle. This was in '47. No, '46, 'cause I met her right after I got outa the Navy. I was twenty-seven. Jeez." Arnie shook his head. "It seemed old at the time. Anyways, her folks didn't think much of me, partly because I'm a Norsky and they were real old-country Sweden, but mostly because they just thought I wasn't the type for their daughter. And I really didn't give a hoot, havin' been through the war and all. But I usta ride up on the Harley to pick Edith up for dates, and before I'd shut the bike down, I'd rev that big engine a few times, really let her rip, just to piss her folks off. Probably made all her mother's china rattle in the cabinet. Anyways, one night, we went out, and she told me her dad had laid down the law. Told her she needed to choose. Either stop seein' me, or move outa the house."

"What did you say?"

"I told her that if she was movin' out, we oughta just get hitched, so we could save the rent money. I dropped her off that night, and she didn't say nothin' to her folks. The next day, I got the boss to give me the afternoon off. I picked Edith up at lunchtime, and we got a marriage license. Three days later, we got married at the courthouse, with my best friend and her best friend as witnesses." Arnie hooted and slapped his leg. "Then we went and told her folks! My folks was dead by then, so there wasn't anything to deal with there, and they woulda loved Edith anyways. But her mother, hoo boy! She just about had kittens right on the floor when Edith told her! Her dad was yellin' a buncha stuff in Swedish that I won't repeat. It was a helluva scene!"

"This is amazing, Arnie." Vishnu sat back. "Edith on a motorcycle, and—"

"She ain't always been old, boy!" Arnie slapped the table so hard the glasses almost tipped over, the strength of the memories running hot in his blood. "You look at her and all you see is an old woman, but lemme tell you, she was a ball of fire in her day!" He looked off across Puget Sound. "Damn, Vishnu," he said quietly. "Goddamn, we had us some times..."

The waitress returned with their drinks. Arnie looked up at her. "What do you think of my car, Missy?"

"Pardon?"

"The Plymouth! The red one out front. Big fast machine." He jerked his thumb at Vishnu. "I'm lettin' my nephew drive it today because it's his birthday." Arnie leaned towards the waitress. "Maybe after I drop him off with his mother, I can come back and pick you up for a spin."

"Well, hon, I'd love it, but my husband hates it when I go driving in fast cars with good looking men."

Arnie nodded as though this was a reasonable prejudice. "Well, we'll bring him along, too. You just call me if you want a ride in a real speed machine."

The waitress walked away, laughing and shaking her head.

Vishnu was still grappling with the revised vision of his elderly friends. "So how'd it work out with Edith's parents?" he finally got out.

"Oh, hell, you know." Arnie took a long pull off his beer. "They got over it. I always half suspected her old man said what he said just to light a fire under us. I was twenty-seven, and Edith was twenty-five, and we was pretty sure to get hitched sometime. Her old man wasn't a bad sort. Actually, him and me got pretty close, in spite of him bein' a Swede and all. And after the girls was born…" Arnie trailed off. "Course, by the time we had our first, Maren, in '48, I'd bought a Ford coupe, and was only ridin' the bike sometimes on weekends, and I'd given up the hillclimbs. And then came Anna and Lisa. I had that old Harley until about 1960, but ya know, when you're a married man with three kids, you can ride a bike like that and nobody thinks nothin' of it.

"So, given your checkered past, you think my car's OK"

"Ja, sure," said Arnie, picking a piece of cod out of his front teeth with his thumbnail. "Just don't be pickin' up my daughters in it."

Arnie walked up his porch steps as the sun hit the horizon. His new shades were still perched on his nose.

Edith met him at the door. She moved to give him the customary peck on the cheek, then pulled up short. "Where on earth did you get those?"

"Those what?"

"Those sunglasses. Are those Vishnu's?"

"Hell, no! These are mine. Whaddaya think, Dee Dee?"

Edith studied him, a mixture of skepticism and intrigue in her clouded old eyes. He hadn't called her 'Dee Dee' since Lord knows when. The name triggered memories from an earlier time when a young woman with curly blonde hair and a piss-and-vinegar sense of humor was going out with a good-looking sailor boy, fresh out of the U.S. Navy.

Before Edith could respond, Arnie kissed her smack on the lips and walked past her with an affectionate pat on her ample behind. "By gosh, I'm gonna have me some pie," he said. "You want a piece?" He laid his shades down on the fireplace mantle as he walked from the dining room into the kitchen.

"Oh, no, dear, that's fine," Edith managed to get out. "Did you and Vishnu have a nice time?"

"Ja, sure, it was a ball!" Arnie's voice came from inside the refrigerator as he rummaged around. "We drove down to Renton and then all the way up to Edmonds. Had fish for dinner."

Edith walked over to the mantle and picked up Arnie's sunglasses. He was still rooting in the fridge. Quietly, she switched on the lamp that sat on the mantle, slipped the sunglasses awkwardly over her bifocals, and looked at herself in the mirror above the fireplace.

"Vishnu says sorry for frightening you this afternoon," Arnie called, now occupied with cutting a wedge of pie.

"Oh, heavens," said Edith, as through the nearsightedness, cataracts, and dim light, a woman looked back at her from the mirror. A woman who used to laugh and sing songs at bonfire beach parties, and ride home late at night on the back of a big loud motorcycle, arms wrapped tight around her man, blonde curls whipping in the warm night air. "Oh, heavens," said Dee Dee. "You tell him it's nothing. Sometimes I just forget how it is to be young and to want to go fast."

Twelve

Just before three-thirty on Saturday morning, Officer Gina Kowalski of the Seattle Police Department, North Precinct, was rolling her cruiser through the bottom end of south Ballard, in search of something illegal, or at least something to stave off boredom. The bars had closed, and the parties had wound down. She checked the list of people and cars for which she was supposed to keep an eye peeled.

Gina had been with the SPD for about seven months, having spent the previous six years with the City of Tukwila's finest. She liked the SPD and the North Precinct. Better all-night places to grab a bite, less chance of being cut down by random gunfire, and the jets weren't coming into SeaTac five hundred feet above her head.

Gina rolled slowly along Canal Street, intending to follow it up to Third Avenue and back to Leary Way, when her headlights flashed on red metalflake a block away. "Son of a bitch," she muttered, taking her foot off the gas and coasting to a stop at the curb. There was absolutely no mistaking *that* ride. But what the hell was Sonny doing this far north, out of his home turf and horning in on the Ballard meth action? She turned off her headlights and contemplated the situation, leaving the motor idling.

As it turned out, just before three-thirty on Saturday morning was a sleepless time for Vishnu, who had gone to bed early only to wake up in the middle of the night, his head filled with ideas, projects, and random thoughts rolling around like cat toys batted by the paws of his restless brain. Entertaining visions of a dawn bike ride, he rousted himself from his bed, put the coffee maker into action, and checked the fridge. Crap. Out of milk.

He pulled on a pair of jeans and a pink t-shirt with a yellow smiley face, grabbed some change and his wallet, jammed his feet in his sandals and padded out the side door. In spite of the disturbance to the neighbors, he couldn't resist the chance to fire up the 'Cuda for the ten block drive to the Stop-N-Shop on Leary.

Gina went on full alert when she saw the figure slip from the shadows towards the car, then got a surprise as the dome light illuminated Vishnu's unshaven face. Who the hell is that? she thought. Certainly not Sonny. Maybe he'll give me a chance to pull him over and find out what the hell he's doing up here.

Unaware of the following cruiser, Vishnu turned westbound onto Leary then took a right into the Stop-N-Shop parking lot, neglecting somehow to use his turn signal.

"Right on," Gina said with a smile. She picked up the radio mike. "This is Car 70 requesting backup at the Stop-N-Shop on Leary Way just west of Seventh Avenue."

"Car 32 to car 70. What's up, Gina?" Car 70 was Hank Collins, one of Gina's better buddies on the force.

"I got a potential bad boy up here from Tukwila, just pulled a moving violation. I recognize the car. Not sure what's going on, and I want some help just in case."

"Car 32 turning onto Leary from Market," Hank said, coming into Gina's view.

"Let's move on him," she replied, splitting the darkness with her party lights.

Vishnu stepped from that darkness into the billion-candlepower landscape of the generic American all-night convenience store, blinking, and blissfully unaware of the other light show entering the parking lot. He made his way back to the dairy case, grabbed a pint of milk, and started back to the cashier. The cashier was stock-still, staring at him. Guy looks like he's on drugs, thought Vishnu, as he pulled a handful of change from his pocket. At that moment, the double doors swung open, and Gina and Hank strode in. Hank moved to Vishnu's right flank, while

Gina squared him off. Vishnu looked over his shoulder, expecting to see a freak with a ski mask and a gun. Seeing no one, he turned back to Gina. She was looking straight into his eyes. He searched for something to say. "Hi," he mustered.

"That your car?" said Gina.

"The red one?"

"Yeah."

"Yeah."

Gina gave him a hard look. "You got some ID?"

"Uh, yeah. Hang on. Vishnu tried to extract his license from his tattered billfold. In his nervousness it flipped into the air. "Shit!" yelped Vishnu. He shot his hands out to catch it, succeeding only in throwing his handful of coins against Gina's chest.

"Watch it!" snapped Gina. She dropped into a crouch, her hand going to the roughened grip of her sidearm. The store clerk dove to the floor behind the counter.

Vishnu, keenly aware that his next move might be his last, dropped very slowly to his knees, found his license among the personal debris and held it up to Gina with both hands like a religious offering. "Here," he got out with a crooked smile. "Sorry."

Gina reached out with her left hand and took the license. She studied it and looked critically at Vishnu's face. "Tensleep, Vishnu Patrick."

"Yes?"

"That's you."

"Yes."

"Officer Collins, would you run this?"

"Sure thing, Officer Kowalski." Hank took the license out to the cruiser.

Vishnu fumbled with the contents of his wallet, still on his knees. "Can I stand up?"

"Slowly," said Gina. "What are you doing up here from Tukwila?"

"What?"

"You heard me."

"I did," said Vishnu. "I just don't know what you mean."

"How's Sonny these days?"

"Sonny?"

"Yeah."

"I don't know," admitted Vishnu. "Who's Sonny?"

"You don't know."

"Huh uh."

Hank came back in. "License is valid. Car was registered yesterday to a Vishnu Patrick Tensleep."

"That's me." Vishnu offered Hank a hopeful smile.

"Mr. Tensleep says he doesn't know what's going on in Tukwila, Officer Collins," said Gina, taking the license back from Hank.

"That a fact?" said Hank.

"No, sir," said Vishnu, trying to sound friendly. "I mean, yes, sir, I don't know what's going on in Tukwila."

Gina studied him closely. "Nice car you got there. Where'd you get it?"

"Today. This afternoon. I mean yesterday afternoon. Oh. You said where. Sorry. A place up on Aurora. Tony's Tigers."

Gina glanced at Hank, who looked out the window. "Where do you live?" she asked Vishnu.

"Just down on Canal Street."

She studied his license, noted the address, and looked up at him. "In the garage?"

"Yeah. Actually, it's a bike shop. And my music studio. And I live there. I fix bikes."

"I didn't see any bikes outside. You ride?"

"Yeah."

"What do you ride?"

"What do I ride?" Vishnu replayed the last seconds in his head. He was sure he'd uttered the phrase 'bike shop' in there somewhere.

"Yeah. What do you ride?"

"You mean what kind of bike?"

Gina's face tightened. "I'm asking you," she said very deliberately, "what kind of bike you ride."

Vishnu managed a small, unconvincing smile. She's flipped her wig, he thought. And as he thought this, Vishnu noticed for the first time that she was kind of cute, although he usually didn't go for deranged, well-armed women. Against his better judgement, he wondered what she looked like without body armor. He turned his thoughts from that; she was obviously expecting an answer to her question. Vishnu thought of the ride he'd intended to take that morning. The plan seemed to have been hatched several lifetimes ago. "What do I ride," said Vishnu. "It's kind of hard to say."

"Try me."

"Well...I mean...my main bike isn't really a brand. It's kind of a melange. I have a vintage Eddy Merckx 531 double-butted frame, but I bent the rear stays to accommodate a cassette hub. It's got mostly Campy components, although currently the rear derailleur is a Shimano because I've been experimenting with a modified index shifter I fabricated. It's mint green." He looked at her like a fourth grader waiting to hear the verdict from the teacher. "The frame is green, not the shifter," he added for extra credit.

Gina's eyes tensed at the corners. "Are you jerking me around? I think this guy is jerking me around, Officer Collins."

Vishnu glanced at Hank desperately. Hank cocked an eyebrow. "Officer Kowalski, I think he's talking about a bicycle."

"A bicycle?" asked Gina.

"A bicycle," replied Hank.

"A bicycle!" confirmed Vishnu. "A bicycle! My bicycle!" He smiled at her. "I ride it!"

"Oh," said Gina. She glanced at his license again. "I thought you were talking about motorcycles." It had begun to dawn on her that there was a chance, however slight, that Vishnu may not be connected with Sonny, in spite of being the proud owner of Sonny's car. It also dawned on her that he was kind of cute, although she didn't usually go for gibbering, wiry guys who wear dopey shirts. Against her better judgement, she wondered what he looked like in a racing jersey and a pair of those tight black biking shorts.

"Look Officer, uh, Kowalski?" said Vishnu. "Is there something I can help you guys with? I mean, you guys seem pretty hopped up, and your flashers are still on, and this is kind of freaking me out. I mean, all I wanted was a pint of milk." Vishnu held up the carton.

"You made a lane change and a right turn without using your turn signal," said Gina. She glanced at Hank, who looked out the window again.

Vishnu felt an array of sarcastic responses rising in him, but restrained himself in honor of being the only unarmed conversant. "No turn signal? Oh, gee, officer, I'm sorry. There wasn't anyone for blocks. Except you, of course. But that's no excuse. I guess you'll be giving me a ticket?"

Gina sighed. "Maybe not. Let's check out the car." The three of them trooped out into the parking lot. Hank turned off the blue-and-reds in both cruisers. "We probably don't need these," he said to no one in particular.

Gina shone her flashlight around the cockpit of the 'Cuda. "I guess it looks OK." She handed Vishnu's license back to him. The first hint of dawn was evident in the eastern sky. "Tensleep," she said. "Interesting name. Indian?"

"Cheyenne, but way way back. I'm basically American mutt."

"And Vishnu Patrick?"

"Vishnu because my beatnik dad said it was a geologic joke, but I never got it. And Patrick for Saint Patrick, for my Mom's side. She was Irish." Vishnu shrugged. "You know parents."

"Yeah." For the first time in the interchange, Gina smiled.

"Do you want to see my shop?" asked Vishnu.

Gina looked at Vishnu in surprise. Behind Vishnu, Hank's smirk widened into a grin. "Why would I want to do that, Mr. Tensleep?"

Vishnu looked surprised himself, as though he couldn't believe what had just come out of his mouth "Oh, I don't know. I mean, you seemed kind of interested in it. I mean, it's just my shop. And the studio for my band. And my apartment. There's coffee!" Vishnu realized he'd said all this previously. He held up the milk. "I needed milk." I must be going crazy, thought Vishnu. First she wants to shoot me, and now I'm inviting her and Andy Griffith over for a date. "Pay no attention to me," he rambled on. "Sorry. I got up a little too early this morning, and I guess I'm not really awake yet."

Hank, amused as he was, decided it was time to step in. "Actually, Mr. Tensleep, that's awfully kind of you, but Officer Kowalski and I need to get back on patrol. Don't we, Officer Kowalski?"

"Right. Yeah," said Gina. "Sorry about the confusion, Mr. Tensleep."

"Vishnu."

"Gina. Gina Kowalski." She held out her hand, and Vishnu shook it. They paused, looking at each other. Hank stuck out his hand. "Hank Collins."

"Vishnu Tensleep," said Vishnu, shaking his hand.

"I know," said Hank. "Well, I think that's that, don't you, Officer Kowalski?"

"Yes. Yes, I guess it is. Well, good night, Vishnu."

"Good night, Gina. Good night, Hank."

"Good night, Vishnu," said Hank. "Shall we go, Officer Kowalski?"

"Right, Officer Collins," said Gina. "Bye, Vishnu. Nice meeting you."

"My pleasure."

Hank and Gina climbed into their cars and drove away. Vishnu watched them disappear from sight before skulking the few blocks home. He went inside and poured himself a cup of coffee. Opening the milk carton, he froze. "Oh, *shit*!" He had just shoplifted a pint of two-percent.

Thirteen

Several hours later, standing in the shower after his ride, Vishnu contemplated the last five hours. What a weird morning. Indeed, the weirdness had been turned up for the last two days, but this morning had twisted the weirdness knob right off whatever cosmic apparatus it was attached to.

After a quick breakfast and some illegally lactified coffee, Vishnu rolled up the shop door, put out his sign, turned on the radio, and took on the day's first repair. He returned from his around-the-block test ride to find a blue minivan parked in his driveway. A thirty-something woman was removing a kid's bike from the back seat. A soccer ball came out with the bike and rolled to Vishnu's feet.

"Is this your bike shop?" asked Soccer Mom, as he handed her the ball.

"Yep."

"Do you fix kids' bikes?"

"Sure do."

"Well, this one's got a flat tire."

Vishnu inspected it. "Do you want to wait while I fix it? It'll take about fifteen minutes."

"Can I leave it?" she asked. "I'll just run up to the store for a few things and come back, if you don't mind.

"Sure thing," said Vishnu. "Here." He fished a repair card and pen out of his apron pocket and handed them to the woman. "Fill out your name and phone number while I put this bike back in the shop."

As he came back out she gestured at the 'Cuda. "Is that your car?"

"Yep," said Vishnu, feeling like he'd been getting that question a lot lately.

Soccer Mom looked at the car coolly. "When I was in about third grade, my big sister's boyfriend had one of those. Maybe a different kind. Like that anyway. Big tires in back. We called it a stinkbug. He finally went to jail." She climbed into the van and flashed Vishnu a smile. "Have a nice day!"

Vishnu took the bike into the shop and removed the back wheel. He extracted the offending tube, found the hole, and applied some glue to it. As he worked, he mused about the 'Cuda. It had clearly seen a lot of miles at hands that hadn't worried much about clutch adjustments, regular oil changes, or suspension checks. "You just wait, little lady," he cooed to his car through the door. "Papa Vishnu is going to make sure you get all spruced up." He thought about flat tires. Hell, he thought, I bet the spare is flat. Come to think of it, there are two different tire sizes. If there is a spare, which one would it be?

With no customers in sight, and the glue on the tube still drying, Vishnu strolled out and opened the trunk. It contained a dank assortment of garbage, a broken boom box and some things that had once been jumper cables. Pulling the trash can over and discarding the first layer of detritus, he uncovered the spare tire, an almost bald recap on a rim that didn't match anything on the car. Vishnu poked the tire with his finger. Flat as a pancake.

Vishnu lifted the tire out, hoping to find a jack and a lug wrench underneath. Instead, he found an old gym bag. Putting the tire down next to the car, he picked up the bag, noticing that it did not seem to contain a lug wrench, although it was uncommonly heavy. He put the bag down on the sidewalk and unzipped it. He was prepared for a variety of things, but he was not prepared for what he saw. "Holy fucking shit mother-fuck!" He leaped backwards and fell on his butt.

Five large handguns. Big and sort of square-looking. Four of them a dark gray-blue color, and one bright and shiny. And a plastic bag containing three plastic-wrapped tubes of pinkish powder, each about the size of a jumbo burrito.

Vishnu's bowels swam. He swiveled his head wildly. Nobody was in sight, but he heard a car approaching. Scrambling to his feet, Vishnu zipped the gym bag shut, threw it into the spare well, threw the flat tire on top of it, slammed the trunk shut, and sat on it, just as the blue minivan pulled around the corner and parked in his driveway.

Soccer Mom hopped out. "Is it done yet?"

"Done?"

"The bike."

"Oh! The bike! Yes! No! Just about! The glue's drying!"

Vishnu ran inside, and tapped his finger in the glue. "Totally dry! Yessir, totally dry! Dry as a bone!"

Ms. Mom had ventured as far as the door. "Is everything OK?"

"OK? Oh, yes! I'll just patch a pop, uh, pop a patch on here!"

"Oh, good," said Ms. Mom. "I thought it might be shot."

Vishnu choked. "Are you sure you're OK?" Ms. Mom asked again, peering anxiously at him.

"Yes, yes," croaked Vishnu. "Just a little spit down the wrong pipe. Let me just test the patch here." He filled it with air. By the grace of all the benevolent powers available to him, it held. "Looks good. And on with the tire." The wrench flew in Vishnu's practiced fingers as he reinstalled the wheel. He wanted to get this woman out of here as soon as possible. He wanted to lock himself in a closet. He wanted his mama. Unclamping the bike from the stand, he forced a smile onto his lips. "That'll be seven dollars even."

"That's a good price," said Soccer Mom, pulling a bill from her wallet. "Most places charge twelve or more."

"Well, I try to keep my prices reasonable."

"I'll be sure to send all my friends to you."

"Thanks. I repair all kinds." He loaded the bike into the van.

Soccer Mom smiled at him. "It seems like a nice shop. I've always liked bicycle shops. Somehow to me they always say 'Family Values.'"

"Family Values," echoed Vishnu.

"Yeah. You know, the kind of place you would want your kids to hang out."

"Send 'em down any time," said Vishnu with a crooked grin.

Soccer Mom pulled away with a cheerful wave and a final Betty Crocker smile. "Send 'em on down," he said to the empty street. "We can get whacked on magic dust, go for a cruise in the mobile crime scene, and later on I'll teach them how to shoot the lights off moving cop cars. It'll be just like Leave It To Beaver."

Fourteen

At four o'clock Saturday afternoon, Tony was sitting in his office, stuffing the remains of a meatball grinder (extra marinara, extra onions) into his maw. The sound of a throaty engine distinguished itself from the general traffic noise, approaching from the south. Through the window he saw a black Fiat Spider convertible make a fast turn into the parking lot, tires protesting on the asphalt. The driver transitioned perfectly into a four-wheel drift on the gravel near the trailer, sliding to a halt ten feet from the office. A short athletic woman, black hair, black sunglasses, black leather jacket, and blue jeans, leaped from the car.

"Christ," muttered Tony. "I should dig me a fuckin' escape tunnel." He took a deep breath. "Gina!" he called as she flung the door open. "Gina!" he repeated in a happy voice, as though he hadn't seen her for over a year. "What a surprise!" He heaved himself from the chair and moved to meet her, arms raised for an embrace.

Gina planted her hands on her hips. "Tony, can you possibly, *possibly*, explain to me just what the *fuck* you keep in that fat *fucking* head of yours where other people keep their *fucking* brains?"

Tony dropped his arms and cocked his head. "Gina? I–"

"Of all the *stupid fucking* things to do! One of these days you are gonna go too far even for *you*, and it's gonna be your *fucking* funeral, and I'm gonna wear a red dress and dance on your *fucking* grave. *Jesus!*"

"Gina! What have I done that you would say these things?" Tony manufactured a look of hurt angelic innocence.

"Don't treat me like some stupid *bimbo*, Tony! Do you think I'm *stupid?* Is that it? That's it, isn't it! You think I'm *stupid!*"

"No, of course not, my little sweet Gina."

"I'll *sweet* you, you lying shit!" She picked up a magazine and threw it on the floor. "Hey Gina!" she said in a faux baritone. "You think your uncle Tony can get me a car like that one for undercover action at the high school?" She snatched up a handful of receipts and shook them at him. "*Christ*, Tony! As if it isn't hard enough for me to establish credibility on the force just being a woman!" She hurled the receipts at the wall.

Tony stepped past her, shutting the door. "Gina, sweetheart, amorosa, keep it down a little. The customers will hear you."

"Customers my ass. Just what the fuck do you think you're doing fencing a drug dealer's car?"

"Now, Gina, you're going too far. We got papers on that car. Vito assures me that there was no funny stuff."

"Vito! Vito assures you! Oh, I am *so* relieved." Gina placed her hand on her breast, rolling her eyes. "You can't imagine my relief. Do you know who used to own that car? I note with interest you don't seem to need an explanation of exactly *what* car we're talking about."

"Some punk named Sonny from your old beat, is what I hear. So what?"

"And, how, might I ask, did it end up here?"

"Like I said, we got papers, so it ain't none of my business. But, since you're asking, what I heard was this putz Sonny borrowed some money from some people, and put his car up as collateral. I guess he didn't pay his debt, and they snagged it. Vito knows some people who know these people, and he picks it up for a good price yesterday morning. He calls me about unloading it, and I'm standing here talking to some numbnuts who says he's looking for a Plymouth. Vito drives it over, and Numbnuts buys it. Bada bing, bada boom." Tony gave Gina a beseeching look; Gina leaned on the doorframe, clearly unimpressed.

"Look, Gina," continued Tony. "I made Numbnuts a very happy man. He loved it. I didn't even screw him on the price! Listen. How come you got such an interest in this affair?"

"I spotted Sonny's car about three this morning in Ballard. Hank and I gave this guy a hard time he didn't deserve." She looked out the office window. "Vishnu was pretty rattled." She sighed. "I don't think he knows what he's got himself into."

Tony studied her side-lit profile. "By the way," he said. "How's Chuck?"

Gina's head snapped around. "Chuck?"

"Ain't that your boyfriend's name?" He tipped his head back, and looked at her from hooded eyes.

"Chuck is *not* my boyfriend. He's just a guy I've gone out with a couple of times."

Tony grunted. "Maybe I got it wrong. I thought your mother said he was your boyfriend."

"Oh for God's sake. Mom says that about every guy I make eye contact with. She's been trying to fix me up since I was sixteen. You know that." She cocked her head. "And why are you so interested in Chuck, all of a sudden?"

"Just a feelin'. Forget it."

"What?" Gina demanded.

Tony looked at her for a moment. "What I mean, if you need me to spell it out, is I get the feeling you like this guy."

"Which guy?"

"This Vishnu guy."

"Like him? I don't even know him! He's just some guy we pulled over in Ballard. I recognized his car, and thought he was one of Sonny's crew. Vishnu's just a bike mechanic who owns a shop in Ballard. What do you mean, I *like* him?"

"He's a biker? Whose shop does he work at?"

"*Bicycle* shop," clarified Gina. "He owns his own *bicycle* shop."

"Bicycles!" Tony barked a laugh. "Now that fits! Perfect for a numbnuts!"

"And what's wrong with bicycles? It's a perfectly legitimate business. Unlike some." Gina glared at Tony.

Tony laughed again, and then grew serious. “Look Gina. Two things. First, the car sale was legit. It may not have come about in the usual manner, but the paperwork was straight. I’m not lyin’ to ya on this, OK?” He looked her in the eyes until she nodded. “Second thing. Don’t mix business with pleasure. It’s bad luck. Third thing. Tell me straight. Do you like this guy? I mean, *like* him?”

“That's three things, not two.”

Tony raised his chin and gave her his hooded-eye look and let the silence hang. Gina hesitated. She couldn’t say that she didn’t like Vishnu. She couldn’t say that she did, really, since she didn't really know him. But there *was* something about him that stuck in her mind.

“Gina.” Tony's voice was uncharacteristically soft, conveying how much he really cared for her. “Gina, sweetie. Look, maybe he ain’t a numbnuts. Maybe he’s OK. But I don’t see how he’s got anything in common with you. Listen to me. I know people. It’s my business.”

“It’s my business too, Uncle Tony,” she said with a little smile. “Maybe that’s why we get along.”

The door swung open, and Vito stepped inside the office. He looked from Tony to Gina. “Hiya, kid.”

“Hi, Uncle Vito,” said Gina. She and Vito looked at each other like two cats in an alley. The three of them stood in an awkward silence. “Well, I gotta go,” said Gina finally. Bye Uncle Tony.” Gina gave him a hug and a kiss. She turned to Vito. “Bye Uncle Vito,” with a hug but no kiss.

“Bye, kid,” said Vito as Gina walked out the door. “Trouble?” he said as Gina roared out of the lot.

“Nah,” said Tony, staring out at Aurora. “She just stopped by to say hi.”

Fifteen

Orange sparks showered down like the Fourth of July as a man on a scaffold modified a davit twenty feet in the air. He flipped up his goggles and yelled something in Russian to his mate on the deck of the big seine boat. His mate tossed him a welding rod. The welder caught it with one hand, began to turn back to his task, then said something else to his friend. They cast appreciative looks at the dark-haired woman walking slowly up the C dock at Fisherman's Terminal. They assumed she was just one more curious tourist who had wandered out to where the bigger boats were moored.

In fact, Gina knew every inch of these docks.

Her dad, Janusz Kowalski, had been a fifth-generation fisherman, a second generation American, and a Seattle native. Starting on his father's boat on Puget Sound hardly past learning to walk, by age twenty-one he'd firmly established himself in the highrolling Alaskan fisheries. To Jan and everyone who knew him, it seemed the fates had woven him a life of salt air and pitching decks. No one anticipated that this man of nets could himself be ensnared, three days before his sixth trip to Dutch Harbor, by a black-eyed, black-haired girl at a backyard party. A girl who matched his every jest and gibe with a better one of her own, delivered in a New York accent with full-force Italian hand waving. Fate, heritage, and plans be what they may, but when the Lucky Lady sailed out of Fisherman's Terminal into the May sunset three days after that backyard party, Jan was waving from the dock, his arm around the black-haired girl.

As for twenty-two-year-old Remilda Ivelia Romano, when she came west to Seattle from the Bronx to stay for a couple of weeks with a wayward friend, she hadn't planned to stay, and she sure as hell hadn't planned to fall in love. Not with a city that was tiny and parochial compared to The City, not with the mountains and clean water, and certainly not with a young fisherman whose claims to fame were a rapier wit, a winning smile, and a left hand missing a pinkie from a dispute with a power winch. But somehow, in the same way that Jan had missed his planned departure on the Lucky Lady, Remi was nowhere near the Greyhound station when her bus rolled back to New York.

The Seattle summer melted away, and by September it was clear that neither Jan nor Remi was going anywhere. By September, Jan had opted for a share on a local gillnetter and the opportunity to step off the dock into his new wife's arms. One September later, their first and only child was born, and Jan had permanently given up the rolling decks for the relative safety of a welder's apron at a Salmon Bay shipyard. Even so, for years after Jan quit fishing, he and Gina still knew most every captain and boat at the terminal, and Gina was the queen and mascot of many.

But life is fickle. Jan, who left one of the most dangerous occupations in America to increase the odds of a long and happy life with his family, died in a run-of-the-mill conflict with a dump truck on the way home from work, two weeks after Gina's twenty-fifth birthday. Remi remained in the Greenwood house she had shared with Jan, but she never went down to the docks after he died. Gina, however, went there whenever she needed some time to think, or just to commune with her dad. For her, it was like going to the park where she'd played as a kid. The salmon fishery was basically gone from Puget Sound well before the end of the '90s, and by then few of the boats were familiar, but that was immaterial. The docks would always be Gina's.

Sitting at a vacant slip near the end of the dock, Gina rested her elbows on her knees, her chin in her hands, watching the water, the gulls, and the traffic on the Ballard Bridge. She'd intended to define whatever it was that was bugging her, using her typical no-nonsense manner, splitting it into workable pieces, whittling them down until she could cleave each in twain with a clean stroke of logic. The trouble was, she couldn't seem to get past the first step.

The obvious problem was Tony, up to his usual dirty dealings, but he'd sworn his dealings with Sonny's car were on the up-and-up. And she believed him, as far as she could, although anything that involved both Tony and Sonny was unlikely to be squeaky clean. But that didn't feel like the real problem. Her mind went back to the convenience store, Vishnu standing there in his jeans and dopey t-shirt, smiling nervously at her as he described his bicycle. Her mind, as it had the night before, replaced the jeans and t-shirt with a pair of black Lycra shorts and a tight green jersey. "Jesus, get a grip," she muttered, pushing the image away. It was replaced by the memory of Hank's voice over the radio as she drove away from the store. "My pleasure, Vishnu!" he'd yelped, losing himself in hoots of laughter. "Would you like to see my shop, Officer Kowalski? Oh, yes, Mr. Tensleep! I'd *love* to see your tools!" It was going to take months to live that encounter down.

As she invariably did in these circumstances, Gina pulled her cell out of her jacket pocket and dialed her mother.

"Hello?"

"Hi, Mom. It's Gina." Gina always said this, as though she was not an only child, and there were lots of people who called Remi 'Mom.'

"Gina, honey! Where are you?" Remi always said this, as though Gina sometimes rang her up from Thailand.

"I'm down here at the dock."

"Mmm. Something on your mind?"

"It's Tony. Tony and Vito," began Gina. "They drive me crazy, Mom. They're always pulling some bullshit and one of these days they're gonna go too far."

"Really."

"I'm not kidding, Mom."

"I know you aren't, honey. I'm sure you recall that I've been watching them pull their bullshit, as you call it, for around fifty years now. Ever since they delivered it in diapers, as a matter of fact." Remi sighed. "Is it the same old thing, or is it something special this time?"

"I don't know. I really don't. Actually, it's probably just the same old thing. I don't know why it's got my goat this time." Gina heard Remi light up a cigarette. "Mom. Goddammit, are you smoking? You told me you quit!"

"Yes, dear, I did tell you that. And yes, I'm smoking. Will it make you feel better if I put it out? Here, I've put it out."

"Goddamnit, Mom! Why are you doing that? Don't you know it's dangerous? Why do you want to do something you can die from? Don't you know I love you? *Jesus!*"

Remi was silent for a moment, then said softly, "You know, that's just what I used to tell Tony and Vito. Vito would make some smart remark, and Tony would just look at me with those big eyes and tell me he loved me too, and to mind my own business, big sister. And it used to make me so mad. It still does." Another pause. "So, have you seen Chuck lately?"

"*Chuck*? What *is* it with everyone asking me about Chuck?"

"Sorry, honey, I just thought I'd ask. Who's been asking you about Chuck?"

"Tony, for starters. And he said you told him that Chuck was my boyfriend. I mean, what the hell's up with that, Mom?"

"Did I say that? I don't think I did. I think I told him that you'd gone out with him a couple of times, and that you seemed happy. And you brought Chuck by to meet me, remember? I thought you wanted to introduce him to me."

"Oh, for God's sake, Mom, I was returning the coat you'd left at my place! Like you asked me to. Remember? I wasn't bringing Chuck by for a Romano clan inspection. Sometimes I feel like you and Tony are putting me up on the auction block, with my dowry chest and a sprig of basil in my hair!"

"Sweetie, is this what you called to talk about?"

"No," groaned Gina.

"Then what is it, honey?"

"Oh, Mom, I don't know. Maybe it's nothing. Yesterday Tony and Vito sold this guy a car that used to belong to a drug dealer, and this guy doesn't know it, and I'm worried that the dealer is gonna come after this guy, and, oh hell, I don't know. I'm just worried."

"Tell me more, honey."

"I'm not sure how much more there is. Hank and I pulled this guy over last night because I recognized the car. I don't think he has anything to do with the previous owner."

"How do you know, honey?"

"Well, I can just tell. He's just not the type. In my business, you get to know people, and I'm sure this guy's just what he says he is. He owns a bicycle shop, and plays in a band, and lives down on Canal Street."

"And you found all this out from a traffic stop? Does he have a name?"

"Kind of. I mean, it was kind of a traffic stop. And his name's Vishnu. Vishnu Tensleep."

"Interesting name. He sounds Indian."

"Actually, he looks Italian, if you can believe it. Or maybe Greek. Or maybe just American. I mean, he *is* American, he just looks Italian. He's got dark, curly hair, and is built like a bike rider. Sort of wiry, kind of tall. He's into bikes. Bicycles. And…" Gina suddenly felt she was wading into the muddy bottom of Too Much Information Bay. "But this really isn't why I called, Mom."

"Whatever you say, dear."

"Look, Mom, he's just a guy I met. I only met him last night. It's not like we even *met*, really. Hank and I just pulled him over."

"As you say, honey. It just sounded like you got to know a little more about him than your standard turn-signal violator, that's all. He sounds nice. Is he nice?"

"Look, Mom." Gina was standing now, alternately waving her right hand and parking it defiantly on her hip. "Look, Mom. How would I know if he's nice? And who said anything about a turn signal. For all you know, he ran a red light and flattened an old lady!"

"Of course, dear. What *did* you pull him over for?"

"Turn signal," Gina muttered.

"What was that, honey? I couldn't hear you." Not for nothing had Remilda Ivelia Romaño Kowalski been raised by Sophia Ivelia Collecini Romano.

Gina covered the phone with her palm and and howled pure inarticulate frustration to the skies. "*Turn Signal*," she shouted into the phone. "*Turn*! *Signal*! *T—U—R—N—Signal*! Honest to *God*, Mom, you drive me crazy! How could you *possibly* know that?"

Remi laughed. "You don't have to yell, honey. I can hear, you know. And it's called motherly intuition. Don't ask me how it works. But if you're worried about this Vishnu fellow, why not just call and tell him. You don't have to make it personal. You could just tell him your concerns. It's his business what he does from there."

"Yeah. I guess I could do that," allowed Gina, eager to quit while she was behind. "I could just look up his number in the book."

"Or you could just stop by on your way home and leave him a note," offered Remi, sounding like she'd just thought of it. "Didn't you say he lives on Canal Street?"

"Uh, yeah, I guess so. I mean, right, that's where he lives." Gina thought about it. Did she really want to see him again? A phone call was business. On the phone, he would automatically think she was Officer Kowalski, even in her bathrobe and pink bunny slippers. A personal visit, off-duty, in civilian clothes, was ambiguous. It required her to take the initiative to define just what the hell she was up to.

"Gina? Are you there, honey?"

"Yeah, mom. Sorry. I got a little distracted."

"Well, you just think about things," said Remi. "I'm sure everything will work out fine. Thanks for calling, honey. You have a good evening. Give me a call in a few days to let me know how things work out, OK?"

"Yeah, Mom, sure thing. Bye."

"Bye, sweetie."

Gina slipped the phone back into her pocket, and walked back down the dock, slowly at first, then more quickly. I'll just stop quickly by his house, and tell him about the car, she thought to herself. I can do that. I don't need to get into anything personal. But he really should know about this, as soon as possible. If he isn't there, I'll just leave my card, and he can call me at work tomorrow. And if he's there, it will be no big deal, she thought, trying to ignore the fact that she hoped he'd be home.

Sixteen

Remi hung up the phone and looked out into the little front yard of her Greenwood house. The climbing roses glowed pink on their metal arbor, which had been Gina's swing set in a former life. Behind it was the apple tree Jan planted the first year they'd bought the house, the first year of their marriage, the year before there had been a Gina to have a swing set. After Gina flew the nest, they'd left the swingset in place, planning for the day when they'd refurbish it so another generation of dirty-faced kids could squeal with delight as Jan pushed them higher and higher. Neither she nor Jan had planned on what happened that September afternoon. He'd refused to get rid of his old pickup on the grounds that nothing could best it in a wreck. Jan...

Remi sighed, picked up her pack of Winstons, and mused about what Gina had said about Tony and Vito. She and Jan, bless his soul, had spent enough breath to blow up a zeppelin trying to get the Romano brothers to change their ways. Ricky, the baby of the family who had stayed in New York, was the only straight one of the three brothers, earning the thinly veiled mocking of Tony and the open derision of Vito. But there was more to Gina's call than a complaint about her uncles' behavior.

Placing the cigarettes back on the table, Remi picked up the phone and dialed.

"Yeah?"

"Tony, is that any way to answer your office phone?"

"Whaddaya mean? It's after hours. Jeez, sis, how's about hello?"

"Sorry, honey. I just thought I'd call to see how you were. How was your day?"

"OK. Pretty good."

"Make any good sales today?"

"Not too bad. A nice Caddy and a piece of crap Chevy."

"That's nice. How about yesterday?"

"'Bout the same. Coupla rice burners, and a...yeah. That's about it. Hey! Did I tell ya I seen Warren Poggioli's mom? She's lookin' great for, what, must be eighty-five years old?" Tony's voice was packed with enthusiasm about a fictitious meeting with a notoriously foul-tempered old woman.

"Really. How wonderful. I remember she always used to give Gina candy," Remi lied in turn. "Speaking of Gina, have you seen her lately?"

"Gina! Funny you should ask, Sis. She stopped by the lot just this afternoon. We had a real nice chat. Real nice."

"Talk about anything special?" asked Remi. "I hardly hear from her anymore. Ever since she started seeing Chuck," she added, as if by afterthought.

Tony snorted. "I don't think that's goin' anywheres fast."

"Really. Why is that?"

"Sounded like they had a fight or somethin'. I asked her about him, and she was all over me. Course, she probably just pissed Chuck off. Nothin' like a Romano woman for that."

"Now, Tony, you should speak nicely of your niece."

"I'm only jokin', Sis. Least about her. Heh heh."

"Nobody else?"

"Say again?"

"Gina didn't mention anyone else besides Chuck?"

"No. Nobody but—no. Not that I recall."

"That's funny. Somehow I think I remember her talking about someone else."

"Huh. Don't ring a bell."

"Really. She said it was someone who bought a car from you."

"From me?"

"Yes. Yes, it's coming back to me now. It was yesterday."

"What was?"

"When you sold this man a car. You sold it to him yesterday."

"I did?"

"Yes, you did. And she said there was something funny going on. Let me think. Yes. She was worried, about something bad happening to the car. Or maybe it was something bad that might happen to the man who bought it?" Remi gave Tony a moment in which to comment; he declined the offer. "Now, little brother," Remi went on, "is Gina just being a little worrywart, as you sometimes call her, or is there something you'd like to tell me?"

A clock ticked in Remi's kitchen as she listened to Tony trying to figure out where the conversation went into the ditch. She pulled a Winston out of the pack and lined it up neatly next to her lighter on the table. A victory smoke, for later.

"What'd *you* tell her?" Tony finally got out.

"Oh, you know. I told her it was probably nothing to worry about."

"Is that right."

"Pretty much." Remi waited until she thought she heard Tony relax his breath. "Yes, that was about it. I just told her it was probably nothing, and she ought to just go over to the man's house and tell him there was nothing to worry about."

"You *what?*"

"Sorry, honey, I'll speak slower. I Told Her To—"

"I heard you already!" Tony cut her off.

"Why, honey, is something wrong? Is there some reason Gina shouldn't go see this man? Is he a *dangerous* man?"

Tony chuckled mirthlessly. "Not fuckin' likely."

"Then what is it, dear?" questioned Remi, unable to disguise her own enjoyment. She rarely got the chance, within the span of an hour, and handed to her on a forked stick, to meddle helpfully in her daughter's love life and also grill her kid brother over some of his dubious activities. "What is it dear?" she repeated. "Is it something about the car? Something Gina shouldn't know?"

"Feh. Ain't nothin' she don't know already. Look, Sis, since you've obviously been diggin' into this with Gina, I'll tell you what I told her. The car is legit. Usta belong to some putz from her old beat. Vito got it legal, and we sold it to a numbnuts named Vince."

"Vince. Now that's interesting. I could swear Gina said his name was Vishnu." Remi visualized her little brother squinting in frustration.

In fact, at that moment he was gesturing obscenely at her smiling face in the family reunion photo on his desk. "And just *how* the fuck do you know all this if you never talk to her?" he got out through clenched teeth.

Remi laughed musically. "Almost never. You know how Gina is. But back to the car, little brother." Remi's musical tone took on some steel. "Is there, or is there not, some reason for Gina to be worried? Don't lie to me. I can see right through you. You and Vito both. Always could, always will. And remember, I'm talking about my daughter now. If there's anything you need to tell me, you'd better spill it."

"Look, there's nothin'! Nothin' beyond Gina always wantin' to stick her nose in where it don't belong." Tony waited for Remi to say something indicating acceptance. "Look, Sis, I ain't lyin' to you!"

Remi let Tony twist in the wind for a few moments. "OK, little brother," she said finally. "I'll take your word for it. I'll find out the truth anyway. I always do." And with that said, her voice shifted back to Benevolent Big Sister. "Well, sweetie, thanks for the chat. You have a nice evening. Say hello to Vito for me. Don't stay up too late."

"Yeah. You too. Right. G'night, Sis." The line went dead.

Remi returned the receiver to its cradle and leaned back in her chair. Immediately the phone rang. She picked it up. "Hello?"

"Remi! This is Bev. Listen, hon, you got a bored divorcee on your hands. There's open bowling at the Sunset tonight, and I won't take no for an answer!"

They'd teamed up as young parents in the neighborhood: tall lanky Bev from eastern Oregon with her cowboy boots and rodeo-queen blond bouffant, and short black-haired Remi from the Big Apple. Grade school parent meetings, high school dance chaperoning, Bev's divorce. Bev had practically saved Remi's life when Jan died, and got her a job at the same little law office where she worked. The two of them had run the show there for almost fifteen years now. "When are you picking me up?" asked Remi.

Bev let out a whoop. "Hot dang! I knew I could count on you! I'll be there in twenty."

"I'll be on the porch. We've got some girl talk to do."

"Nothing bad, I hope?"

"I don't think so. Just the usual stuff with Tony, and Gina's involved somehow. But the bright side is, I think there's a man in the picture for Gina."

"Oooh, Lordy! I can't wait. See you in a few!"

Remi hung up the phone, picked up the cigarette, smelled it, lit it, and gazed out the window into the evening sky, exhaling luxuriously out of her nose like some forgotten Italian cinema queen.

Seventeen

In Seattle, in mid-July, the sun drops below the horizon at about nine o'clock, but because the city is actually farther north than the northern tip of Maine, true darkness doesn't come until about ten-thirty.

For some people, the gradual transition between sunlight and darkness is a time for sitting outside, talking of this and that with a friend, or just contemplating life while the night drifts slowly in on warm breezes. For others, it is the time for preparation, a last-minute adjusting of armor, a quick brush-up on one's lines, a final equipment check before heading out to do business in the night.

At nine-thirty on Saturday evening, the gravel lot of Tony's Tigers was bathed in a surreal, garish glow of waning daylight mixed with mercury-vapor streetlamps. Shadows were cast in unexpected directions, and colors were slightly askew.

Out on Aurora Avenue, the daytime people had gone home, and the night people were emerging from their holes and clefts. The freaks, the predators, the misfits, the hookers, the johns, the thrillseekers, the curious, the distorted, the lost. All arriving for the night shift on the old highway. It was a study sketch of Hell by Hieronymus Bosch, with angelic lighting courtesy of Maxfield Parrish.

Aurora Avenue is a world unto itself. Interstate 5 is the young road, a freeway conceived in the Eisenhower era and finished in the '60s. Interstate 5 transports more people than Aurora, but I-5 is limited-access. The old road, Aurora, has no limits to access; it is fair game to all who come, and all who come are fair game. Sometimes people die on I-5, but nobody lives on I-5. On Aurora, people live, and die, twenty-four hours a day.

In the cluttered office of Tony's Tigers, Tony had completed his day's work, and was sitting in his padded leather-look chair, his feet on the desk, his chair back leaning against the wall. His eyes wandered out the window, across the lot, and came to rest on Aurora, with its battered bus stop and mix of auto-accessible sleaze. Not exactly heaven, but OK, all things considered. It wasn't pastoral; it was closer to the old 42nd Street in Manhattan. But on a good day, it was almost Madison Square Garden, and he had a ringside seat.

1967. That was the year Sergeant Tony Romano had arrived in Seattle, just discharged honorably from the United States Army's First Infantry. In the Big Red One, Tony had been given the chance to visit fascinating new places with names like Ap Taou, meet interesting people, and kill them before they could return the favor. Unlike many of his less fortunate comrades, Tony came through his tour without major change to his emotional makeup. It wasn't that he hadn't seen things that no one should have to see, or done things he wished he didn't have to do; if you were at the battle of Ho Krignou in 1966, you probably did both or you didn't go home. But in many ways, the jungle just south of the Cambodian border wasn't much different than the jungles of the South Bronx or Hell's Kitchen where he'd run as a kid with Vito. Life was tough, and there were a lot of tough people out there, and smart ones too, and you had to be tougher and smarter than them or they'd kick the shit out of you. Nothing personal, friend. It's just how it is.

Vito had come out to Seattle before Tony, in 1965, to see what their oldest sister Remi was raving about. By the time Tony hit town, Vito had made connections. Remi's husband Jan had introduced Vito to a number of his fishing-boat friends, and Vito had taken it from there. Jan was as straight as they come, but you can't work as a commercial fisherman without rubbing elbows with a few people who've figured out that fish are only one of many things you can carry in the hold of a fishing boat, and that it's a big, big ocean out there, and that it's useful to have good people to meet you at the dock when it's time to unload the catch.

Between Vito's dockside connections and mechanical skills, Tony's facility with people, and a few old family friends who had previously emigrated west, there was enough in place in 1967 to launch Romano Brothers, Ltd., a full-service automobile repair, sales, and transport company. Of course, if certain valued customers needed to repair, transport, or sell a car, or some other piece of equipment, without the need for pesky questions or cumbersome paperwork, the Romano brothers were always willing to oblige. Vito handled the nuts and bolts, and Tony handled the people. It was how they'd always worked, and it was a winning combination.

Were those early days in Seattle the good old days? Hard to say, thought Tony, as he scratched himself in a personal spot and gazed out into the growing darkness. Things seemed simpler in the old days. Things were complicated now. Or maybe he was just getting soft.

Tony was fretting. He'd been fretting since Gina came by and gave him the idea that she might be interested in Numbnuts. In and of itself, this conversation wouldn't have stood much of a chance against Tony's ability to rationalize away his concerns. But the call from Remi had really twisted his tail, not only confirming Gina's interest in Numbnuts but giving Tony the news that she had probably taken Remi's suggestion and gone over to his place. Jesus fucking Christ, what was Remi thinking?

Tony wasn't used to fretting, and he didn't like it. He was used to making crisp, quick decisions. Life was a fast game, played hard, and he enjoyed it. He liked winning, and didn't worry much about the losers. Even when he lost, he didn't worry about it much; he just tried to figure out why, and to make sure he had a chance to even the score.

This was not to say that Tony only lived his life for himself, or that he had no loyalties. On the contrary, he was to-the-death loyal to his tribe, which consisted of his family and a few close friends. If he'd learned one thing in an Italian family in the Bronx, and in the Big Red One, he'd learned that blood was thicker than tar, and that in the jungle, whether concrete or tropical, a person needs to be able to count on his buddy to watch his back, and that meant watching his buddy's back.

But this view of life implies that there is a boundary to the tribe. A person can't trust everybody, and there isn't much of a game without an opposing team. Tony accepted these facts, consciously and without question. In this way, he was the complete opposite of a politically-correct, I-love-everybody, standard middle-class Seattle liberal like Heather. Heather's actual tribe was just about as big as Tony's, but she wouldn't admit she even had a tribe. Heather wept for the oppressed in the abstract, but avoided looking at the "Made In China" tags on her underwear because she didn't want to think about where they really came from. Compared to Heather, Tony was a hell of a lot clearer to himself, and everyone else, about who was in his tribe, who was not, and what anyone could expect from Tony in either case.

Tony lit a cheap cigar and clamped it in his teeth, eyes slitted against the smoke. A minor drug deal was going down at the bus stop, providing a welcome distraction for Tony. He smirked, made a derisive noise in his throat. Fuckin' punks. Let 'em rot their brains. Every brain cell they waste is an opportunity for me.

Such were the words Tony told himself. But way, way down inside, there was another voice. His conscience was talking to him. The sound was very soft and distant, like the sound a king might hear when a prisoner in the dungeon banged a stone on a rusty pipe. Tony had ignored that sound for so many years that he had come to hear it as just another banging, like a dented can rolling down the street in the wind. But tonight, the part of him that was fretting was also listening to that sound, and the voice behind it.

Tony turned his thoughts to the day's conversation with Gina. So what's the big deal, he thought? I gave Numbnuts a good deal on the car. A great deal. (Bullshit, said the faraway voice. You unloaded it because it was trouble.)

What's his name? Vishnu Tensleep. Not such a bad guy, I guess, for a numbnuts. Gina's worried about Sonny looking for his ride. But what's the chance of that? And even if he did, what's the chance he could find it? (Probably not much less than if you were looking for it. And you could find it in forty-eight hours, anywhere on the west coast.)

No, the real problem is Gina. Why's she always gotta have a thing for charity cases? (The real problem is that you put someone in danger, and this time the danger followed you home. Followed Gina home.)

Gina's always been like that. Like that time she brought home that wormy puppy from the box outside the Safeway when she was ten, and pitched such a fit that Remi and Jan let her keep it. Gina will get over it. No sense in worrying about it. (Maybe so, but you're worried anyway.)

Outside, the light was almost entirely artificial now, except for a deep blue stripe of twilight on the top of Phinney Ridge. On the far side of Aurora, in the southbound parking lane, two teenage prostitutes were leaning into the window of a beat-up pickup. The truck windows were tinted; Tony couldn't see the driver. One of the girls climbed into the truck, and it roared off. The other girl backed up onto the sidewalk, standing alone under a streetlight, looking expectantly up the road. Skinny, dark hair cropped short, clutching a small pink purse.

A wisp of cigar smoke rose in front of Tony's face, and by a trick of mind and eye the girl became Gina. It was just for a moment, but in that moment the thought flashed across Tony's mind that he should go out there, find her a safe room for the night, give her some money, buy her dinner. Just for that moment, he was worried about her; about her friend in the truck; about Gina. And then it all started to slide, and he worried about Vishnu; about various other people he'd screwed in deals big and small. About Salve Fortunado, his childhood nemesis, who had broken Tony's nose with a brick in an alley fight in '61 and who ended up in Sing Sing. About the Vietnamese woman whose guts he had blown out on that jungle trail outside of An Loc in '66. About that woman's little daughter, maybe five or six years old, who'd stood there beside the trail and just looked at him with those bottomless black eyes. Eyes just like Gina's.

And then the moment passed, and the smoke cleared. It was just too much for Tony to bear, and he sent the jailer down into the dungeon of his soul to shut that goddamned prisoner up.

"What am I thinkin'," he said aloud to himself in the darkness of his little room, looking at the girl under the light. "That chick's gonna make more money tonight than I clear in a week. Besides, we all make choices. It's not my problem. It is *not* my problem."

Tony stubbed out his cigar and hoisted himself out of his chair. It was time to roll back to the condo, grab a shower, maybe head up to one of the roadhouses to see where the action was. Time to pack it in for another day.

Eighteen

As the early evening cast its golden glow over the fair and gentle Emerald City of Love, Vishnu hunkered behind locked doors with curtains drawn. He hunkered in his office by the lone light of a reading lamp, nursing a cup of coffee, scared and trying to figure just what in the hell he was going to do.

Right on the face of the situation, Vishnu was scared simply by being near the guns and the drugs. Previous to the last fifteen hours, and ignoring standard childhood stuff, Vishnu's forays into lawbreaking had gone no farther than minor recreational drug use. Even this had tapered off dramatically in the last decade to a few tokes per year at a backyard barbecue or outside a tent high in the Cascades. He generally figured it was best to carefully marshal all of his remaining mental resources. Now he was in possession of a big wad of powdered who-knew-what, and not one, not two, but five hairy-looking firearms. Vishnu had a healthy respect for guns of all kinds. He wasn't handy with them, but as a mechanic they were interesting devices. A lot of force precisely channeled by a mechanism less complicated than a two-speed coaster brake hub. But appreciating clever applications of engineering principles was one thing, and ending up with a bag of handguns in the back of his car was quite another. And Vishnu didn't know a lot about guns, but he knew enough to know that the main purpose of the ones in the bag was to blow big holes in human beings from close range. He was also acutely aware that the rightful owner of these items probably wanted them back, and the owner might not cheerfully accept Vishnu's statements about how he had acquired them.

For that matter what would have happened if the cops had searched the trunk during last night's Stop-N-Shop escapade? Vishnu imagined himself face down on the asphalt of the parking lot, the barrel of Gina's sidearm against the bony knob behind his ear, while Hank yanked his arms up behind him to slap steel cuffs on his wrists. His stomach churned.

But these concerns, large as they were, were only the surface. One level down, Vishnu was scared by the feeling that his life was spinning out of control. Two days ago, he was fixing bikes, having a beer with Hans, talking about garden-variety girlfriend problems. Now he was driving around in a bad-ass car, sparring with the local cops, and harboring a small arsenal and enough drugs to give whatever effects they gave to half of Ballard.

Deeper yet, Vishnu was worried about ethical deterioration. In his decision to buy the 'Cuda, he'd casually shrugged off his own concerns that it didn't fit with his poorly-articulated ethical system, telling himself that anyone who had trouble with his choice was a tightass. And Evan, who had embraced Vishnu's new car like long-lost family, had delivered his diatribe about vehicular / personal image half in jest, and certainly not as a moral imperative. But in the last day and a quarter, Vishnu had frightened Arnie and Edith, ended up in a rhubarb with the police, and nearly alienated a paying customer, all for the selfish and purely illogical pleasure of a silly car. Could he be a socially thoughtful, environmentalist, bike-loving, carbon-footprint-minimizing kind of guy, and at the same time drive a loud, obnoxious, gas-guzzling, fume-exuding, populous-offending car for the simple reason that the car was exactly those things? And how did the guns and drugs tie into this? Did not the Great Traditions of the world, each in its own way, hold that deed follows thought, and that overall form of life follows deed? That we attract precisely that upon which we meditate? That a slopdolly approach to the daily particulars was the same as standing in life's whaleboat with your foot, Ahab-like, in the coil of fate's rope, waiting for the Big Whatever to give a well-timed pull on the other end? Was ownership of a nasty-ass muscle car a harbinger of moral decay? Was it maybe even a sign of deterioration already so advanced that Vishnu couldn't even be trusted to self-evaluate? Were the guns and the drugs a test, or were they his scored exam paper, marked at the top with a big red F?

Vishnu might have stopped at this level of discourse and settled into a thoroughly enjoyable bout of moral self-flagellation, followed by a gratifyingly smug decision to rid himself immediately of his new car and all of its contents like a dieter swears off chocolate cream pie, were it not for the deepest feeling: it wasn't just the car. He was enjoying all the hoopla. It was a hot and spicy desert wind, long overdue, blowing some of the leaves off his little well-tended tree of life, but blowing the dust away as well. Some long-standing itch was being scratched, and it felt good, and this feeling was sapping his commitment to do the obvious.

He tried to turn his mind from abstractions to the need for a plan of action. He obviously couldn't keep the guns and the drugs, but what the hell should he do? He could wait for dark and just toss the gym bag in the canal. But what if the former owner of the 'Cuda located it and wanted the merchandise back? Vishnu visualized a compulsory diving expedition, hog-tied and sporting the latest in concrete footwear.

He could call the cops. Oh, right. Drive up to the North Precinct in a car apparently on the shit list of the local police, fish a big bag of drugs and handguns out of the trunk, walk in and drop them on the desk. "Hellooo! Can I talk to Gina? I forgot to show these to her last night. Someone must have left them in my car before they sold it to me. Well, I've got to hop. Toodle-oo!" And, as with the previous option, this approach wouldn't solve the problem of possessing a car that some drug lord might be looking for.

He could drop the bag into the canal and sell the 'Cuda to the first used car dealer he could find, which would solve all of the problems. But, as the Bard wrote, "Aye, there's the rub." Vishnu had a car he couldn't keep without drawing either the cops or some unknown drug dealer down on him, and he wasn't going to get rid of it. He studied the shadows cast by his little desk lamp. "You've really got a screw loose, my friend," he said aloud.

As he cast about for another option, he heard a car pull to a stop in the driveway. A car door opened and closed, and someone knocked softly on the roll-up door. His balls retracted into their sockets. Beads of sweat popped out on his face. Tears welled in his eyes. The drug dealers had come for him. They had come to kill him. They couldn't afford to let him live, knowing what he knew.

Again the knock, and a voice. "Vishnu?" A female voice. "Vishnu, are you in there?" Not Heather. Vaguely familiar. "Vishnu, it's Gina."

So it had come to this. Gina and Hank had captured the drug dealer, hung him upside-down in a concrete room until he'd confessed about the dope, and now they'd come to finish the job. Vishnu's mind replayed the last scene in Butch Cassidy and the Sundance Kid. Vishnu flinging the side door open, desperately tearing up the street on his mechanical steed into Bolivian Ballard, only to be shredded into hamburger and bone fragments in a hail of lead.

"Vishnu, I need to talk to you. Are you home?" Gina knocked again.

He was a dead man. Or at least imprisoned. What did they do to thirty-nine-year-old bicycle shop owners in the state pen? Vishnu didn't want to know. Yet what was there to do? They had him. Resigned to his fate, he made his way quietly to the front door. "Gina?" he said.

"Vishnu! You're there!"

"I'm opening the door now."

"OK."

"I'm going to open the door slowly. With my right hand."

"OK."

"I'm alone in here. Just so you know. There's no one else with me."

"Vishnu, are you OK?"

"I'm fine. I'm opening the door now. Nice and slow. Here I go now, opening the door."

And true to his word, he rolled up the door, nice and slow, expecting to see a squadron of police cruisers, lights blazing, with about forty high-powered weapons of all description trained on him. Instead, of course, he found one black Fiat Spider, devoid of emergency lights, and one pretty woman wearing civilian garb.

"Was there something wrong with the door?"

Vishnu had no prepared response. He had gone in about sixty seconds from death by a pack of drug dealers, to five years in the pokey, to a visit from a single (and good-looking, and possibly single) female cop. Further, she was out of uniform. It dawned on Vishnu that maybe she knew nothing about his dirty little secrets. Maybe. "You came alone," he ventured.

Gina made a show of looking around. "I guess so."

They stood there looking at one another. "Would you like to come in?" he asked finally.

"Yes."

"This part here is my shop," he explained as she followed him. "I live in the back. Could I offer you something to drink, maybe some tea or coffee?"

"Coffee would be nice." Gina looked around at his apartment as Vishnu went to pour her a cup of coffee. "You really do have a band," she said, looking at the amplifier and the drum kit compressed in a corner.

"Yeah. Just some friends who come over to play jazz."

"Jazz?"

"Yeah."

"I've never known anyone who played jazz."

"Well, now you do."

"I guess so."

Vishnu fumbled with the cups and the conversation. "So, uh, Gina, what brings you by?"

"Funny you should ask."

"Do you take anything in it?"

"Hmm?"

"Your coffee."

"Milk would be nice," she said.

"Milk I have. As long as you don't mind stolen milk."

"What?"

"The milk. When we walked out of the store last night so you could inspect my car, I had it in my hand. I was so nervous I just drove home with it. I didn't even think about it until I got back here."

Gina laughed. "Well, given that we walked you out to the parking lot, I guess it's fair game. I won't take you in for this one."

"Oh, I paid for it. When I left for my ride this morning I went up there and paid first thing." He looked at her. "I'm not a thief."

She appraised him, still smiling, but a different smile now. "No. No, I didn't guess you were."

"Would you like to sit down?" He gestured to the small kitchen table.

"Yes, thanks."

They sat in silence for a few moments, then simultaneously started, "There's something I should—."

"Guests first," offered Vishnu.

Gina took a sip of coffee and a deep breath. "It's about your car, Vishnu. There's something you should know about it. It used to belong to a drug dealer."

"Don't tell me. Let me guess. Sonny."

"Sonny." Gina smiled sheepishly. "He's kind of a nut case. I know him from my old beat in Tukwila. And your car left Sonny's possession, in, well, let's just say what might not be normal circumstances." She rotated the mug on the table. "I'm not totally sure about that, and if there's a problem with legal ownership you don't have any real liability, but...basically, I'm concerned that Sonny might come looking for it. If what I hear is right, he lost it for not paying a debt, probably to some people who are worse than he is. They're basically the only people who Sonny could end up owing anything to." Gina felt like she was babbling, and noted with discomfort that Vishnu was staring at her. “I just wanted to warn you about this, Vishnu. That car sticks out like a sore thumb, and the guy who owned it is a real whack job. He might do nothing, or he might try to find it. If you’re around when that happens, if it happens, well…I just…I wouldn’t want that.”

“So all this is pretty much known to the police?” he asked.

“Yeah.” Gina hesitated. “Pretty much. Like I said, I’ve had first-hand dealings with the guy who used to own your car. And I...I know some people.” There was another pregnant pause. She pushed her cup towards the middle of the table, looking embarrassed. “Well, I bet you're busy, so I should prob—”

“This is why you came here, to tell me this?” interrupted Vishnu.

“Yeah.”

“Wow.” He leaned back in his chair. “Man.”

“What?”

“Well, I guess I can trust you.”

“Well, sure. I mean, about what?”

“About a problem I have,” he replied. “Come on, I'll show you.”

She followed him back out through the shop and into the driveway. He popped the trunk lid, pulled out the spare, and unzipped the gym bag, exposing its contents. “Officer Kowalski, I place myself at your mercy.”

“Jesus!” said Gina in a low voice.

“I doubt these relate to what Jesus would do.”

“These were in the car?”

“Right like this. In the trunk.”

“When did you find them?”

“About eleven this morning.”

“Eleven. After we met.”

“Hours later.”

“What made you look in your trunk?”

“I wanted to see if the spare was flat,” said Vishnu. Gina looked at him curiously. “I was fixing a flat on a bike,” he explained, “and thinking about how many things on this car might need fixing. It occurred to me the spare might be flat." He shrugged. "While the glue was drying on the bike tube, I came out to take a look. The spare was flat, so I pulled it out. The gym bag was underneath it, so I looked in it."

"Can you describe for me exactly what you did? Exactly?"

Vishnu thought a moment. "I picked the bag up out of the trunk by the handles, put it down on the ground, squatted by it, unzipped it, and looked inside. Then I fell backwards on my butt." He grinned weakly. "I said some bad words, too."

"And the guns and the drugs were inside."

"Uh huh."

"Did you touch anything inside the bag?"

Vishnu thought again. "No. No, I didn't. I was sitting on the ground, and heard a car coming, so I zipped up the bag, threw it in the trunk, threw the spare on top of it, and slammed the trunk shut. I just about shit my pants," he admitted. "The car was my customer, coming for her kid's bike. A classic mom, with a minivan and everything. It was a weird scene. She was talking about how wholesome bike shops are, and I was wondering how many felony charges I had in my trunk." He paused. "What do I do now?"

"Well, my recommendation would be to call the cops. You're sure you didn't touch the guns or the drugs?"

"Yeah."

"That's good," said Gina "Just makes it easier to sort things out if your prints aren't on them."

"What do you think the stuff is?"

"Meth, I'm guessing."

"Pink? I always pictured it as white."

"If the guy who used to own this car was involved, it's probably what we call a Beavis and Butthead operation. They crush up generic Sudafed, run whatever solvent they can find through them. Paint thinner, gasoline, anything. There's some other steps, but if the pills were pink, the powder's pink. There are high-tech labs, but the fact that it was somehow left in the trunk kind of says it all."

"And the guns?"

"These are screwed up people, Vishnu. You want to avoid them."

Vishnu let out a long sigh. "Wow," he said.

"What?"

"It's all kind of hard to keep track of. But I'm glad you didn't search the trunk last night."

"Yeah. If you didn't touch the merchandise, you would have gotten off ultimately, but it wouldn't have gone well in the short run."

"No. But it's not just that. I mean, I just, uh." He paused. "What I'm trying to say is, if you'd have found them last night, you wouldn't have come by this evening. We wouldn't have had the chance to have a cup of coffee, and, you know, just talk."

"No," she agreed. "Several of today's conversations would have been different."

"Huh?"

"Never mind. Just thinking out loud."

"So we just call the police?"

"That's usually the best thing to do when you discover a bag of drugs and five guns in your trunk. Especially if somebody else left them there by mistake."

"Will you wait until they come?"

Gina smiled. "The cops are already here, Vishnu. But of course I'll wait until an on-duty patrol gets here, if you like."

"How will you explain your, uh, your presence?"

"I'll just tell them that my friend found these things in a car he just bought, and he wanted my advice about what to do. We'll answer some questions. They'll probably look through the rest of the car, to see if there are any more surprises. Then they'll take the stuff and go."

"Then what?"

"Then we could finish our coffee, and, you know, just talk."

Nineteen

Heather stood alone in a field and looked straight up. From the middle of the twenty-three acres of the Mystic Heart Retreat Center on Lopez Island, the Saturday night sky was a riot of stars, the Milky Way a skunk stripe across the cosmos.

When she'd arrived at the retreat on Thursday, Heather's psyche had been knotted and wrinkled about the apparent web of problems with Vishnu. But now, two days later, those knots and wrinkles had been smoothed gently away by the influence of multiple chanting circles, hours of meditation and yoga, sweat lodges, smudges, wonderful organic food, quiet, and, perhaps most importantly, separation from Vishnu. What had appeared to Heather on Thursday as faults of Vishnu now seemed as quirks; his quirks, amusing traits; his amusing traits, loveable basic essences of his being that separated him from other men she knew. Besides, she knew him to be honest to a fault, and devoted to her.

It was with this frame of mind that she had entered the final circle a few hours before. After a smudge, each participant had invoked his or her guardian spirit with the intent of channeling a universal guiding message. Each participant had written the received message using a quill feather from a non-endangered species dipped in organic beet juice on a piece of handmade parchment, and placed it in a large wicker basket passed around the circle. The basket was then passed around the circle once more, and each member took from it a piece of parchment, the idea being that the message one needed would be guided divinely to one's hand.

The message Heather had taken from the basket read: Your intimate relationship is on a threshold. One of you holds tightly to the future, the other holds tightly to the past. Let yourselves merge in the Now, and let the energy thus released transform your souls.

Standing barefoot in the grass under the stars, Heather thrilled to this admonition. It wasn't clear which of the two of them was clinging to what, but that seemed a minor point. The releasing was the key; Heather felt sure of that.

She thought of seeking out a clandestine cell phone, in order to call Vishnu, to hear his voice, to tell him what she was feeling, but she didn't want to leave her place under the beautiful night sky and subjugate her inner being to the spoken word. It will wait, she thought, and wrapped her arms around herself against the slight chill in the air, savoring the sense of order in the universe brought by the admonition on the parchment. Savoring the feeling of universal happiness brought by a couple of days of yoga, meditation, and the company of kindred spirits. Savoring the anticipation of seeing Vishnu at lunchtime the next day. She and Vishnu had so much potential to unlock together. She could hardly wait to get started on the project.

Twenty

As a sole proprietorship, Vishnu's business gave him a lot of quality one-on-one time with himself, time he generally used for unfettered rumination. It wasn't the orderly method of problem-solving employed by Gina's dockside meditations. Instead, while Vishnu's hands mended various bicyclic ills, his mind flowed along fractal paths, exploring every possibility related to whatever was on his mind. He saw it as a good thing, which produced useful insights and new ideas.

There were other views. Once, when such mulling had led to his failure to make weekend reservations at a bed-and-breakfast out on the coast, a deeply frustrated Heather complained that he chewed on things the way a termite chews on a wooden porch, producing nothing but a big pile of sawdust, and that it was nothing more than narcissistic mental self-abuse, and a glorified cover for avoiding anything he wanted to get out of. Since Vishnu hadn't really wanted to go to the beach that weekend, he had found himself in a weak position to argue general virtues.

Irrespective, whatever else could be said about Vishnu's deliberations, the process wasn't speedy. It took days, sometimes weeks, to maul a dilemma into submission. Which was in itself a dilemma at about ten minutes to noon on Sunday. Vishnu had about ten minutes before the ever-punctual Heather was due to arrive for lunch, and he was flummoxed.

His divestiture of the gun and drugs had come along with its own complication, in the form of a couple of hours spent with a woman with whom there seemed to be a real spark. A cup of coffee, a walk, the brief clasp of hands at parting, and the mutual statement that it would be nice to do it again. A sweet, innocent, Doris Day interlude, except that it was not with his official girlfriend, a girlfriend who was supposed to show up way too soon, who wasn't expecting to hear about anything of the sort, and who wasn't going to be very sympathetic when she found out. For that matter, Vishnu had somehow neglected to mention Heather to Gina; funny how those things happen.

The problem was a classic in the course of human affairs, and it really wasn't even that complicated. While the long-term prospects with Heather were uncertain, Vishnu wanted to keep open whatever possibilities there were. He also wanted to explore whatever was going on between him and Gina. And he wanted to do it all relatively pain-free, without inciting a riot or being a lying, two-timing butt. He just wasn't sure how to get from here to there.

The challenge of how to solve the problem in ten minutes was solved eight minutes later, as Heather's little Toyota pulled to a stop at the curb. She walked up the driveway, her totemic bag overtopping with organic vegetables. She cast a puzzled look at Val, the hood left ajar and a drip pan under the engine. Her nostrils flared as she examined the 'Cuda. She had radiated sunshine as she arrived, but she seemed under a cloud as she approached the door.

Vishnu was looking up to greet her as she walked into the shop. In the absence of a better idea, he had decided on the duck-and-cover approach. "Hi, Heather! You're back!" He gave her a dazzling smile.

"Vishnu, what is that *car* doing in your driveway? It looks like you're starting a junkyard. It's Evan's, right?"

"Actually, Heather, it's mine."

"Well, Hans, then," said Heather, looking for a grease-free spot to set down her bag, "but if he can't find a place to park his car, that's not your problem."

"Heather, it's really mine. Val finally gave up the ghost. I bought it on Friday. It's a '70 'Cuda! Isn't she grand?"

Heather gave him her full attention for the first time. "You're kidding, right?" She looked out at the driveway. "Look, Vishnu, I know you like to help your friends out and Evan is a good guy and everything but I just don't think you should let him park a car like that in front of your—"

"Heather."

Heather looked at the 'Cuda, then at Vishnu. "You're serious?"

Vishnu wasn't happy the conversation had started with this topic; alternatively, he could think of worse ones. "Look," he said, "repairs are light today. Why don't we go for a spin? We can head up to the Sunbeam for a salad."

Heather's nostrils flared again. She held up her bag, trying gamely to regain her earlier mood. "I brought some salad stuff for us to have here. For the two of us."

"Hey, that's great!" Vishnu was happy to find something to agree about. "How about I wash up. Just put the veggies in the kitchen and I'll be out in a sec."

As he stood at the bathroom sink lathering his hands, he looked his reflection in the eyes. This is going to get out of hand real fast, he told himself. You better take the initiative early. Honesty is the best policy. It's not fair to Heather to act like nothing's changed. Best not to put off until tomorrow what you can do today.

Stepping from the bathroom into the kitchen, he was met by Heather, a glint in her eyes and a coffee mug in her hand. Apparently, there's no rest for the wicked, thought Vishnu.

"What is *this*?" demanded Heather.

Vishnu reflected that he could run, but he couldn't hide. His life was a collection of aphorisms, and he was tiring of it. "That's a mug."

"I know it's a mug," snapped Heather. "What the hell is *this*?" Heather pointed to the red smudge on the rim.

Shit, thought Vishnu. Here we go. "I'd guess that's Gina's lipstick."

Heather was caught off guard. Her question about what was on the cup was rhetorical; she knew lipstick when she saw it, and knew what such things implied. She had, however, expected the conversation to build slowly and with many rich subthemes, like the 1812 Overture, to a point near the end of the final movement, when she would extract this confession with pliers and a blowtorch. Now the orchestra had jumped to the cannon fusillade, and she had barely raised her baton.

Vishnu spoke while he had the chance. "Look. Heather. A lot of stuff has happened in the last couple of days. My car died, I bought a new one, some other crazy stuff you wouldn't believe." He paused. "And I met somebody. A woman. We're just friends, but..." He searched for how to continue.

Heather stared at him. "How long have you known this – this – *Gina*?"

Vishnu did a quick calculation. "About thirty-three hours," he said, hoping such an answer would throw Heather off.

Heather did her own quick calculation. "What are you telling me? You met her at three o'clock Saturday morning?"

"That's pretty close."

"And *what*, might I ask, were you doing at three o'clock Saturday morning that would result in your meeting women named Gina who leave lipstick on your dishes?"

"The lipstick's actually from later that afternoon." Heather's eyes narrowed into slits. "I mean, it's not quite like that," Vishnu said quickly. "It's kind of a long story."

"I have time."

"Look, we're just friends," said Vishnu, casting about for words that wouldn't serve merely as shovels. "And anyway, you're the one who said you weren't sure that we had a future. And might I remind you that it was you who said you needed to think things over." He tried for a look of indignance, managing only indigestion.

"Well, you listen up, *bucko!*" Heather pointed her finger at Vishnu's breastbone like a spear. "*Me* saying I want to think things over does not give *you* the right to go chasing after skanks in the middle of the night!"

"Gina's not a skank! She…" Vishnu stopped, and began again more softly. "I'm sorry, Heather. Look. I'm not lying to you. Gina and I are just friends. At least for now. But look at us, Heather. You and I, I mean, we really aren't any more than friends, either. I didn't know that until now, or wouldn't admit it. All we do is argue, and, and...coincide. I'm sorry." He paused. "I want more."

Krishnamurti wrote that true renunciation is when you give something up without knowing what is going to happen, what you will get in return. Vishnu hadn't read this, but for him this was a moment of true renunciation. Heather had, in fact, read this, but it didn't come to her mind. What came to her mind was the memory of the previous night, standing in the field beneath the stars, thinking of Vishnu and her plans for their future. What came to her mind was a vision of Vishnu's freshly decapitated head skewered on a wooden pole. Her rage stripped away any composure she still had. Heather, the politically correct, astrological-chart-making, Nepalese-prayer-flag-flying, New-Age vegetarian chai-tea-drinking Seattle good girl, delved deep into her past and the summer afternoon training received from her older brothers, wound up like Bill Lee on the mound and uncorked a fastmug at Vishnu's head. The mug grazed his left ear and continued past him into the bathroom where it introduced itself to the mirror. Fragments of glass and ceramic cascaded to the floor like the windchimes of relationship hell.

"Coincide?" Heather shrieked. *"Coincide with that, motherfucker!"* She whirled about, grabbed her bag, and stormed from Vishnu's apartment out to the shop. *"Coincide! I'll show you fucking coincide!"* She shoved an orderly row of eight bicycles into a tangled mess on her way out the door. She paused by the 'Cuda, hawked up a loogie that would have done her brothers proud, and spat it expertly on the windshield. *"You fucking sleazy SHITBAG!"* She hurled her vegetables one by one at Vishnu, who had followed her from the kitchen. A red onion caught him full in the chest with surprising force. He took cover behind the toppled bikes. A head of Romaine lettuce wedged itself in the spokes of a wheel right in front of his face. A very ripe tomato clipped the doorframe and dispersed itself broadly.

An old man in a blue nylon tavern jacket was shuffling down the street towards the shop. He stopped in his tracks about fifty feet from

Heather. She caught sight of him out of the corner of her eye. *"Fuck YOU!"* she screamed, spinning to face him and swinging her upraised middle digit up so violently that she came out of her left Birkenstock and almost fell over onto the pavement. The old man turned tail and hustled away.

Tears streaming down her face, Heather ran to her car door, yanked it open, and jumped in. She jammed the key into the ignition, turned it until the running engine was grinding against the starter motor, slammed the transmission into gear, and careened out onto Canal Street. A pickup truck lumbered towards her. She leaned on the horn and floored it, staring the driver in the eye and driving straight for the center of the truck's hood. Vishnu ran to the door just in time to see the pickup swerve over the curb and onto the sidewalk, avoiding Heather by the smallest of margins. A banshee's scream of astounding obscenities came from the Toyota as it barreled up the street. The driver of the pickup backed quickly off the sidewalk, and sped past Vishnu, flipping him off as he went.

Vishnu stood in the peaceful sun for a moment, wiped a few tomato seeds from his forehead. A crow, possibly the same one he had seen on Thursday, landed on top of Val. It looked at Vishnu, cawed twice, preened under its wing, and looked again at Vishnu. Vishnu shrugged. "I don't know. I think that went pretty well, all things considered."

Twenty One

When Vishnu found himself in times of trouble, Mother Mary did not come to him. Then again, he'd never seriously requested her intercession, so She couldn't really be faulted. Instead, when Vishnu wanted words of wisdom, or just to shoot the breeze over a cup of instant joe, he'd wander up the hill to St. Thorfinn's Lutheran Church, to see what sort of no-good Pastor Bob was up to.

There were a number of reasons Vishnu liked Pastor Bob Randall. To begin with, Pastor Bob wore a disguise. On the short side, plump, balding, clad in a standard-issue Lutheran Church brown corduroy jacket, sensible slacks, and nondescript loafers, and accessorized with wire-rimmed bifocals, Pastor Bob looked just like a Lutheran minister. Moving around in public, he often topped the disguise off with an ancient Julie-Andrews-style Raleigh three-speed, the kind with a spring-cushioned seat, upright bars with an attached metal basket, and a twingly little bell.

His appearance was the perfect disguise for a man with a Mephistophilean sense of humor whose main passion was the theatre of the absurd known as the human condition. To this end, Pastor Bob was like a kid at a county fair, intent on seeing every exhibit and sideshow, and hearing the spiel of every barker, carny, and shill.

Not that Pastor Bob was an irreligious charlatan, or an uncaring person. Quite to the contrary, he was a deeply religious man who had surrendered his soul and life to the service of his Savior. He just felt that his Savior had a vast, wonderful, sometimes raucous sense of humor, and allowed His children a fairly long leash so they could tangle themselves up in it once in a while. If they got a few scrapes or bruises, well, that's what this life is about. Bob's role in the whole mess, as he saw it, was mostly to listen to people talk about their troubles, and occasionally offer some limited observations.

Vishnu had once asked Bob what it was like to be a minister, to which Bob had replied, "It's like being a stand-up comedian with a tough crowd, most of whom don't get the jokes, but who insist that you finish your routine and keep coming back week after week."

The tough crowd Pastor Bob faced each week consisted of old-school Ballard Scandinavian Lutherans: thrifty, hard-working, middle-class, conservative Seattle natives, who generally viewed the world as centered around Market Street and 24th Avenue, declining in overall quality and moral fiber as distance increased therefrom. Pastor Bob enjoyed roasting them from the pulpit now and again, but his favorite game, akin to biblical Jeopardy, was one in which he would make passing reference to some obscure but incriminating verse during a discourse about a seemingly milktoast topic. Several church members prided themselves on their knowledge of Biblical arcana. If any of these folks looked dour or scandalized during the sermon, Bob knew that the offended had caught on to his goad, in which case Bob felt he hadn't done his homework. Alternatively, if the scholarly crew assumed a bland, inscrutable mien, he was confident he'd gotten their goats. Departing conversation at the door with them would be short, because they'd be itching to get home and search their references in order to decode his latest excoriation. He was unabashed about the amusement he derived from stirring the pot with the congregation. "Besides," he once told Vishnu, "they keep paying me in hard cash, so they must like it."

All this was reason enough for Vishnu to like Pastor Bob, but there was also the matter of the Five Foot Jesus.

For the last several years, Pastor Bob and an unidentified group of local youths had taken turns altering the appearance of a five-foot-tall statue of our Lord and Savior that guarded the door of St. Thorfinn's like a Chinese temple dog.

The whole thing had been initiated by the youths during the wee hours of a Monday night. Tuesday dawned to reveal a depiction of fourth-grade-quality male genitals just below the belt on Jesus' robe, and a corresponding obscenity on His upraised right arm, both of them rendered in permanent black felt pen.

The parish was outraged, and proposed a stakeout of elderly Clint Eastwood wannabes armed with their old twelve-gauge Remington Model 32 over/unders. Claiming Divine inspiration, Pastor Bob quelled the militia, and with the help of some weatherproof acrylic paints, he transformed the penis of the Five Foot Jesus into a stylish pair of blue gym shorts. The 'Suck Me' on His arm became an unusual Celtic-style tattoo. In a final stroke of genius, Bob left a bundle of paints and brushes out in a box at His feet.

While most of the parishioners didn't think Pastor Bob's artwork was one bit funny, the youths got the joke. Most of them were simply trying to provoke real communication with anyone who would take them halfway seriously, and this was beyond their wildest expectations. Two nights later, they added a bright red bikini top and some rather daring Melina Mercouri eye makeup, which made Jesus look like a hippie transvestite raccoon. Bob altered the bikini top into a bustier complete with leather laces, and turned the eye makeup into wraparound shades. Sunday morning found the gym shorts changed into lederhosen, His feet sported snow boots, and His head was crowned with a Canadian-style fur-lined cap complete with ear flaps (the real item, not a painted reproduction). He now looked like a Bavarian tourist straight off the midnight bus from the Calgary Winter Olympics.

St. Thorfinn's was in an uproar, and a few members called for Pastor Bob's resignation. Others, however, who had suspicions or direct knowledge that the perps were blood relatives, tolerated it. Bob called it Youth Outreach, and bought more supplies out of the church fund dedicated to that effort (a hundred bucks a year, hitherto unspent and duly reallocated to the Easter Coffee Fund).

Since that time, the operation had continued unfettered, and the parish as a whole had to grudgingly admit that some of these kids had gotten to be pretty good with a paintbrush and had quite an eye for Goodwill fashion. Further, some of the young artists came to enjoy the work so much that they felt limited by having only one statue, and over time they added other pieces, to the point where the courtyard looked like a cross between a diorama depicting the life and work of St. Frances di Assisi and the croquet game from Alice in Wonderland.

Such was the setting that greeted Vishnu when he reached the church courtyard several hours after Heather had departed from his shop in so spectacular a manner. The scene was completed by Skippy Sullivan reading his latest poetry aloud, while Pastor Bob added a final detail to the day's adornment of the Five Foot Jesus. Vishnu leaned on the brick archway of the courtyard, unnoticed by Bob as he applied the last few strokes to a Groucho Marx moustache, and unnoticed as well by Skippy, who was reaching a crescendo.

"Freed! from the frisson of fission, and fishin' in the indigo/
Mood of the false conundrum. The moon, skewered like a cocktail/
Onion on the Seventh Cavalry saber-tooth of/
The Tigris, shone tears of translucent sorrow, while Custer hopped/
A midnight Euphrates southbound, leaving only penumbra numba/
Three. I turned to my right, and what was left said – Vishnu!"

"Hey Skip. Hey Bob." Vishnu entered the courtyard.

Pastor Bob smiled up at Vishnu. "Skippy always inspires me to greatness."

"The moustache?"

"Well, the moustache for today. But, now that you mention it, the whole Jesus fashion show." Pastor Bob placed his brushes in a pan of water. "Do you know, when those kids first defaced our statue, the whole congregation was angry. I was, too. But then again, I couldn't abide the idea of posting armed guards, or locking it inside, like we were putting Jesus under house arrest for his own protection. But I didn't know what to do. So I prayed, and got my answer."

"And the answer was?" asked Vishnu.

"Skippy."

"Skippy?"

Skippy shrugged. "All I did was call Bob on the phone and ask if he wanted to come with me on my annual pilgrimage to dress up the dog statue down by the Fremont Bridge, in honor of Charles Mingus' birthday. I had no idea that God was speaking through me."

Pastor Bob laughed. "We never do."

Vishnu looked at Bob. "I never heard this part of the story."

"You never asked."

"How could I ask a question I didn't know I had?"

"Hold on!" Skippy dug around the pocket of his overalls for a pen, and began scribbling on his paper. "What you said, man!"

"It's probably a good thing that they didn't alter your little 'sermon-of-the-week' advertising board," commented Vishnu. "You might have left a bunch of spare letters out, and God only knows what sort of blasphemy they would have written."

"Don't think I didn't consider it." Pastor Bob began swishing the brushes in the pan of water. "Come to talk about muscle cars, I presume," he added without looking up.

"How did you know about that?"

"Come now, Vishnu. You don't think you can sneak a big red Plymouth past the neighborhood sentries in broad daylight, do you?" He shook the brushes in the air to dry. "Besides, you drove it right to the Arnesons."

"I didn't know Arnie and Edith are members of St. Thorfinn's."

"They aren't. But Edith is a friend of Myrtle Ricci's, and Myrtle is married to Eddie Ricci, whose sister is Edna Anderson. Edna is married to Gus Anderson. Edna and Gus are members of St. Thorfinn's. You know Gus."

"Yeah."

"Not only that, but from what I hear, Edith Arneson lives directly across the street from Ida Helmdorfer."

"I don't know her."

"No," replied Pastor Bob. "And she doesn't know you either, but she doesn't like your looks, and she doesn't think much of Edith Arneson. Which is why she called her sister Agnes to report that the neighborhood was going downhill, and now those Arnesons were letting disreputable types come and go as they please, and Arnie was driving around with them." Pastor Bob paused for rhetorical effect. "Ida's sister Agnes is Agnes Sandstrom, whose husband is Carl Sandstrom. You know Carl."

"Yeah." Carl owned a '69 Dart, the Dodge equivalent of a Valiant. For what felt to him like the twenty-seventh time since Thursday morning, Vishnu felt woozy from the effects of reality. For nearly four decades, he had been under the impression that he was fairly anonymous in a metropolitan area of over a million people, and that his comings and goings went essentially unnoticed even in his stomping grounds of Ballard. Apparently, the truth was that a network of elderly people, some of whom he'd never met, were trading phone calls about his activities and moral character. He wondered how much of the rest of his life had been catalogued without his awareness, and by whom.

Pastor Bob did not miss the look on Vishnu's face, and went on with visible amusement. "Carl and Agnes attend St. Thorfinn's, and Carl knows Arnie Arneson. He called Arnie yesterday. Apparently you and Arnie had quite a nice car trip on Friday afternoon. I think Carl is a bit jealous, although he was trying to sound good-natured about it while talking with his pals before the service this morning. Were I you, Vishnu, I'd prepare for a minor flood of phone calls from old men intent on wangling a ride in your hot car. And I should warn you," Pastor Bob said as he wiped his brushes on a rag, "I heard mutterings in the receiving line about the ultimate disposition of your Valiant. There are those among the flock who I fear are being tempted into covetous thoughts."

Pastor Bob turned to Skippy. "The world's not as big as we think it is, is it, Skippy."

Skippy looked up from revising his verses. "Indeed it is not. Witness Bob and me. It is written in the cosmic parchment, Verse One Million and Seven, that once a man partakes of Skippy's fried potatoes, he must orbit in their influence forevermore."

Vishnu pondered this as Skippy scrawled and Pastor Bob packed the paints into their box. "How did you guys meet, anyway?" asked Vishnu.

Pastor Bob and Skippy traded glances. "Lucky accident," said Bob. "God provides."

"Like I said, man," Skippy picked up the thread, "I was grillin' my pommes frittes, ensuring a crisp golden brown crust with just the right amount of oil to keep a man lubricated in all the right places, while sealing in the life-giving moisture that—"

"In Seattle?" interrupted Vishnu.

"Oh, no, man, much farther afield, lifetimes ago—"

"Several, at least," Pastor Bob chimed in. "West of the Pecos, east of Eden, north of the—"

"OK, OK," Vishnu held up his hand. "But one of these days I'm going to find out the truth. And if you're not going to tell me now, I'm going to tax you with my own tales of woe. At least the parts that haven't been published in the Ballard Observer," he added, looking pointedly at Pastor Bob.

The three of them settled down, Pastor Bob and Vishnu on a bench in the shade of an overhanging cherry tree, and Skippy flat on his back in the postage-stamp lawn amid the outlandish statuary. Vishnu related the events of the preceding three days, finishing with Heather's fiery departure from his shop.

"Sounds like you've been a busy man," remarked Pastor Bob, after Vishnu had finished. "What think you, Skippy?"

"On Thursday, I cooked some pancakes. On Friday, I cooked some pancakes and had a nice visit to the Japanese Gardens. Yesterday, I cooked some pancakes and some waffles, and wrote poetry in the shade of the Fremont Troll. Nothing to compare with Vishnu's adventures, which sound inspirational. I envision a sculpture, maybe fifteen feet tall, with razor-sharp blades of stainless steel to symbolize the perils of romance. Of course, I'm just the cook, so don't look to me for spiritual guidance. And my marriage counseling license was revoked."

"That's what Hans said when I talked with him on Thursday." Vishnu picked a branch off of the ground and traced patterns aimlessly in the grass. "And that was before I met Gina. What do you think, Bob?"

Pastor Bob shook his head. "Quite a tale. I'll restrict my advice to saying that you've got a muddle with Heather, and you need to straighten that out. It's only fair to her. And to Gina. Provided I'm correct in my assessment that you intend to pursue something in that direction."

"Yeah. I feel bad that it happened the way it did. I wish I'd straightened things out with Heather before I met Gina."

Skippy held one hand aloft, index finger pointed at the sky like a Roman senator. "The oft-proclaimed regret that one had seen things more clearly while in the light of reason shining from Apollo's chariot. Fuzzy-minded hogwash! Pine not for Helios! Selene, the moon, is full, and she beams down on Morpheus, demigod of dreams, who doth dance the boogie-woogie in her glow!" Skippy lowered his arm and stroked his gray beard, looking immensely pleased with himself.

"Speaking of dreams, I did have a weird one last Thursday night. Heather and I were riding bikes, and she kept going away from me, or maybe I wasn't keeping up with her. Then we got separated. And then a dark-eyed woman pulled me into a dance at some kind of festival." Skippy had turned his head to look at Vishnu. "But don't you get carried away." Vishnu pointed the stick at Skippy. "That was *before* I met Gina, not after."

Skippy had raised himself up on one elbow. "Pish-posh! Feel free to discount it, but my assessment, as the monk of the sacred flapjack, is that you met Gina Thursday night, and it took twenty-four hours for your reason-hobbled daylight world to catch up. How else can you explain the fact that you met Gina so conveniently in a convenience store?" He held his oratory finger up again. "Remember how earlier you asked how you could ask a question you didn't know you had? Well, think about this. Gina is the answer to a question you didn't know you'd asked! Wait a minute!" He reached his hand behind his back and tugged his notebook out of his hip pocket. "Wow!" he said, writing furiously. "Sometimes I even surprise myself!"

Pastor Bob shrugged. "He may only be the cook, but he's also the resident mystic. I'm just the purveyor of dogma."

"Well, then," said Vishnu "just for the record, where does the Lutheran Church come down on prescient dreams?"

"That's an interesting question." Pastor Bob rested his chin thoughtfully on the fingers of his right hand. "The conservative approach would probably be to warn the faithful away from such slippery slopes, lest they fall to their death in the pit of miracle-revering Papistry."

"Straight to Hell in an icon-encrusted bucket!" interjected Skippy, who was again flat on his back, flapping his hands in the air. "Millions of good American burghers quitting their day jobs to crawl on their hands and knees to an east Los Angeles taqueria, where the Virgin Mary appeared in midair, handing out paper cartons of frijoles with the winning loteria number! Only one step up from league bowling for eternity!"

Pastor Bob continued, unflustered by Skippy. "On the other hand, one could take the broader view, espoused by Skippy, that a dream could come in answer to a prayer. As Skippy's phone call came to me, apparently unbidden, but inspiring all this." He waved his hand at the mind-bending array of figurines. "But I think spending too much time wondering how and why the message came is a distraction. The real question is, what does one do with the message?"

"The holy man, ears wrapped around the peal of the church bell, ignores the sound of the door on its hinge, a squeak so fecund with potential enlightenment!" Skippy was on a roll. "The scholar demands that the solution to the unified field theory take the shape of a Twinkie, ignoring with profound effort the obvious fact that the hole in the middle of the universe is exactly the shape of the Ding Dong he spurns. Oh,

Lord!" he wailed. "How much longer must conditionless happiness go unmanifest because of snack-food delusions?" He raised himself on an elbow again, pointing his finger at Vishnu. "Vishnu!" he commanded. "Do not ignore the symbols dropped lovingly at your feet by Hermes himself, god of thievery and gymnastic exercises." He let himself flop back on the grass, arms at his sides.

Pastor Bob applauded. "Bravo, Skippy! I'm not sure that it's as serious as all that, but you get a ten for zeal. Then again, I must admit I have a can of 3-in-1 oil that I use on my hinges to keep them from squeaking." He turned to Vishnu. "So we come to a question I ask a lot in my profession. How are you doing?"

Vishnu leaned back on the bench and flipped the stick in his hand across the courtyard. It bounced off the antlers of the Virgin Mary disguised as Bullwinkle Moose, holding the Baby Rocky in her arms. "Good," said Vishnu. "Great, actually. It's weird. All this stuff going on, and I feel like I should be freaking out, but I feel like it's all leading to something good." He looked at Pastor Bob. "Thoughts?"

"None that add value. As Skippy so eloquently points out, you're the one who had the prescient dream about an unhappy Heather departing, and a mysterious dark-haired woman leading you into a dance."

Vishnu got up and stretched. "So I did. Guess I need to let it fester for a while. You coming to the show tomorrow night, Bob?"

"Wouldn't miss it. I'll dream a packed house tonight, to ensure tomorrow's success."

Vishnu picked a dandelion and placed it on Skippy's forehead. "Dream of Coltrane, Skip."

"And Mingus for you, man. Mingus like he played Goodbye Porkpie Hat on the night Lester Young left this realm for greater possibilities."

Vishnu walked from the courtyard and disappeared down the street.

"Interesting tale," said Pastor Bob.

“That it is,” agreed Skippy. “A fast car with a load of contraband, a faceless thug, and a mysterious dark-haired woman. What more could you add? A duel, fought by comely women over the honor of our young friend. A criminal mastermind. Clowns and jesters. A cosmic reckoning at the feet of the Great Mother. Waffles, cooked by someone other than me.”

“True love is at stake, and all you can think about is food.”

Twenty Two

East Marginal Way.

Do names foretell the future? Do they actively shape it? For humans, motivated as they are by symbols, there is great power in names. As it is said, in the beginning, there was the Word.

In this case the word was Margin, referring originally to the east bank of the Duwamish River, along which East Marginal Way lies. At one time a major artery for indigenous people in the area, the Duwamish River was mutated, mutilated, and otherwise improved by Whitey into industrial thralldom, to the extent that it became not a River but a Waterway. As a final comment on the transition to oblivion, the southern terminus of East Marginal Way is actually on the west side of the Duwamish Waterway, where proclaimed marginality becomes municipal anonymity, and the road becomes simply 40th Avenue South.

Sonny lived in a trailer behind a defunct gas station near the south end of East Marginal Way. The area was flanked on the east by the heavy industry of the Waterway, and on the west by a hill crowned with the tawdry strip development of State Route 99. An area deceptively bucolic and verdant to the untrained eye, the local cops tended to see it as a typical low spot in the bushes where people can hunker down and do their illegal activities. Aptly, State Route 99, or '99' in the parlance of Sonny's neighborhood, was the same road that passed in front of Tony's Tigers not twelve mile to the north, where it went by the euphonic name of Aurora Avenue.

At about eleven o'clock Friday morning, approximately the same time that Vishnu first laid lustful eyes on the 'Cuda, Sonny was trudging across a gravel parking lot towards the entrance of his local tavern, a few blocks from his trailer. A squat building of unpainted cement blocks with small windows like gun slots, the place advertised all the cheer of a hanging in winter. The lot was empty save for two battered choppers parked by the front door. Only sixteen hours before, Sonny had been hauled off for brawling in this very tavern. His car had been in the lot when he'd left.

Sonny pushed open the door and squinted into the dim light. Two men with a combined weight close to six hundred pounds were playing eight-ball in the far corner. Sonny walked to the bar.

"Howdy, Sonny." The moonfaced bartender made lazy circles on the bar with a discolored rag. His accent was as mild as his face, a good ol' boy drawl that evoked the Gulf Coast sun slowly roasting engine blocks in the front yard. "They letcha go for good behavior?"

Sonny glowered at Moonface. "You fucking know what happened to my car?"

"Lessee." Moonface suspended his attempts at public sanitation and gazed at the ceiling. "Nope." He resumed his wiping.

"It was here when I left, man. You fucking tow it?"

"Nope," repeated Moonface, shaking his head slowly. "No, sir, I did not have your car towed."

Sonny leaned forward, hands on the bar. "Look, man. Don't fuck with me."

Moonface turned his back to Sonny and began to rinse the rag in the sink. "Now, Sonny, don't get all het up." He glanced in the mirror behind the bar to the reflection of the two men at the pool table. One had his thumbs hooked through the motorcycle chain he wore as a belt. The other held a pool cue in his right hand, pointed the wrong way around. Moonface called to them. "Hey there, Manny, Sledge. Mightn't you fellers know anythin' 'bout Sonny's car gone missin'?"

Sonny turned to face them. Sledge's broad, flat features were impassive; he just fingered his chain belt. Manny's expression indicated he was hoping for a chance to break a pool cue.

"Guess not," interpreted Moonface. "Mighty sorry 'bout that, Sonny. Y'all want me to call the po-lice?"

Sonny scowled at Moonface, then at Manny and Sledge. "Ah, fuck it," he said finally, and headed for the door.

"I could put up a sign or somethin', if'n you think it might help," Moonface called after him.

Sonny stomped his way across the gravel, the raucous laughter of Manny and Sledge burning in his ears as he went. There was only one explanation. Tiny had his car.

Several days earlier, Sonny had expanded his line of merchandise to include guns. Since his boss, known only to Sonny by the campy moniker of 'The Man,' sold guns as well as drugs, and since the people who bought drugs from him carried guns, and used guns, and sold guns, and other people Sonny dealt with carried and used and sold guns, it was one of the most sound decisions Sonny had ever made. The only hitch was that The Man wouldn't front Sonny any guns, because he (correctly) didn't think Sonny could be trusted with them. Further, Sonny could have bought a few cheap Saturday Night Specials on the side with what cash he had, but Sonny wanted to deal in style. No punk-ass crap for him.

Enter opportunity in the form of Tiny, a bear-like man with a leadership role among the local bikers. Tiny could see his way to fronting Sonny some quality merchandise, with arrangements for a reasonable payback. Of course, there was the matter of collateral, and the only thing Sonny had of any value was, of course, the 'Cuda. Tiny had taken an ignition key as collateral.

One day after this deal was done, Sonny had instigated a fight with some equally volatile character, or maybe it had been the other way around. Such a fight would usually go on until someone suffered real damage, but Tiny had, perhaps out of some latent spark of compassion, given the order for Manny and Sledge to restrain Sonny and the other fellow, and asked Moonface to call the cops. As Sonny had been hauled out of the bar in cuffs, he'd seen Tiny laughing in the corner with his two lieutenants.

At the time, Sonny hadn't paid much thought as to why Tiny had squelched what might have turned into a healthy bloodletting, but now he knew. Tiny had sent Sonny to the can so that he could just drive the 'Cuda away without any interference. The fact that Sonny still held the title was of little consequence. Neither man was the type to quibble about paperwork. If Tiny had Sonny's car, he had it, and it was up to Sonny to work things out.

Sonny didn't have much in the way of life's external trappings, and he didn't generally give a shit. His car, however, was a different matter. It wasn't just the inconvenience of getting another set of wheels. The red 'Cuda was Sonny's personal statement, pure and simple. It rankled Sonny mightily that his personal statement was probably being made by someone who, in Sonny's eyes, and irrespective of body mass and beard length, was markedly unfit to make it.

To right this injustice, Sonny needed to move some guns, and he needed to move some drugs before The Man fucked him up for being late with his proceeds. But all of this was fixable, now that he was out of the can. Sonny would go back to his rathole trailer, arrange some deals, maybe even move a couple of the guns, pay off his boss, pay off Tiny, and get his car back, with enough cash to do it all over again. And the next time around, instead of a cheap .32 for backup, he would have his own primo piece, a stainless-steel Colt .45 automatic, the pick of the litter from the ones he'd been fronted by Tiny. It was all going to work out.

Sonny stopped at the corner and peered around the bushes towards his trailer. Nobody was visible, no cars moving in the street. He crossed the road quickly, entered his trailer, and went straight to the one little closet in the back. He removed the rubber welcome mat (his idea of a joke) exposing the hole he had cut in the floor (his idea of a place nobody would look). He reached his hand in to grab the gym bag. He found a paper sack.

It was a surreal moment, even for Sonny. There was supposed to be a paper sack, but there was also supposed to be a gym bag. He yanked the sack out of the hole, dove to the floor, and shoved his arm into the hole up to the shoulder, reaching this way and that. He pulled his arm out and stuck his head down the hole. It was dark, too dark to see. He yanked his head out of the hole, giving himself bloody scrapes behind his ears. He grabbed the sack and dumped out its contents. Several rolls of cash bundled with rubber bands rolled across the floor, but nothing else. He spent the next thirty seconds savagely dismantling furniture, kitchen drawers, and piles of rubbish and random objects. Nothing. He picked up his mattress off the floor and flung it across the trailer. His little .32 lay there.

He grabbed the .32 and spun around in a complete circle, slapped at the light switch, and ran into the bathroom. Squatting against the wall beside the filthy toilet, sweat running down his face, he held the gun in front of himself, listening to the pounding in his temples.

He had no wheels. He didn't have the drugs or the money that was supposed to come from them. He was into The Man for about eight big ones in drugs he couldn't locate, and he didn't have eight grand worth of anything. He didn't have the guns. The guns were in the gym bag. His total assets amounted to about a thousand bucks and a cheap pistol that wouldn't even bring fifty on the street. Where the fuck was the bag?

He tried to cut through the haze in his head and recreate the previous twenty-four hours. He had been in a fight at the tavern before he made his run. No, he'd gone to the tavern after he got back. No, wait. He was going to have a beer, then take off on his run. No, wait. It was on the way back from his delivery, but before he went home. He didn't remember putting the gym bag back down the hole. It had to have been before. No. *Shit!* It was before he'd made his run, but he'd decided to drive to the tavern, instead of walking. He'd loaded his shit in the car and was on his way to the drop, but he'd never made it. He'd stopped at the tavern first. And that little skinhead fuck had fucked with him, and he'd–. Sonny wiped the sweat off of his face. He hadn't made it to the drop.

The meth was in the gym bag. With the guns. Under the spare tire. In the trunk of the 'Cuda. Which was with Tiny.

Sonny spewed a remarkably pungent and original curse. Suddenly he froze, a new thought clanking into place. Would Tiny have looked in the trunk? He might have, but he didn't know the meth and guns were there, so he wouldn't have any reason to. If Tiny had the 'Cuda, and Sonny could get it back... Sonny fished out his cell and called Tiny's number.

"Yeah?" said Tiny.

"This is Sonny."

"Yeah?"

"Sonny. From the south end."

"Yeah?"

"You guys took my car." Silence. "I need it back."

"Yeah?"

"Listen. If you let me have the car back for an hour, I can pay you back."

"Hang on." Tiny's voice moved away from the phone, telling people in the background something Sonny couldn't make out. A wave of beery laughter broke against a seawall of screaming guitars; it sounded like walruses mating at a Megadeth concert. Then only voices in the background, and the guitar.

Sonny waited ten seconds or so. "You still there?" he asked finally.

"You listen, punk," said Tiny. "First, you're lucky I'm busy, or I'd come over right now and cut your dick off and stuff it down your fuckin' throat. Second, your jerk-off ride is gone."

"Gone?"

"Gone. Listen up, fuckface. Don't call me again. If you call me again, I'll rip your nuts out by the fuckin' roots. If I ever even see you again, you're a dead man. Dig?" The line went dead.

Sonny's heart raced. Putting his head on his knees, he breathed deeply, trying to figure out what to do. As far as he could tell, he had only two options. The first one was to run. He had run before. Maybe he could get away before The Man found out he was gone. Even to Sonny, that option seemed hopeless. The only skills he had were drug sales and unorganized mayhem, both of which required visibility. The Man was better organized, had a whole crew of people, and was even more violent than Sonny. The other option was to try to find his car, with the hope that the bag was still in it.

And maybe he had one advantage. The Man might not know he was out of the joint yet. Sonny still had his .32, a cell phone, and about one G in cash. He could get a set of cheap wheels and hole up somewhere while he tried to locate the 'Cuda. If he got it, and the bag was still there, he might still be able to work something out with The Man. If he found his car and the bag was gone, or if he didn't find his car, well, Sonny's planning abilities weren't really geared for more than one goal at a time. His plan was far-fetched plan, but it was the only one he had. Besides, to the extent that Sonny could love, he loved his nasty, greasy, loud, red 1970 Plymouth 'Cuda with the minor exhaust leak and the chrome pistol-grip shifter more than he had ever loved anything. He was going to find it. The main thing right now was to get out of his trailer before The Man found him.

He gathered up the .32, a box of bullets, and the rolls of bills off the floor, stuffing them all into pockets of his fatigue jacket. He surveyed the scene outside from the edge of the front window. No one was around. He could go back up to 99, hop on a bus, and find some place to lay low for a couple of days. He would make some calls to people he knew, and one of them would call him back telling him where his car was. As Tony had said, unbeknownst to Sonny, the ride wasn't exactly nondescrip'.

He walked up the hill to 99. His luck had already taken a turn for the better, in the form of a northbound #174 pulling up to the bus stop. He hopped on and slumped into a seat near the back. As he sat down, a black Camaro turned onto the street he had just walked up, heading down the hill towards his trailer. A surge of adrenaline made him twitch. It was just before noon on Friday, and they hadn't caught him. Not fucking yet.

A kid of about sixteen got on the bus and sat down on the sideways-facing jump seat. He glanced briefly at Sonny, then looked away.

“Fuck you lookin’ at, bitch?” snarled Sonny. The kid stood up and walked up to the front of the bus. Sonny watched him go, feeling better than he had in days.

Twenty Three

Romano Brothers Ltd., the umbrella company owned by Tony and Vito, consisted of Tony's Tigers Pre-Owned Classics, managed by Tony, and Apollo Precision Automotive Repair, managed by Vito. On the surface, each was a lucrative and straight-up enterprise, but Tony and Vito were men of strong ambition and varied interests, and at any given time they had one or more side ventures not directly relatable to Romano Brothers Ltd. Ventures that could be executed from an auto repair shop or a used car lot without attracting the wrong kind of attention.

Such was the case involving the 'Cuda. One of Vito's associates had let him know early Friday morning that a client had come into possession of an auto that, for some reason, the client had decided to part with. Perhaps the color did not match his décor. Whatever the case, the client was once again disenchanted with an automobile, and Vito's associate was offered the chance to take it off the client's hands. No reason to trouble anybody with a report about the final disposition. Vito's associate had taken the offer, and in turn called Vito.

The following Sunday morning, Vito received a second call from his associate. The associate hated to bother Vito on the Sabbath, and to trifle in the affairs of others. But, as one gentleman to another, he offered the advice that, if Vito had not already disposed of the 'Cuda, it might be wise to do so as expeditiously as possible. It seemed the car's previous owner had taken leave of his residence sometime on Friday, following a ruckus at a local pub and a night with the constable. Gone on holiday, perhaps. Bit of an unpredictable chap. But it appeared that the lad might have dipped his hand in the till before he departed, and now his employer had an eye peeled. It was probably a tempest in a teapot, but just the same there wasn't any reason to borrow trouble. In case the lad, or his employer, or for that matter the police wanted to start a silly row with whoever had the car, it may as well be with someone other than Vito, mightn't it? Well, that's as that is. Regards to the mum.

And so it happened that at about six o'clock Sunday evening, Vito strutted into Tony's office, cackling like a raven.

"You wanna hear a good one?" asked Vito.

"Lemme guess." Tony looked up from his paperwork. "You got a dick implant and it looks like Uncle Carlo."

"Very funny. No, this is rich. I got a call this morning from my friend Jimmy who turned me on to that 'Cuda. The red one we sold Friday to that jerk-off?"

"Yeah?"

"You remember it belonged to some putz from the south end named Sonny? Remember we was jokin' about how Sonny might come after it? Well get this. Turns out Sonny got out of the can on Friday, and called Jimmy's friend. Said he wants his car back. As if Sonny the dickweed is gonna tell Jimmy's friend what to do."

"And?"

"And Jimmy's friend tells him to stick it where the sun don't shine!"

"So the fuck what?"

"Wait, wait, it gets better! So right after this call, Jimmy's friend's cousin calls Jimmy's friend. Sonny works for him."

Tony squinted at his brother.

"The cousin," explained Vito. "Sonny works for the cousin. And the cousin tells Jimmy's friend to let him know if he hears from Sonny. Turns out Sonny was thrown in the joint before he could sell his shit, or at least before he could turn the proceeds in."

"Will you get to the fuckin' *point*?" The concerns Tony had battled the previous night had started to bang on the dungeon walls.

"Yeah, yeah. Jesus, you ain't got no sense of humor. So Jimmy's friend tells the cousin that Sonny just called and was real anxious to get his car back, like maybe the shit was still in it. So the cousin goes over to the shithole where Sonny lives, not fifteen minutes later, and Sonny's not there. And the place looks like it's been hit by a fuckin' bomb. And no Sonny. Somewheres out there's either a pile of money or some free product rollin' around. And everything points to Sonny's car."

"So I presume you told him there wasn't nothin' in it when we got it."

"He didn't ask, and I didn't say nothin' about it. I didn't check."

"You *what?* The fuck do you mean you didn't check?"

"Jesus, bro, cool your jets! Bobo didn't even have the car out of the van when I called you, and you said drive it over as soon as I could 'cause you had some numbnuts ready to roll on it, so that's what I did. Whatsa big fuckin' deal?"

Tony closed his eyes and shook his head. "Sorry. No big deal. You're right, you did just what I asked. But did these guys think Jimmy had the shit? Do they think we got it?" asked Tony.

"I can't see how. If they hadda thought that, they wouldna called Jimmy on the phone. And Jimmy's solid for us. He was just givin' us a courtesy call to let us know that both Sonny and Jimmy's friend's cousin is lookin' for some missin' shit, and one or the other of 'em might think it was in the 'Cuda."

"So what'd you tell him?" Tony tried to sound casual. He didn't want to explain his concerns to Vito, not right now anyway.

"I told him we sold it to some local jerk-off."

"How'd you know he was local?"

"I thought that's what you told me. You're the one who did the paperwork with him. But he didn't have no trade-in, remember? He took the bus. Or maybe his mama dropped him off." Vito's good humor had returned. "I'd hate to be Jerk-Off right now! What's his name? Vince. Sucks to be Vince!"

"Jimmy ask you for Vince's address?"

"Nah. I think his buddies think Sonny sold the shit and stashed the money somewheres. They're mainly lookin' for him, and they'll take it outta him one way or the other. Jimmy was just callin' to let us know that if we ain't sold that 'Cuda yet we might wanna move it or chop it, in case somebody wants to mix it up. And I agree. Ain't no point in gettin' it on if there ain't nothin' in it for us. But it ain't no big thing. Jimmy knows us, and who we got backin' us. If he's any kinda friend to his biker punk buddy, he'll let him know if he fucks with us he's askin' for two in the hat. Any case, it ain't our problem now. Sonny and Jimmy's buddies can go look for the car if they want, and if they don't find the shit, they can talk to Vince about it. Can't you just see his face if these baboons come knockin' on his door in the middle of the night? Probably drop a load in his pants before they even ask his name!" Vito looked as though he couldn't imagine anything more hilarious, and rested his vocal cords. The conversation had been quite a workout for a man of few words who usually left the talking to his little brother. "Whatsa matter?" he asked at last. "Don't you think this is funny?"

"Yeah, yeah. It's a hoot."

"The hell's eatin' you? Y'actin' like your piles is on fire."

"Nah," said Tony. "Sorry. I'm just cranky today. It's nothin'. Listen, bro, I got some stuff I need to handle. I'll call you tomorrow. Better yet, come on by and I'll have lunch waitin'. Large pepperoni, extra cheese. OK?"

"You got it," agreed Vito. He turned to the door, opened it, then looked back at Tony. "You sure you're OK?"

"Yeah. I'm OK. Thanks, bro."

Vito walked out the door, leaving Tony rolling a pencil back and forth in his fingertips, deep in thought.

Twenty Four

The band at Barker's billed itself as Cock Robin; the name said it. A lead guitar player with two feet of permed Roger Daltrey ringlets was doubled over his instrument like a man in the throes of severe abdominal distress. His mouth was open in a silent scream. The sound from his amplifier was somewhere between three tomcats in a barrel and plate steel jammed into a bench grinder. The singer, Robin, strutted and pouted in the finest tradition of 1980s butt-rock. His pancake-and-glitter makeup did little to conceal the crow's feet at the corners of his eyes and the creases in his cheeks, but he laid everything he had on the line. It beat the hell out of selling paint, which was what he did eight-to-five to pay the mortgage and his daughter's orthodontist bills.

Gina rested her elbows on the sticky table, chin in hands, waiting for Chuck to return with a couple of beers. A few couples gyrated on the dance floor. Single men sat at tables and laughed raucously, or stood solo along the walls and the bar, leering at the women. The women, outnumbered about two to one, preened in groups at tables or hung on their partners' arms.

Why am I here? wondered Gina, reviewing the afternoon's conversation with Chuck in hopes of finding some reason to blame him.

"Hello?" she'd panted into the receiver, having come in from her afternoon run to find the ringing telephone.

"Pick you up at six?"

"Chuck!"

"Who'd you think it was gonna be?"

"Nobody. I mean, I just got in the door. I was out running."

"You didn't forget, did you?" Chuck's husky voice held the slightest touch of accusation.

"No, no," Gina fibbed. "Six is fine."

"Good." Chuck sounded mollified. "I thought we'd grab a steak and then head up to Barker's. There's a band the guys at the station say is hot!"

"I'll be ready." While Gina wasn't sure she shared the musical tastes of the boys at the University District Fire Station, Barker's usually booked bands that could at least manage a danceable beat.

"Great, baby. See ya then."

"'Bye, Chuck." She'd hung up the phone, half-tempted to call him back and cancel. She was irritated at Chuck's growing sense of presumption; she'd only gone out with him three times, and now he was calling her baby. And after the couple of hours she'd spent with Vishnu the night before, she wasn't sure she wanted to go out with Chuck at all. But a steak and some rock-and-roll did sound like fun, and Chuck was easy to look at if you went for the blond linebacker type. And apparently she had already agreed, and didn't feel like going to the effort of canceling. Basically, going out with Chuck for the night was the easy route, and Gina took it.

True to his word, Chuck had arrived at six on the dot, and had even brought her a small bouquet of flowers. His pickup had seen some recent attention from a vacuum cleaner, and the rearview mirror sported a new air freshener (Tall Timber Scent). And dinner had been pleasant. Chuck was clearly trying to be attentive. He even managed to initiate a discussion about a book he had just read, and though basing a critique of Clinton's foreign policy on a Tom Clancy novel might seem like thin soup, Gina had to give Chuck high marks for effort.

Consequently, the simple existential question Gina had put to herself – Why am I here? – had two undercurrents. One was: What am I doing sitting at a roadhouse waiting to drink beer with a guy whose main attraction is his ability to bench-press twice his weight? The other was: What am I doing taking advantage of this poor guy's money and time when I'm not really interested in him? In either case, the answers Gina came up with were not very flattering to her.

Chuck returned from the bar, two bottles in beer in each broad hand. He set two down in front of Gina, two in front of the chair next to her, and squeezed himself into it.

“Two?” asked Gina, half-shouting to be heard.

“Bar was crowded. I figured we'd drink 'em both before the night was through. Band's cookin', huh? Mick told me that the drummer used to tour with Foghat. Hey! Speak of the devil! Mick! Randy!” Chuck raised one of his bottles in salute.

A pair of burly, crew-cut men moving toward the bar waved and altered their course. Gina recognized them as firefighters she'd met at some emergency services mixer, and gave them a smile. Randy leaned over to Chuck. “Be sure she tells you about her big drug bust!” He winked at Gina, and the two men resumed their course for the bar.

Gina spluttered on a swallow of beer. “How the hell did you hear about that?” she yelled to Randy.

“Jungle telegraph!” he called back over his shoulder.

Chuck looked at Gina, eyebrows raised. “It wasn't a bust,” she explained, wiping stray droplets from her upper lip. “A guy I pulled over Friday night discovered some drugs in his car on Saturday, and I helped him turn them in.”

Chuck's big forehead rumpled. “How’d that work? He found drugs, and called you up?”

“Not exactly. I knew that the car used to belong to a drug dealer, and I was concerned that there might be some funny stuff with it. It's nothing, really.”

“So if he didn't call you up, how did you find out about it?”

“Like I said, I pulled him over on Friday night, and went back over to his house on Saturday.” She took a sip of beer, and gestured to the floor. “Want to dance?”

But Chuck was high-centered on the non-drug-bust, and ignored the question. “I don't get it. You went to his house before you knew whether there were drugs in the car? Did you call for backup?”

Gina shrugged and smiled her most disarming smile. “It wasn't that kind of a thing. There wasn't any danger. It's kind of complicated.” She waved her hand dismissively. “The long and short of it is that he'd found some drugs and guns and wanted to turn them in, and that's what happened.

“Guns? You didn't say anything about guns!”

“We haven't talked about it until now! C'mon,” she smiled, a little thinly. “Let's dance.”

She tugged at his arm, but Chuck was the immovable object, hunched forward, elbows solidly planted on the table, determined to dig at this situation until he was satisfied. “I still don't get it. You go over to some guy's house, alone, without knowing about the drugs. And then there’s guns. Why would you go to his house if he didn't call you? How'd you know where he lives?”

“I pulled him over about five blocks from where he lives. I watched him come out of his place. I *saw* where he lives before I even pulled him over! Look, Chuck, don't get all wrapped around the axle over this. I knew where he lived, and stopped by to tell him that I was concerned, and–“

“Were you off duty?”

“When?”

“Saturday.”

“What difference does it make?”

“You were off duty, weren't you.”

“Yeah, but it wasn't like it was dangerous or anything. He told me he'd found a bag with this stuff in it. We called the precinct and had someone come and get it and take a statement.”

“And that's all that happened?”

Gina started to respond, then held the words. “Wait a minute. I get it. You're trying to sound like you're worried about me, all this crap about calling for backup, but you just want to know whether I went out with him. That's really it, isn't it!" Chuck shifted in his chair, but said nothing. "Well, as a matter of fact, Chuck, he made me a cup of coffee and we went for a walk."

"A walk! Oh, right!" Chuck turned his sulky gaze to the band, ranting its way through an old Stones tune.

"Yeah, Chuck, a *walk*! You might have heard about it. You use your legs to move around the surface of the planet. It's quite the rage these days. Some people actually learn how before they're potty-trained. Girls, mostly."

"Well, I don't like it."

"*You* don't like it? What the hell is that supposed to mean?"

"It means I don't like it. I don't want you seeing him."

"Are you kidding me? Screw what you don't like! I don't remember getting a phone call from *you* asking for permission to go hot tubbing naked all night long with a bunch of women EMTs last month. As a matter of fact, I didn't even hear about it from you. I heard about it from Alice. She said you put on quite a show with the bath toys."

"That was different," said Chuck, peevishly. "That was a work retreat."

Gina rolled her eyes, snorted a disdainful and unladylike snort, emptied her beer, and banged the bottle down hard on the table. "Look, *buster*." She jabbed her forefinger hard into Chuck's bicep. "Don't you be giving me a bunch of your double-standard bullshit, and talking to me like I'm your property! When I'm ready to wear your brand on my ass like a cow, you'll be the first to know! Until then, you can go hot tubbing, mud wrestling, or naked skydiving with anyone you want! Have fun, and don't bother to call me to ask if it's OK. As a matter of fact, don't bother to call, period." She stood up, grabbing her purse and jacket.

Chuck looked up at her, genuinely surprised. "Where you going?" He wasn't used to women who stood up to him, especially to make an exit in front of a crowd.

“Home, as if it was any of your business!” Gina's eyes narrowed. “I've had it with this! I've had it with you, and my uncle, and my goddamn mother, and everybody and their frigging cat telling me who I should or shouldn't call on the phone, or who I can or can't go out with, or whose permission I have to get to take a pee!”

Chuck almost apologized. Would have apologized, if he had been in a neutral setting. But instead, he was in a noisy bar, with Robin crowing, “She's under mah *thumb*” to Randy, Mick, and fifty-three other beer-enhanced and proudly-testicled yahoos, who were waving their opposable digits in the air like one hundred and six pieces of testimony to all that was right with the world. And under this influence, Chuck fell into familiar habits, and dealt with Gina like he always did when he was in trouble with a woman, which was to try to placate her in a schmoozy, patronizing way. “C'mon, baby, sit down. You have my permission to pee anytime you want.” He patted the chair she had just left. “As long as I don't have to put the seat down.” He gave her an oleaginous grin, as though his remark could have been found endearing.

Gina looked at him, slack-jawed, then found her voice. “Good luck, Chuck. You'll need it.” And she stalked away from him across the bar, dialing for a cab on her cell, leaving Chuck sitting all by himself.

And Chuck, a big, cute, chauvinistic, oafish, forty-one-year-old little boy, who just wanted to have a good time, and get his way, and not make Mommy mad, watched Mommy walk out the door into the Aurora Avenue night. He shook his head, and stole a glance around to see if anyone had noticed Gina's departure. Nobody seemed to have paid it any mind, which made him feel a little better. “Must be that time of the month,” he said to himself, and looked around the bar for Mick and Randy, or maybe a lonely babe who wanted a beer.

Twenty Five

Tony pulled up to the curb, shut off the engine, and scanned the vicinity. There was the 'Cuda, sitting next to an old Valiant with the hood cracked open. A sandwich-board sign and mural on the front of the building verified that this was the place. A cat lay on the sidewalk in the noonday sun, tail twitching lazily. The quiet street and surrounding area contained nothing to indicate trouble, and everything to indicate that Numbnuts' story was for real. He checked his jacket to make sure he had everything he'd need, took a breath to focus himself, and left the car to do this thing.

Nobody was visible as he entered the shop, and he paused just inside the door. The smell of coffee mixed with the ambience of vulcanized rubber and penetrating oil, and voices, those of Numbnuts and another man, were coming through a doorway to a back room. Tony took a few steps forward, listening.

"...can't come tonight because she's working. But she said it would be fun another time," said Numbnuts.

"Well, now. That's interesting," said the other man. "Skippy owes me a waffle for losing that bet. And what about Heather. Have you called her?"

"No. I decided to let the dust settle. But I can't imagine she'll show up. I spent about an hour cleaning up yesterday, and I'm still finding bits of broken mug on the floor and little vegetable parts in every bike I put on the stand. She's got a hell of an arm."

"Well, if we go zero for two, Skippy owes me *three* waffles. He gave me odds. But Heather not coming makes it less complicated, I suppose."

"Yeah," agreed Numbnuts. "Yeah, it sure does. But I'm going to call her today before the show. Try to clear the air."

"Yes, you should."

Tony thought about all of this. Zero for two could be two women, one named Heather. Was Gina the other one, the one who couldn't come to some show tonight because of having to work? Was Gina working tonight? He could find out. He walked silently to the counter, looking around the shop. A stack of pink papers sat on the end of the counter, flyers advertising a band playing a show on that very night. Vishnu's face grinned from the photo. Ah ha. Now to do what he'd come to do. Forcing himself to think of Numbnuts as Vishnu, he called to the doorway. "Hello?"

"Be right with you!" Tony heard the sound of a chair scraping on the floor, and a second later Vishnu emerged from the back room. "Tony!" He looked out the door past Tony, as though to see if Tony had accomplices stationed in the street.

"Hiya, Vishnu," said Tony. "Nice place you got here." He looked around, walking slowly towards the counter, nodding approval, hands clasped behind his back. "Real nice. Did I come at a bad time?"

"No. This is a fine time." Vishnu walked around the counter to meet him, picking up a big crescent wrench as he went. "What can I do for you?"

"Oh, I was just in the neigborhood and I—good afternoon." Tony addressed the other man, who had emerged from the back room.

"Good afternoon." The man smiled at Tony.

Vishnu turned back to the man and then gestured to Tony. "Bob, this is Tony, of Tony's Tigers. He sold me my new car. Tony, this is Pastor Bob Randall."

"Nice to meetcha, Father. Tony Romano." Tony gave a deferential nod, and Bob came forward to shake his hand.

"Actually, it's just Bob. I'm not a priest. I'm the pastor at St. Thorfinn's Lutheran Church, just up the hill."

"Well, you'll have to excuse me. Where I come from they're all Fathers."

"Fine with me. So you're the gentleman who sold Vishnu his new car. It's made quite an impression on a number of people already. It was the hot gossip among my congregation yesterday." He turned to Vishnu. "You go ahead and take care of business here. I'll just go back and poke through your bookcase, maybe find something interesting. It was a pleasure to meet you Tony." He nodded farewell and went back through the rear doorway.

Vishnu waited until Pastor Bob had left the shop. "If you're looking for the gym bag, I don't have it anymore."

"Gym bag?"

"The one in the trunk of the 'Cuda. Under the spare. I turned it in to the lost-and-found. At the police station." Vishnu emphasized the last two words.

Tony generated a look of bland approval. "Well, that's the best place to turn in lost items. Probably just some old socks or something."

"Yeah. Socks. Or something. So tell me Tony, how's Sonny these days."

"Sonny?" he asked.

"Yeah."

"Who's Sonny?"

"The guy who left the bag in my car."

Tony shrugged. "Don't know him."

"You don't know him."

"No idea. Vito got the car through one of our auction agents. I could call Vito and have him call the agent, tell 'em you took Sammy's box to the police station."

"Bag."

"Bag?"

"Sonny's gym bag."

"Gym bag," repeated Tony. "You want me to call Vito?" Tony pulled his cell phone from his jacket.

Vishnu sighed, turned the wrench over in his hands, and slipped it into the thigh pocket of his overalls. “No. Whatever. So if you weren’t looking for the bag, why are you here?”

Tony smiled as he replaced the phone in his pocket. “Like I said. I had some errands out this way, and thought I’d stop by. I know you were lookin’ for a Valiant, which is a very reliable car. I wanted to make sure you’re not havin’ any trouble with the ’Cuda.”

Vishnu cocked an eyebrow. “Trouble? No. Thing drives like a champ.”

“I'm glad to hear that, Vishnu. But, you know, I just got to thinkin' about the engine in that car, and did a little research after you left on Friday. That V-8 is a lot less reliable than I’d thought. Certainly not anything like the slant-6. Fact is, with the miles on that engine, and the type of drivin’ it’s had, the main bearings could go at any time.” He paused for emphasis, looking concerned. “I'd hate to see you stranded, Vishnu. That ’Cuda’s a great car for its day, but let’s be straight, that one’s been around the block a few times. And you've already had one Plymouth pass on. I know how it feels,” he said, nodding like an uncle comforting his nephew over the death of a beloved dog. “So before you had any more troubles like that, I thought I'd offer the possibility of something in trade. I looked around my lot, and noticed a ’92 Firebird with only about eighty thousand miles. Really good shape, too. Fact is, I drove it over here so’s you could take a look at it.”

“You want me to trade the ’Cuda for a newer Firebird? With less mileage? And you drove it over here so I could look at it?”

“Well, it don't need to be a Pontiac. I know you're a Plymouth man. And with the Firebird I got here, I couldn’t ask you to trade straight across, I know, given the price you paid for the ’Cuda. I’d need to make it worth your while. I could offer you, say, the Firebird and four grand cash.”

“Hold on a second. Let me get this straight.” Vishnu looked like he’d caught a whiff of old fish. “You want to give me four thousand and the Firebird for the ’Cuda. An eight-year-old Firebird, with lower miles.

Basically, you're offering to sell me the Firebird for three thousand dollars."

"Yeah, I guess that's about right," said Tony, as though he hadn't fully worked it out for himself. "Of course, I'll throw in tax, license, and any fees. I've got the paperwork right here with me." He pulled a sheaf of papers out of his inside breast pocket.

"Wait a minute. Not so fast. My friend Evan says I could sell the 'Cuda for more than the seven thousand I bought it from you for. What do you say to that?"

"I'd say your friend Evan might have a point. There's always a market for a classic. On the other hand, you'd probably have to sink some money into it, and some time. If you cleaned it up a little, you might get another grand or two outta the deal. Kinda depends how much your time is worth. But you got smart friends, Vishnu. Tell you what, let's say Evan's right. How about I go five grand and the Firebird?"

"Five thousand dollars, and the Firebird?"

"Yeah. I think it's a good deal I'm offerin' you."

"I don't know, man," said Vishnu. "It's a little too good."

Tony almost smiled in spite of his worries. This wasn't the same Numbnuts he'd played so easily on Friday. Friday's Numbnuts would have gone for anything Tony suggested. Today's Vishnu was going to be a harder fish to land. Finesse, he thought. Let Vishnu run some line off the reel, and set the hook later. Time for a little diversionary tactic. Tony picked up one of the flyers from the counter. "Hey, Vishnu! Is this you? You didn't tell me you was in a band. Mind if I take this?" Tony had already folded the flyer and was tucking it into his jacket pocket. "Maybe I'll come tonight. What kinda music you play?"

"Jazz, mostly."

"Jazz! My favorite!"

"Your favorite. Really."

"Really."

"Who's your favorite pianist?"

"Bud Powell," said Tony, without hesitation. "You play any Bud Powell?"

Vishnu looked surprised. "Uh, actually, we do play a number by him. Bouncin' with Bud."

"No kiddin'! And people say the youth of America have no appreciation of fine music!" Tony beamed at Vishnu, who now looked if not pleased, at least less suspicious. Perfect, thought Tony. Rapport reestablished. "About the car, Vishnu," he continued. "It's really a matter of customer satisfaction. I just wouldn't want you to have any trouble with a car you bought from me. Our relationship could be damaged. Loss of trust. My business is built on repeat customers and word of mouth. Best advertising there is. I always want my customers to say 'Tony looks out for you.' That's what I'm doin' now. Just tryin' to look out for you. You wanna take a look at the Firebird?"

Vishnu looked at the 'Cuda, walked to the doorway to get a look at the Firebird, then looked back at Tony. "No," he said. Then, with more resolution, "I think I'll keep it awhile longer. Maybe your offer is good, but... I just like it. I'll take my chances."

Tony cast about for another angle. This whole situation had turned into a real friggin' rat's nest. Vishnu clearly thought Tony had known about the drugs all along, and probably still thought that, although Tony had euchred him in the conversation about the gym bag. Vishnu also still thought, at least to some extent, that Tony wanted to get the 'Cuda back strictly for business reasons, which could only mean to Vishnu that he'd get screwed. The supreme ironies of the situation were that Tony, for once, had known a lot less than he should have at the outset of the deal (why the *fuck* hadn't Vito checked the car before bringing it over?), and that, for once, there was no business involved. Tony would gladly refund all of Vishnu's money and give him the Firebird for free, if that's what it took to minimize the chance that Gina and the 'Cuda would cross paths. But there was no way to explain any of this without making things worse. What could he say? *Lemme straighten you out, kid. This ain't got nothin' to do with your car, it's got to do with my niece. See, this drug dealer named Sonny and his bosses and maybe some other goons is lookin' for the drugs that was in your car. And now you don't have the drugs, which is gonna piss all of 'em off, and they ain't likely to believe your little story about turnin' anything in to the cops, so if they find you they're gonna be givin' you a little squeeze, which ain't gonna be pretty. But I digress. My niece, Gina – you remember her from Friday night, and maybe Saturday night too? The good-looking cop? I think she's sweet on you, see? Don't ask me why, 'cause it sure as hell don't make no sense to me. I told her you're a numbnuts, but my goddamn sister won't keep her busybody mouth shut, and Gina is stubborn as shit, so if I tell her I think she shouldn't see you, she'll just want to do it more. Sorry. I digress again. Anyways, the main thing is, I don't want Gina to get hurt, so I figure the best thing to do is to get the 'Cuda away from you, on the long shot that Gina could be around when whoever it is comes to get it. Don't get me wrong, kid. I don't give a shit what happens to you. It's Gina I care about.*

It was a truthful explanation, but not helpful. But, Tony was nothing if not a pro. All these things ran through his mind, while he just nodded and spouted genialities, waiting for an angle to come to him. "Well, I respect your decision, Vishnu," he said. "The 'Cuda is a fine car, and there's always a market for those. And I know how it is to get attached to a certain brand. I've always been a Chevy man, myself. Had me an El Camino for twelve years, and that was a hell of a thing. Nothin' impresses the ladies like an El Camino. But Plymouth made some great cars, too. Tell you what. Maybe your engine will go for another million miles, but if you have any concerns, or hear any funny noises, let me know. Vito can take care of it for you. Free of charge. As a matter of fact, why not let Vito take another look it for you, just to make sure. Free, of course. You could bring it by this afternoon." If there was to be an engine problem, thought Tony, it may as well happen today. Vito could arrange that.

Vishnu gazed out the door at nothing in particular for more than a few moments, then shook his head. "I'm kind of busy this afternoon. How about I get back to you on that."

"Fine, Vishnu, fine. I'll be in early. You call anytime." The big man thrust out his hand to Vishnu. "Give my regards to the Father."

Twenty Six

Vishnu went back to his kitchen. Pastor Bob was thumbing through a well-worn copy of The Lyre of Orpheus, chuckling to himself. He looked up at Vishnu. "A madman art-thieving Anglican priest! I should expand my horizons. Maybe I should buy a hot car like yours! I could smuggle stolen Botticellis under the floor mats!"

"That was really weird!" Vishnu exclaimed. "People are amazing! First, he says he doesn't know anything about the drugs or the guns, which I just don't buy. Then he's offering me ridiculous amounts of money for my car! What the hell do you make of it?"

Pastor Bob laid the book on the table and sipped his coffee, saying nothing. Finally he agreed, "People are amazing."

"Come on, Bob. Out with it."

"Out with what?"

"Whatever you're thinking. You think he's the drug dealer?"

Pastor Bob shook his head. "I doubt it. I was eavesdropping – a terrible habit, but useful in my line of work – and it was a fascinating act. But you're right, it doesn't make sense. If I was a drug dealer, and I left my drugs in my car, then lost control of the car, and then found it days later, I wouldn't try to buy the car back from you. Either I'd assume you didn't know they were there, in which case I'd just break into the car or steal it, or I'd assume you would have taken them out, in which case I'd try to rob you but leave the car alone. And if it was about the car, and I was Tony, I'd just steal the car, or rather, have someone steal it. But I don't think this is about the drugs or the car. Tony is obviously a smart man. If he's a drug dealer, I don't think he's the type who absentmindedly leaves his drugs in the trunk of a car, and then sells it by mistake." He took another sip of coffee. "No, there's more to it, I suspect."

"You think I should have sold him the 'Cuda? He was offering me a lot of money. Probably about as much profit as Evan says I could get if I found the right buyer."

"So why didn't you take it?"

Vishnu scratched his head. "Good question," he said at length. "I think I might have, a couple of days ago. Maybe I didn't want Tony to think he could push me around." He thought a bit more. "That's not it, really. I guess I just like the 'Cuda. I'm on some kind of ride with it, and I'm just not ready to get off yet."

Pastor Bob smiled. "People are amazing."

Twenty Seven

If, in the year 2000, you had walked south on Ballard Avenue, you would be looking up at three-story brick buildings that told a story of more than a half-century of commercial bustle, several more decades of hard times, and recent discovery by the Seattle urban chic. While a few of the original businesses remained, most had been replaced by the new jacks.

Mostly gone were taverns with concrete floors, an old pool table with three cues as crooked as a dog's hind leg, fifty-cent schooners, a jukebox that had all of your favorites as long as you liked Hank Williams, and, most distinctively, no windows, because who in the hell wants to look out the window while sitting at the bar drinking a beer? In their places stood ale houses with recycled plank floors, a couple of top-end billiards tables with a fine selection of straight cues, a state-of-the-art sound system pumping out World Music, lots of windows framed with actual living green plants, and, most distinctively, schooners of all the best microbrews starting at a mere three clams apiece. Think globally, get ripped off locally.

Gone were the office supply stores proudly stocked with adding machines, typewriter ribbons, chlorine-bleached paper, all of the toxic products needed to run a normal American office. They had gone the way of the dodo, supplanted by shops with names like InnerVisionSanctuary that sold fine journaling parchment made from the recycled rinds of organically grown vegetables, dead from natural causes.

Nearly nonexistent were the cafes and hash houses where the Tuesday special was always meatloaf, mashed potatoes with gravy, and green beans, because that was what the Tuesday special had been since God invented dirt, served by a waitress named Gladys who had, permanently mounted in the corner of her mouth, an unfiltered Pall Mall that dispensed ashes on your table while she took your order. Prevalent were bistros where the Tuesday special was never the same but tended to be something like *Tillamook Bay sand lance filets, steamed in the vapors of distilled Evian spring water and Absolut vodka, served on a bed of negative-ion-enhanced organic kelp polyps, and drizzled with a durien root viniagrette ($37)*, served by androgynous waitrons named Jason and Melissa who wore name tags that read 'Gladys' as a little retro joke.

And, of course, there were the true harbinger of urban renewal: galleries presenting exhibitions of objects and behavior so cutting-edge, so avant-garde, that even the most cutting-edge, avant-garde of the Seattle intelligencia needed printed guidance and proper critical reviews to alert them to the fact that these exhibitions were, indeed, art.

The particular gallery at which Aguirre was to play that night was located in what had once been a truck repair facility, and had thus been christened 'Honque' by the new owners. Vishnu had mixed feelings about the circumstance. On the one hand, he worried that this kind of gentrification would ultimately force out all of the low-budget sidestreet denizens, like oddball musicians who run little bike shops on Canal Street. On the other hand, it was nice to get gigs at places where the patrons wouldn't throw beer bottles if they couldn't relate to Skippy's muse.

Vishnu arrived at Honque about five-thirty, time enough to set up his gear, get the vibe of the place, and go grab a bite before the music began at eight. He wrangled his amp, bass, mixing board, and bundles of cords and whatnot into the front of the gallery, and looked around at the art. Surprisingly traditional charcoal and ink renderings of larger-than-life-size human figures lined the walls, and found-object sculptures in the tradition of Marcel Duchamp stood on black pedestals throughout the room or hung from the ceiling.

The gallery manager hustled up, an appropriately arty-looking fellow with the obligatory short-cropped but ragged 1950's-nerd haircut, three earrings and a lower lip stud, black hornrims, and an off-center soul patch, no doubt a neo-Dadaistic comment on the moustache. The manager extended his hand to Vishnu. "Alex 3. You must be Vishnu."

"Alex—".

"3. My partner told me all about the band. This will be exquisite. The installation is by a man named German. Isn't that marvelous? With your band named Aguirre and all."

"3?" repeated Vishnu.

"Yes," said the manager, through a sigh of practiced weariness. "And Vishnu. What prompted you to take that name?"

"Actually, it wasn't me. It's my real name."

"I see," said Alex 3, although he didn't. "Well, let me know if there's anything you need. Set the band up on that riser." He pointed to a corner. "The bar will be over there."

"Great," said Vishnu, as Alex 3 hurried off to harangue the caterer, who had hired some performance artists to serve trays of hors d'ouvres. "Don't let them get too funny," Alex 3 told the caterer. "This is a serious installation. I don't want it undermined by humor."

Vishnu began ferrying the pile of equipment onto the stage. Gallery denizens had begun to condense like dew from moist air. Gaunt people dressed in variations of black ranging from twisted Donald Trump elegance to Max Shreck vampirism drifted aimlessly like plankton in a slow ocean current. Alone or in pairs, silent or in voices that never rose above a murmur, they gazed with sophisticated absence at the art, each other, or nothing at all.

"Vishnu! My main man!" Hans came through the door with his drum kit on a dolly. He stripped off his leather jacket, unveiling his sheetrocker's body encased in a white tank top. Vishnu watched the female energy in the room align towards Hans like iron filings around a magnet. Hans proceeded to the stage and began to unload drums from their cases. "I assume that's your car parked out front," he said. "Sweet! And Skippy tells me you've been a very busy lad since Thursday."

"It's been a little wild. What did he tell you?"

"Only that you'd been terrorizing the elderly," said Skippy, coming up from behind and setting down his sax case. "And alternately bear-baiting and charming the constables, causing interpersonal geography to shudder with phreatic blasts not seen since Krakatoa."

"By which I think he means all this stuff with Heather and this other woman," said Hans. "Janine, is it?"

"Gina."

"Gina," said Hans. "See what happens when you don't follow my advice? I tell you to buy a truck, a simple instruction. Go buy a little truck, just like a million other little trucks. Why can't you just listen to me?" He turned to Skippy. "I thought you were on duty this weekend to keep him out of trouble."

"Ah, you forget the Tao of Vishnu," said Skippy, adjusting the reed in his mouthpiece. "The Tao of Hans is to clarify, to bring order to the chaos, to exfoliate the extraneous and thus reveal the rhythm of the quantum. That's why you're the drummer. The Tao of Vishnu is to take that order and refract it into a fretless frenzy, a complicational continuum. His particular genius is to add complication where not even the gods could have foreseen it." He put his lips to his mouthpiece and blew a long wavering quack. "Perfect," he pronounced, and fitted the mouthpiece onto his instrument. "At any rate, my good Aguirre, you know I abhor the very idea of avoiding trouble. The propagation of jazz depends on cosmic tension, which we channel through our muse. And one person's trouble is another's fortune." Skippy placed his sax in its stand. "Where would you be without damaged walls? Where would our friend Vishnu be without flat bicycle tires?"

"Hungry," said Vishnu, "which is where I am now. I'm heading out for a bite. Any takers?"

Hans shook his head. “I think I’ve got a couple of things to go take care of before the show.” He made eye contact with a redheaded woman in the crowd.

Skippy looked appreciatively at the hors d’ouvres trays, filled with trendy nimnams. “Those are being underutilized, I think. As a chef, I know how hard it is when people don’t appreciate your work. I’d hate to have the caterer feel unloved. And the price is right for poetical-minded house musicians. I do believe I'll stay here and ensure that our staff members don't fall prey to sloth.” He indicated the waiters, who were walking as though underwater in imitation of the patrons as they carried trays of food to and fro.

“Well, I'm going to go get some grub,” said Vishnu. “Final tuning at quarter to eight?” Hans and Skippy nodded, and the trio dispersed.

Twenty Eight

About half an hour after returning from Vishnu's shop, Tony sat in his office, willing would-be customers away while he figured out his next move. Vishnu hadn't fallen for his ploy with the Firebird. Maybe he'd been too clumsy. Maybe he was losing his touch. Maybe he was overreacting. Maybe Sonny had flown the coop. Maybe there wasn't anything between Gina and Vishnu. Maybe. Maybe Gina and Vishnu were in the 'Cuda right now doing the hokey-pokey, and Sonny was walking up to it with a sawed-off shotgun and trouble in mind.

"Shit," Tony muttered. "How do things like this start?" He rolled his cigar from one side of his mouth to the other. His overall plan was simple enough – get the 'Cuda away from Vishnu, one way or the other. It was still his plan, but his first shot, always the best shot, hadn't worked. Maybe he should've just had the 'Cuda stolen straight off instead of screwing around like he had, but he'd wanted to finesse the situation because Gina was involved. Now his hand was tipped, and time was running out. Vishnu had been driving the goddamn car all over Seattle, showing it to his friends; the Father had said so. Gina had spotted it, and Christ only knew who else. "There's just too goddamn many people lookin' for that car," said Tony, stubbing out his cigar. And as he said it, he saw the opportunity inside the problem.

He pulled the flyer for the gig out of his jacket pocket and studied it. "Too goddamn many people," he repeated, as he dialed a number on his cell, punched in his own number, and hung up. Usually it was Vito who made such arrangements, but Tony had a few friends of his own. And he didn't want Vito in on this. Not yet, anyway. He stood up and began pacing the office, the plan taking shape in his head. His cell rang. "Yeah," said Tony.

"You called?" said a voice.

"Yeah. My friend wants you to pick his car up." Tony described the 'Cuda, where it would be that evening, and when.

"Where's your friend?"

"He's busy tonight. He's playin' music inside where I told you."

"Inside."

"Yeah. But he's gonna be busy. I'm gonna help him."

"Did he give you the keys?" asked the Voice.

"No," said Tony. "You'll have to use your spare set."

"That will be an extra charge. Five more."

"No problem," agreed Tony. "My friend said the car will be outside the club. If it ain't, I'll meet you on the corner of Ballard and Ione and tell you where it is. You just pick it up by ten, and drop it at the usual spot. If it's picked up by ten, my friend said he'll pay you double your normal fee. Plus the five."

The Voice read back the other information to Tony, who confirmed it. "What if your friend decides he doesn't want it picked up?" asked the Voice.

"I don't expect that. I'll be there to help him so you should have no problem. And if the car ain't available you still get the five for mobilization."

"Double fee, plus five."

"Plus the five."

"It's a done thing," said the Voice, and hung up.

Tony took a deep breath and exhaled slowly. He began to relax, moving around the office with the loose grace of a boxer circling his opponent, running through scenarios in his head. This would work. It was a little tricky, but it would work. If Vishnu could see the street from the bandstand, there could be complications. Vishnu would need to be busy, or at least distracted, and to ensure that Tony would have to be in the club. Which meant that the biggest risk was Vishnu accusing him of involvement. But there was nothing to be done about that, and the rest of the plan was solid. The Voice was the best in the business, and the delivery end was airtight. And the safety valve was inside the original problem – there were too goddamn many people lookin' for that car. Plenty of people. Less careful people. People who weren't as smart. People who the cops would be happy to talk to if they were pointed in the right direction.

Tony started to hum a snatch of Luck Be A Lady as laid down by Sinatra. It was a night for jazz, and the soul of jazz was improvisation. Improvisation was Tony's profession, and he was a master of his craft.

Twenty Nine

Skippy was making some arcane adjustment to his saxophone when Vishnu returned to Honque. Hans was sitting on his drummer's stool, eyes closed as though in meditation.

"Ready?" asked Skippy.

"Yeah," replied Vishnu. "Man, I tell you, this hot weather must be making people cranky. I was getting my dinner, and some guy got all wigged out over having to wait for his food." He shook his head. "People need to relax."

Skippy ran his fingers over the pads of his instrument, nodding. "Well, Aguirre will sooth the savage beast. Nothing but Orpheus and Morpheus, baby."

Hans opened his eyes. "I don't think this crowd needs much soothing," he said, looking around at the murmuring patrons.

"Well, either way, it's about time," said Vishnu. He turned on his amp and rechecked the tuning on his bass. "Wait a minute!" He slapped his forehead with his palm. "I forgot to call Heather. Hans, can I borrow your cell?"

Hans pulled it from his pocket and handed it to Vishnu. "What are you calling her for?"

"I want to clear the air between us."

"I think there's more smog in the air that you can clear with five minutes of your honeyed explanations. Besides, if I know Heather, she's hunkered in the hot tubs down at Breitenbush. Getting back in touch with her inner karma, or whatever. Forget it, man. Everything's done under the sun." He pointed a drumstick at Vishnu's bass. "Just play. You can talk to her later, for what good it will do."

"You're probably right," said Vishnu, handing Hans' cell back to him. He looked over at Alex 3, who gave him an impatient gesture. Vishnu turned to Hans. "Take it away."

Hans picked up his sticks and flashing a smile at the redheaded woman, who looked back at him with doe eyes. "Ladies and gentlemen!" he yelled. The crowd quieted, looking at him with blank expectation. Hans pointed a drumstick at a randomly selected patron. "We are Aguirre!" he cried, and led off with a blistering solo. Eight measures later Skippy and Vishnu kicked into Coltrane's Giant Steps, and the wild rumpus began.

Thirty

At five-thirty Monday afternoon, Sonny's luck changed.

Since leaving his trailer on Friday, he'd been holed up in an Aurora Avenue shithole motel up in north Seattle. It hadn't been a restful stay. He was out of his turf. He had put out the word to everyone he dared trust to call him if they saw his car, but he hadn't gotten any reports on it, and each hour decreased his chances. He was hiding from two groups of people, which was new for him – he was used to being the hunter, not the prey – and in contrast to the situation with his car, each passing hour increased his chances of being found. And the most fucked thing to Sonny was that he couldn't do a damn thing but sit tight, which was driving him batshit crazy.

Sonny was used to constant motion, like a shark. Sitting still made him feel naked and exposed, with too much repeated face time with people he was sure who would turn him for a six-pack of Hamms and a lottery ticket. The motel manager was looking through the office curtains every time Sonny went out to get food. The woman at the grimy little store on the corner was always on the phone, but hung up every time he came in. The guy at the car lot in south Everett where he'd bought the shitty little car yesterday had wanted to talk all fucking day, like he was trying to keep Sonny from leaving. There were just too many people looking at him funny, and he was getting real itchy, and he couldn't do anything but stay holed up or try to make a run for it.

But at five-thirty on Monday afternoon things turned for him. A skinny little tweaker had called Sonny with the news that he had spotted a red 'Cuda outside an address in south Ballard. Sonny got him off the line with an empty promise of future goods, and breathed his first relaxed breath in days. He took a triumphant crap in the rust-stained toilet, delegating the job of flushing for the management. He checked his fatigue pockets for the roll of cash, and checked the cylinder of the .32 to make sure it was loaded. Satisfied, he stuck it back in his pocket, and swaggered out the door past the accumulated litter of fast-food wrappers and beer cans on the floor.

The motel manager's opossum-like face was peering through the office window as Sonny crossed the cracked asphalt, a freshly lit Camel in his mouth. Sonny was sorely tempted to go into the office and yank the manager's chain, menace the wizened little fuck just for the sheer fun of it, give him a good look down the barrel of the .32. It was the sort of inspiration that characterized Sonny's life, but somehow he passed it up, settling instead for a defiant stare at the gap in the office curtains. He was going to find his baby.

Thirty One

The band had been stoking it hot and heavy for about half an hour. Vishnu had just led the band into a trio arrangement of Magical Dog when he caught sight of Tony standing near the big front window. Tony seemed to be watching the door and the street as much as anything, but his head was bobbing to the beat. Before he could think much about Tony's presence, Vishnu's eye was distracted by a tall blonde hottie at the bar. Dressed to kill in a tight red blouse, an even tighter red miniskirt, her four-inch Fuck-Me pumps raised the top of her head above all the women and half of the men. Wow, thought Vishnu, and then recognition made him lose his place for a couple of measures in the land of 11/4 syncopation. He had never seen Heather dressed like that. He didn't even know she owned clothes like that. Further, she was holding a plastic cup of brown liquid and ice cubes, which might be a Coke, except Heather detested soft drinks. On the other hand, Vishnu had never seen her drink booze.

Whatever was in the cup, it swirled wildly with her gestures while she flirted with a couple of gallery rogues. Heather tossed off the contents of her cup at one go and wove her way over to the bar. Planting her elbows on it, she leaned low over the bar, giving the bartender an eyeful. The bartender refrained from ogling her balcony while he poured a generous double-splash of whiskey into a fresh cup. Heather fished around in a tiny black purse and tossed several bills onto the edge of the bar. They teetered and fell to the floor. Paying them no heed, she took her drink, fixed Vishnu with a venomous stare, and veered off to a group of people clustered around a rather phallic sculpture. She gestured at it with her drink, put her free hand on the nearest man's shoulder, and said something in his ear that made him laugh and caused the other two to look at each other behind her back. The lone woman in the group glared at the back of Heather's head.

Well, what the hell, thought Vishnu. It's a free country.

Thirty Two

Gina spent Monday doing household chores in her Northgate condo, her mood oscillating between disgust towards anything on two legs with a Y-chromosome, and curiosity about Vishnu. Her frustration with Tony and Vito was overlaid by a thick layer of indignance at Chuck's behavior the night before. Gina kept trying to paint Vishnu with the same brush so she could enjoy a bout of guilt-free man-bashing. But try as she might, she couldn't quite manage to convince herself that Vishnu was just like Chuck, and had to admit in the end that Vishnu was unlike any guy she'd ever been attracted to.

Her usual pick for a man was a guy with a buff upper body who wore cologne, had a blow-dried hairstyle, was shrewd but not necessarily smart, was suave, and owned a slick vehicle or two. In comparison, Vishnu was skinny, smelled like himself, had no hairstyle whatsoever, seemed smart but little naïve, and owned a car that, while it was many things, wasn't slick.

That was Gina's historical pattern. But now, as she folded her laundry, she explored the idea that maybe the guys she'd been going out with were muscle-bound pine-scented lugs who spent too much time looking at themselves in the mirror pumping in the weight room and primping in the bathroom. Guys who were rather dull-witted, arrogant, and owned a slick car or two. She still liked the slick cars.

Viewed in this light, Vishnu was lithe, smelled like a man ought to smell, had rather nice wavy hair, was considerate, pretty sharp, and drove a fast car that could be cleaned up with a little elbow grease. She was still concerned about him keeping the 'Cuda, but there was a lot of water to go under that bridge before she dropped a boat in it. Besides, in the light of day, her concerns about Sonny had started to seem overblown.

She turned her attention to the music thing, which intrigued her. To a man, her previous beaus' concept of music extended to something that came out of a stereo, and stayed well within the scope of rock-and-roll. She'd never even gone on a date with a guy who knew anything about jazz, let alone anyone who admitted to playing it on an actual instrument. That is, aside from a brief involvement with the trumpet player in high school, who was stuck on himself but had startling kissing technique. Now, she was faced with this guy who not only played an instrument, but was the bonafide leader of a jazz band, and was serious enough about it to put his face on a poster and staple it to a telephone pole telling total strangers to come and listen.

Gina put down the shirt she was folding, and picked up the flyer for the gig she'd brought home from Vishnu's. She examined the band photo. He *was* good-looking. And nice. He'd said the band's name was from some German movie. That was another thing – he was into movies other than the latest action flick. Gina examined the floral border on the flyer, and came to no conclusions.

Her thoughts were split by the feline screams of two crotch-rocket motorcycles blasting down the street. Gina glanced out the window. The riders were at the stop sign, checking out the buttocks of a woman walking down the street. One black visor turned to the other, nodded, and turned back to ogle the woman some more. Then, having their fill for the moment, they shot off down the street in her direction. As they passed her, one of the riders gunned his engine and popped a wheelie, apparently thinking the woman might swoon at the sight of a brief mechanical erection.

Gina's feelings of anger and disgust returned. Men were such a pain in the ass. What was the attraction? Her married friends spent most of their time complaining about their husbands. Her unmarried friends alternated between complaining about their ex-whatevers and driveling on about the guys they were trying to lure into a new half-baked emotional mess. Sometimes, especially after times like the evening she'd just had with Chuck, Gina felt like the whole relationship thing was just more trouble than it was worth.

She walked over to her bed and sat down, chin in hands. Her eyes fell upon a framed picture of her mother and father, and, riding on her dad's shoulders, six-year-old Gina. Her mom looked so happy. All of them did. Gina thought back to when she was a girl. Her mom *had* actually been happy, as far as Gina could tell, and in love with her dad. Had her mom just been fooled all those years? Gina considered her mom and dismissed the idea that Remilda Ivelia Romano Kowalski could have been fooled for over two decades. Was it possible that men, categorically, were not the whole problem?

She picked up her phone and dialed her mother's office.

"Mardin, Pierce and Hamill, may I help you?"

"I hope so, Mom."

"Gina, honey! What a nice surprise! Where are you?"

"Sitting on my bed."

"Is something wrong? Are you sick?"

"No. I'm not sick, anyway. Nothing's really wrong, I guess. Mom?"

"Yes, honey?"

"Do you have a few minutes to talk?"

"Sure, honey. What about?"

"Men."

"Hang on a second." There was a sound of voices muffled by a hand, then Remi spoke distinctly into the receiver. "Do I have a few minutes to talk about men with my only daughter? I should hope so." Gina heard a whoop in the background, and a woman's voice yell, "Rope 'em and tie 'em!"

"Was that Bev, Mom?"

"Mr. Mardin just won a big case, and Bev was congratulating him. So, honey, what would you like to know?"

Gina heard Bev laugh, but continued. "Mom, were you and Dad happy?"

There was a pause on the line. "Yes," Remi said finally. "Yes we were, honey. Terribly happy."

"But were there times when you weren't? Weren't there things about Dad that just pissed you off?"

Remi guffawed. "Oh Jesus Lord! Are you kidding?"

"Like what?"

"Oh, my, where do I start? For one thing, your father was the most infuriatingly pig-headed man I ever met. Don't you remember how he was always after me to let him convert the garage into a saltwater aquarium and raise salmon in big tanks? I wanted a hot tub and a gazebo, and he wanted a fish hatchery. You must remember that! We argued about it for years. He never gave up! We argued about that until the day..." Remi's voice caught. "Until the day he died," she finished softly. "But good Lord, what a wonderful time we had together. Your daddy's infuriating pigheadedness was one of his biggest attractions." She was silent for a moment. "I know you heard us arguing sometimes. It wasn't in your father's nature to hold it in, or mine either, God knows. But is there some reason you thought we weren't happy?"

"No. No, Mom. I remember you being happy, and Dad too. I just...I don't know. I mean, how do you know, though, at the start? How did you know Dad was the one?"

Remi laughed. "You mean besides being young and funny and terribly handsome?"

"I'm serious, Mom."

"I know that, sweetie. But I'm not sure I can answer your question. It wasn't something I really decided, not like other decisions you might. It was just easy with him. He made me laugh. We made each other laugh."

Gina considered that. "Chuck doesn't make me laugh."

"Is this about Chuck?"

Gina thought. "No. No, I really don't need any advice about Chuck."

The two women let the silence pass. Finally Remi spoke. "Sweetheart?"

"Yeah, Mom?"

"Being happy isn't about not having problems. But when you're with someone you can laugh with, it doesn't matter if he drives you crazy. It just makes it more fun."

Gina was quiet for a moment. "Yeah," she said.

"Are you doing OK, honey? You sound down."

"I'm OK, Mom. I'm just trying to figure some things out. But I'm OK. Don't worry about me."

"The day I stop worrying about you is the day I'll die. But I'll take your word for it."

"OK. Thanks, Mom. Bye. Say hi to Bev."

"I'll do that. Bye bye."

Gina set the phone down and studied the framed picture of her parents. Impulsively, she picked up her phone and called Hank's number.

"Hello?"

"Hank. This is Gina."

"Hey! How you doing?"

"Fine. Great. Hey, I've got a favor to ask of you. Can you sub at work for me tonight? I can return the favor later in the week."

"Let me check with Ann." There was a few seconds of background discussion, then Hank's voice returned. "Sure, Gina. I can do that. Is something wrong?"

"Oh, no. Things are great. I just had a chance to do something on short notice."

"Well, it's not a problem," replied Hank. "Just call in and let the sergeant know."

"Will do. Thanks."

"You're welcome. See ya soon."

"Bye, Hank."

Gina stood there holding the receiver. Should she call Vishnu, or just show up? She opted for the latter. She told herself that it was to give herself an out if the music was too horrible for her to even enter the place, but the real reason was a teenager's whim to have the element of surprise.

Thirty Three

Sonny left the Ratbox Inn and drove straight to the address he'd been given, arriving about a quarter to six. He found the building as described, but instead of his 'Cuda found only an old green hulk. A man in coveralls was assembling a bunch of metal scraps and wire in the driveway of the building next door.

Sonny pulled up and rolled down the window. "Hey!" he called, trying to sound friendly. "I'm looking for a friend of mine who drives a red 'Cuda. A big car with big tires. He just got it. You seen it?"

The man looked up from his work. "You mean Vishnu? Yeah, he lives right there." He pointed to Vishnu's shop.

"He drives the 'Cuda?"

The man straightened up to his full height and adjusted a red bandanna holding back what was left of his graying hair. "I don't know from 'Cudas, but he got a new car a couple days ago. Red and loud." The man's sculpture was urban abstract, but his drawl came from somewhere in the sagebrush.

"Is he around?" Sonny wanted to know.

"He left about a half hour ago."

"Did he say when he'd be back?"

"Sure didn't. But I think he's got a gig tonight."

"A gig?"

"You know, his band." The man walked over to Sonny's car and looked at him curiously. "You sure we're talking about the same guy?"

"Yeah, yeah, the band," said Sonny, "I forgot. Hey, where is it? The gig. I should go surprise him."

"Right here in Ballard, somewhere."

"You know the address?"

"Sorry, pardner. But I'm sure it's around here somewhere." He smiled at Sonny.

Fuck it, thought Sonny. "Thanks," he said.

"You want me to tell him you came by?"

"No, that's OK."

As Sonny pulled away, the man's eyes passed across a flyer on a nearby telephone pole. "Hey! Wait a minute, bud! The address is right here!" He yelled and pointed at the flyer, but just a moment too late.

Sonny headed northwest back up Leary and hung a left onto Market Street westbound. He was feeling upbeat. He was closing in on his baby, and before the night was over he'd have it back, one way or the other. For now, he would drive around looking for it. If he found it, he would leave the piece of shit he was currently driving and reclaim his baby when the moment was right. If he didn't find it by midnight, he would just go back to wait for Fish, or whatever the fuck his name was. Fish would come home, go to bed, and Sonny would jack the 'Cuda right there. It wasn't even a real jacking. Sonny felt his pants pocket to make sure he felt his keychain. All he needed to do was walk up, unlock the door, start the motor, and drive away.

But all good things must pass, and as Sonny passed the Chittenden Locks his happiness began to deteriorate into the usual paranoia. Maybe he should just go back and wait near Fish's pad. Just driving around looking, things could go wrong between now and when Fish came home. He could get pulled over by the pigs. He could get in a wreck. On the other hand, Sonny thought, if Fish is busy playing music in a bar, I'll look like any other asshole unlocking a car door and driving away.

Thinking at this level was pretty highfalootin' stuff for Sonny, and between the unusual amount of energy being consumed by his brain and the fact that it was dinnertime, Sonny was hungry. Burgers, he thought. Get me a burger. And some fries.

One of the great triumphs of modern American urban civilization is the constant proximity of low-quality burgers. In Sonny's case, nearby was only a couple of hundred feet ahead, in the form of Cap'n Jack's Burger Hut, a small building on the local historical register of teen-age gutbomb palaces, liberally festooned with faux-Polynesian goo-gaws: plastic palm trees, glowering tiki statues, garlands of garish weatherproof tropical flowers, and an eight-foot fiberglass orca the likes of which had never graced the South Seas.

Sonny pulled into the front parking lot. As he got out, a tall, skinny guy wearing a t-shirt with the message 'Dinky's Donuts - The Hole is Free!' came around from the back parking lot. Donut Man stepped into line behind a teenage girl at the counter, who was gossiping with another girl working the till. The cook, a fifty-something fireplug with a jarhead haircut and a Semper Fi tattoo on his massive left bicep worked slowly at the grill.

Donut Man stood staring at the menu board. The girl at the till chattered to her friend. "...and, like, he was all, like, 'Sure, I can go,' and I was, like, 'Snap!' I mean, he's such a hottie, and Marissa, like, dumped him, and—"

"Jesus Fuckin' *Christ*," said Sonny. Donut Man seemed not to have heard, and the cook was too far away, but the curse silenced the girls.

"Order up!" called the cook, sliding a paper bag across the stainless steel table to the cashier. She handed it to her friend, who moved down to the end of the counter. The cashier looked up at Donut Man expectantly."Can I take your order, sir?"

"I'm torn between the Hula Hula Lollapalooza and the Ham-N-Angus Rebel Rouser," responded Donut Man, as though it was a deep philosophical dilemma. "I've had the Hula Hula and it was good, but tonight I just don't know. Which do you prefer?"

The cashier giggled. "Well, I don't eat red meat." She giggled again, and was joined in this by her friend. Sonny shifted his weight impatiently. "But the Shakespeare's Codpiece is good," the cashier continued. "It's, like, fish, on a bun, like a fish sandwich." She giggled again. "I don't get the name. But it's good. I mean, if you like fish."

"Fish," said Donut Man. "Hmm. Fish." He turned to look at Sonny. "What do you think of fish?"

Sonny looked at Donut Man, then his mouth split into a malicious grin. "I think if I find a guy named Fish, I'm gonna kick his fuckin' ass!" He laughed, a humorless sound, then the smile left his face as suddenly as it had appeared. "Now, are you gonna *fuckin'* order, or what?"

Donut Man turned back to the cashier, who was now looking at Sonny wide-eyed. The cook was looking at Sonny too, impassively. He casually removed a billyclub from a hook on the wall and laid it next it next to the chef's knife on the cutting board.

"Ham-N-Angus it is," announced Donut Man. "And fries and a chocolate shake."

The cashier finished the transaction and turned to the shake machine. The cook began preparing the order with the careful deliberation of a demolitions expert defusing a land mine. The cashier finished Donut Man's shake, set it aside, and turned to Sonny. "Can I take your order, sir?"

"Cheeseburger, fries, and a root beer," Sonny said, looking over his shoulder. Gotta get the fuck outta here, he thought. Little sirens of craziness were going off inside his head. Just being around people was difficult for him under the best of circumstances, let alone being in unfamiliar turf, with The Man and maybe Tiny looking for him, and with the 'Cuda's recovery so close he could taste it. He tried to focus on the imminent success of finding his car, and to ignore the possible consequences of a missing gym bag.

The cashier wrote the order down quickly, took Sonny's cash, gave him his change, and busied herself with tasks near her friend at the end of the counter.

Donut Man turned to Sonny. "I notice you have a Plymouth Reliant. What do you think of it?" He smiled, as though Sonny had indicated he wanted to make small talk about cars with some dipshit at a burger joint. Sonny stared at Donut Man, barely able to restrain the urge to take a swing at him. Oblivious, Donut Man went on. "I had a Valiant. They were like the ancestor of the Reliant. My Valiant lasted thirty years! It just died last Thursday, as a matter of fact." He nodded, as though this explained much, then grinned at Sonny. "But guess what I got to replace it!"

Sonny exploded. "Will you shut the *fuck* up?" He scowled at the cashier. "When am I gonna get my *fuckin'* food?"

"Ham-N-Angus." The cook slid a paper bag across the table to the cashier. "And you watch your mouth, buddy." He stared at Sonny.

Sonny took a step toward the counter. "The fuck *you* gonna do?"

The cook's hand went to the nightstick and he started out around the table. Sonny's hand went to his pocket and wrapped around the grip of his .32.

"Hey, why don't you just take my burger?" All eyes went to Donut Man. "You're in a hurry, and I'm not," he continued. "Why don't you just have mine?"

The cashier quickly handed Donut Man his bag and shake, and backed away from the counter. Donut Man held them out to Sonny, one in each hand. "Go ahead. It's OK."

Sonny looked at Donut Man for a moment, then removed his hand from his pocket and snatched the items. "Fuck you," he muttered, stalked off to his car, and squealed from the lot as best as a Reliant would squeal.

"Jesus *fuckin'* Christ," Sonny said to himself through a mouthful of Ham-N-Angus, as he headed east up the hill from Golden Gardens. "What a buncha fuckin' losers." He chomped and slurped with a vengeance as he started weaving his way south from 85th, cruising every commercial street between Aurora and Puget Sound for a place that had live music and a red 'Cuda.

Thirty Four

Remi rolled things over in her mind as she slipped out of her office pumps and into her walking shoes. Two calls for advice from Gina was about a six-month quota, and Gina had used it in less than two days. At least the girl wasn't hung up on Chuck, which was fine with Remi. Chuck was probably OK if you wanted a couch moved or someone to look good in a suit at a wedding, but the few minutes Remi had spent with him had made obvious that if she'd cracked a joke it would have been fifty-fifty whether he'd laugh or stand there like an ox wondering which weed to eat. Nothing to compare with Jan. Now this Vishnu character, thought Remi. He sounds interesting. Different, anyway. Whatever had happened between him and Gina had been enough to generate the two phone calls. And beyond all that lay the unspecified entanglement of Tony. It was simply too much to expect a woman, a sister, a mother, to let lie.

Remi tapped her pen on her desk, then ran through her phone list to find a number at the SPD North Precinct. As she began dialing, she thought of how to frame the conversation. What, exactly, was she after, and how was she going to get it? She was still pondering these questions when the call was answered.

"Seattle Police, Sergeant Fox. How may I help you?"

"Hello, Sergeant. This is Remi Kowalski, Gina Kowalski's mother. We met at Gina's swearing-in ceremony. How are you today?"

"Oh, yes, Mrs. Kowalski, I remember. I'm fine. How are you?"

"Just fine, thank you. Listen, Sergeant, I don't want to take up your valuable time, but I have a favor to ask. I have a package for Gina that I wanted to get to her tonight, but I don't want to leave it on her doorstep.

Is there any possibility I could leave it at the station so she could get it when she gets off duty?"

"Not a problem, Mrs. Kowalski, but Gina's not on duty tonight."

"Oh, I'm sorry, I must have written her schedule down incorrectly."

"No, Mrs. Kowalski, you had it right, but she called in this afternoon to say that she was going to trade shifts with Officer Collins."

"Oh. Well, how nice. Gina speaks very highly of Hank. It's good to know that she's made such good friends on the force."

"Well, we're glad to have her, Mrs. Kowalski. Is there anything else I can help you with?"

"No thank you, Sergeant. You have a good evening."

"You too, Mrs. Kowalski."

Remi hung up, looking very satisfied with herself. Score one for motherly intuition. Now, what had Gina said Vishnu's last name was? Tenstone. No, Tensleep. That was it. She pulled out the Seattle phone directory and riffled through to the Ts. There it was. Tensleep, Vishnu, on Canal Street. But he could still be at his shop. Gina had said he owned his shop, but hadn't said what the name was. Would he have given it his own name? She flipped through the business listings to the Vs. Score *two* for motherly intuition. Vishnu Tensleep Cycle Works, with the same Canal Street address. Now that was interesting.

Remi turned to Bev, who was logging off her computer. "What do you say we go fishing tonight?"

Bev looked confused. Neither woman had been fishing since Jan had died. "Fishing for what?" she asked.

"Bicycles."

Thirty Five

An hour later, Bev threaded her old Ford pickup through the southbound traffic on Greenwood Avenue like a cutting horse chasing a calf. "Where the hell are we goin' again?" she asked Remi.

"Canal Street. Right down where it runs into Leary."

"You gonna tell me what we're gonna do there?"

"I told you, fishing."

"Oh, come on, girl! It's time to spill the beans! I'm gonna pull over and park until you tell me!" Bev put on the turn signal and took her foot off the gas.

"OK, you win," laughed Remi, and told Bev everything she knew or suspected. "So I'm not quite sure what we're looking for," she finished. "Just fishing, like I said."

"You sure I shouldn't have brought my pistol?"

"I said fishing, Bev, not shooting snakes! And I hope you don't have it inside your jacket, just because you have a permit."

"Well, I always have a rope, just in case," said Bev, referring to the neatly coiled lariat hanging from the gun rack behind her head.

"If he looks like he's going to stampede, Bev, you have my permission to stop him. Turn here."

Bev steered the pickup onto Canal Street and drove a couple of blocks.

"Slow down, there it is." Remi pointed to a building in the next block with a gaily-painted facade below the roof and a sign with Vishnu's name above the side window. A metal sculpture stood in the driveway next door. "Let's park here," said Remi. Bev pulled the truck to the curb about half a block away. "I don't see Gina's car," said Remi. "Let's just go take a quick look."

The two women walked down the street and stood on the sidewalk in front of the shop. Other than a careworn old car in the driveway, it looked like nobody was home. Remi began to walk up to the door. "What are you doing?" asked Bev.

"I was just going to see if he's here."

"What are you going to say if he answers the door? You don't have a bicycle."

"I'll just ask if he'll be open tomorrow. I just want to get a look at him."

"Well, you're makin' me nervous, girl."

"Relax, Bev. He doesn't know us, remember?" Remi knocked on the shop door. There was no response.

"What now, girl?" Bev stood on the sidewalk, thumbs hooked in the pockets of her jeans, looking around and tapping the heel of her boot on the pavement. Remi shrugged and walked back to her. They both looked at the sign on the window.

"May I help you ladies?"

Bev and Remi turned. A tall man in overalls was carrying a box of plexiglass sheets in various colors and shapes. He set the box down beside the sculpture and smiled at the two women. "You all looking for Vishnu?"

"Why, yes." Remi returned his smile. "He doesn't seem to be here."

"He's at his gig. His show." The man pointed at the flyer tacked on the phone pole behind him. "You're the second person to come by askin' for him. Second and third."

"Really," said Remi. "How interesting." She walked over to the man. "I'm Alice," said Remi. "This is my friend Wanda."

"Eldon," replied the man. "Eldon Harper. Wanda." He nodded to Bev.

"Uh, howdy," she said.

"You say Vishnu's show is tonight?" asked Remi.

"Yup. Come see." Eldon led them to the phone pole and pointed to the flyer. "It's a jazz band. They can really play, too. I grew up on country, and I didn't listen to much jazz until I moved in next to Vishnu, but it sounds good to me. You all oughta go."

"We might just do that," said Remi. "You say other people have been by?"

"Just one. A guy came by about an hour ago. Maybe more. I never seen him before. Said he was goin' to the show, too,"

"You didn't happen to see a woman, did you?" asked Remi. "Late thirties, looks like me but a lot prettier?" Remi smiled. "My niece."

Eldon grinned and shook his head. "No ma'am. Guy I saw was all by himself. If I see your niece, you want me to tell her you called?"

"Oh, no, Eldon. But thank you."

"Okey-doke." Eldon's gaze went to Bev, and he cocked his head. "Wanda, huh?" He shook his head. "Funny."

"What?" asked Bev.

"Aw, it's nothin'." He looked down the street, then back at her. "You any relation to a woman named Beverly Hall?" Bev wasn't sure what to say. "Guess not," answered Eldon for her. "I ain't seen her since she graduated high school. That'd be, gosh, 1963. But I swear you could be her sister. Cousin, anyway."

"Isn't that fascinating?" said Remi. "Where did you go to school, Eldon?"

"No place you ever heard of, I bet. Baker City, Oregon. I grew up on a ranch south of there." He looked at Bev again. "Girl I knew in high school looked just like you. Damn, she was somethin' else. Could ride like the wind, rope a barn swallow, and shoot the ass off a cricket." Eldon shook his head and grinned at the memory.

"She sounds like quite a character," said Remi.

"That she was, ma'am, that she was. Truth is, I had quite a crush on her, but she was a year older than I was, so I never let on. Foolish." He chuckled, then raised his index finger. "Youth is wasted on the young, as my friend Skippy would say."

"Sad, but true. Well, it was nice to meet you Eldon," said Remi.

"You too, Alice. And you Wanda."

"My pleasure, Eldon."

Remi and Bev walked back to the truck and drove slowly past Eldon. He gave a standard wave of the hand to Remi, and to Bev he gave the index-finger pistol-shot salute of the desert west. Without thinking, Bev responded in kind. She pulled about fifty feet past and stopped.

"Quick. Roll down your window," she said to Remi, then backed up to Eldon's driveway.

"Hey Eldon!" Bev yelled through the open window. Eldon turned around to look at her. "Go Bulldogs!" Bev popped the clutch and barreled around the corner.

"Eldon Harper!" Bev exclaimed as they pulled onto Leary Way. "Holy shit, Remi, who'd've thought! Straight-A student and star forward on my high school basketball team! Sweet Jesus, I never would've recognized him! He was supposed to go to law school, then come back and take over his uncle's practice. And how in the hell did you come up with Alice and Wanda?"

"Well, I had to come up with something! What, you think I was going to tell him my real name and who I am? Tomorrow, Eldon tells Vishnu, 'Remi Kowalski came by to see you yesterday,' and Vishnu says, 'You mean Gina Kowalski,' and Eldon says, 'No, her mother, Remi, and some crazy cowgirl named Bev.' The poor boy would bar the door the next time he saw Gina coming. He'd think the whole family was after him. Not to mention the fact that Gina would shoot me on sight."

"That's assuming Gina actually went to see him."

"Assuming that. Or that she's going to see him tonight, which is what we're going to find out shortly."

"You mean we're actually gonna go to the show? I don't know, Remi. If Gina sees you, how are you gonna explain that? She'll blow a fuse for damn sure!"

"Only if she's there, which is just a guess. Anyway, we won't necessarily go inside. Just snoop around a little. Maybe there's a window we can take a peek through. Maybe get a look at Vishnu. The flyer said eight o'clock. Let's go get some dinner and we can show up later, say nine or nine-thirty. Give things a chance to get started."

"Whatever you say, Alice."

Thirty Six

Tony drained half of his cup of seltzer water, nodding in time to the beat from his station near the front windows. It was eight thirty-five, five minutes after he had strolled into Honque from his surveillance point at a bus stop down the street.

The setup was nearly perfect. Outside, the 'Cuda was parked at the curb in front of the building next door, out of sight from the stage, but from where he stood Tony could see everything – the stage, the front door, the 'Cuda, and the street in both directions. He was about forty feet from the door, the same as Vishnu, which would allow him to block an attempted exit if it came to that. He took another swig from his cup. He really wanted a double whiskey soda, but that could wait. This was business, of the most important kind. Family business.

He'd already scanned the crowd for muscle and dismissed the notion after a few seconds. This wasn't the kind of joint that needed a bouncer. Bunch of skinny little wussies. The only guy in the place who looked like he was in any kind of shape was the drummer. Tony watched Hans flailing away like a blacksmith in a grand mal seizure. He'd be a buddy of Vishnu's, thought Tony, but it'd take him five seconds to get past his drums and off the stage. Add five seconds from the stage to the door, and another five onto that for a surprise factor. That's enough, thought Tony. That's more than enough.

Tony had also looked for anyone who might recognize him. Vishnu, of course, but that had been a given, and there was nobody else except the priest who had been at Vishnu's shop this afternoon. Not a priest – a pastor. Tony looked at him again. The pastor seemed like a sharp cookie, and Tony thought about potential problems the pastor could cause the operation, but found none. If things went right, Tony would do nothing but hang around unnoticed by the window for another forty-five minutes, then slip out the door in the middle of a song. If the pastor made eye contact, Tony could walk over and make happy talk for the entire show, firmly establishing that he'd been there the whole time.

Satisfied the situation was about as good as it could be, and with a few minutes left before the deal was supposed to go down, Tony reassessed the band. Not bad, for what was clearly a pickup combo booking local art joints. The sax player, a hefty man about Tony's age, was serving it hot off the stove, not seeming to care that the crowd looked like they were on reds. Tony let his eyes take a lazy walk over a hotshot blonde in a red top and a miniskirt, shitface drunk and hanging on the shoulders of two men. He glanced quickly out at the 'Cuda, then rested his gaze on a neutral spot above a painting on the opposite wall. After his business was handled he'd have plenty of time for drinks and broads. The blonde wasn't his type anyway.

The sun was down behind the buildings now, but the street lights weren't on yet. Perfect lighting. Not dark enough yet to bring out a person's natural defenses, but enough shadow to prevent a positive ID on someone you didn't really look at.

Come on baby, Tony prayed. Any time now. Daddy needs a seven. Roll them bones.

Thirty Seven

For most people, searching for a car by driving around would be nothing more than a waste of gas, but Sonny had a preternatural affinity for the 'Cuda, or perhaps it was the other way around. Whichever it was, Sonny spotted his quarry just after nine o'clock. He rolled his window down and drove slowly past. It was parked outside some bar with weird music wailing out the open door.

Sonny parked two blocks away and killed the engine, listening. Nothing but the clinking of the cooling motor and the hum of the city. He pulled his keys out of his pocket, his pulse starting to quicken. A less rash or obsessed person might have reasoned that the 'Cuda did not, in fact, need to be stolen. That the trunk merely needed a little light cleaning. That possession of a flaming red, loud, highly identifiable car had some potential downsides, even if there was no question about rightful ownership. But Sonny was not such a person. He was inherently rash, his brain was fried, and most importantly, he was a man obsessed. He wanted his car, his ride, his baby, and he had found it. He would walk up to it, open the door, start the engine, and drive away. Opposition would be dealt with. He fingered the .32 in his pocket. Whatever came later would be dealt with. It just didn't fucking matter.

Thirty Eight

Gina walked into Honque about a few minutes before nine. She saw Vishnu and the band on the stage. She looked around the room, expecting to see no one she knew, an expectation not met. She made her way to her uncle. "Tony! What are you doing here?"

"Catching the sounds, what else!" He shrugged and gave her his most innocent smile. "I found out our friend was in a band, and thought I'd check it out."

"How did you—" Gina stopped short, not wanting to spoil her own good mood. "What do you think?" she asked instead.

"Pretty tight. Some of the tunes ain't really my style, but this is real music." He gestured at the band making their way through Bouncin' With Bud. "He told me he played some Bud Powell, but I had to hear it to believe it."

Gina thought about pursuing the details of how Vishnu had come to discuss his band with Tony, but decided the better of it. She squeezed his arm. "I'm going to get some wine."

"Great! I'll be right here."

Vishnu had not yet noticed Gina, absorbed as he was in his fretboard. The song ended with a high note from Skippy that encouraged a buzzing sound from the ceiling tiles. Hans and Vishnu continued the swing backbeat, and Skippy bent down to his mike. "Some of you might recognize this melody as an old Zappa tune called Fifty-Fifty. We've tarted it up a bit, and under our care and feeding it's called I Was Aguirre." This drew some hoots from several in the crowd, and Skippy leaned into a Parkeresque solo in response.

About sixty seconds into the tune, Vishnu looked up and saw Gina. She gave a small wave and a smile, which he returned with a thousand-watt grin. Heartened, she made her way to the bandstand. He spent the rest of the song minding his business, although a few of his riffs sounded particularly inspired, and he managed to send another appreciative smile her way.

The tune ended, and Vishnu announced, "We're going to take a short break." Skippy and Hans exchanged knowing looks. Vishnu set his bass in its stand and hopped down off the stage. "Wow, you came!" he said to Gina. "I thought you had to work."

"I asked Hank to cover my shift. I wanted to see—hear your band." She paused. "I wanted to see you."

"I'm really glad you came, Gina!"

"So *this* is Gina! How *nice!*"

Vishnu spun around, colliding with Heather, who barely managed to hang onto her Bloody Mary. Heather stepped around to stand at Vishnu's side. With her spike heels, she had about eight inches on Gina. She leaned down into Gina's face with a nasty smile. "Vishnu tol' me *all* aboutchoo." Heather's breath could have ignited in an open flame. She took a large swallow from her cup and ran her left hand up the inside of Vishnu's right thigh.

"Jesus *Christ*, Heather, lay off!" exclaimed Vishnu, trying to levitate off of Heather's thumb, jammed as it was into his balls.

"Ooooh, lay off! Honey, I'm so sorry. You ushz'ly like t' be laid *on*!" She turned to Gina. "Or d'you favor a diff'r'nt p'sishn?" A drop of spit sailed out of Heather's mouth with the last word and hit Gina in the forehead.

"You leave Gina alone!" yelled Vishnu. "You don't know what you're talking about!"

"Oh I *don', don'* I!" I don' *know*? I don' *know?*" Heather made an expansive gesture with her arm that rocked her back on her heels. "I maybe don' know *mush, Fuckface*, but I know you bin pokin' this li'l *bish* behin' my *back.* You sleazy *fuck!* You—you—" She leaned down to

Gina. "You *slut!* You *filthy li'l cunt!*" And Heather flung the last half of her Bloody Mary down the front of Gina's blouse.

The crowd at Honque, accustomed to ironic detachment, stood transfixed by the raw bleeding hunks of emotion on display.

Gina looked in shock at Vishnu. Tomato juice ran between her breasts and collected in her navel, and dripped from the front of her blouse onto her pants and boots.

Aghast, Vishnu pulled a small towel out of his instrument case and held it out to her. She took it in her hand but made no move to clean herself.

Heather's fierce expression softened, and she began to walk, weaving toward the back of the gallery. About halfway there, she stopped to admire a blue enamel-coated metal bedpan, hung from a nine-foot gallows by several lengths of fishing line. The pan contained a porcelain doll's head and a pocket watch. Heather scrutinized this assemblage for a moment from a distance of about five feet, opened her mouth as if to say something, and closed it. She swayed a little, then opened her mouth again and soundlessly launched an arc of well-masticated tofu, spinach, oat-sesame snack bar, carrots, green beans, and spelt crackers, all emulsified in a matrix of white wine, vodka, tonic water, gin, more tonic water, whiskey, club soda, more whiskey, more vodka, and tomato juice. The crown jewel was an intact lemon wedge that Heather had somehow incorporated wholesale.

Heather's comment landed in the bedpan with a sweet ringing splat. The crowd stood transfixed for a couple of seconds, then a trio of the most well-informed in the audience broke into well-informed applause. Most of the rest, not wanting to look like hayseeds, followed suit. Murmured comments were passed, containing words like juxtaposition and dynamic synthesis.

Gina was one of the few who did not clap. She was simply too mortified to move. In a different venue Gina might have met Heather face to face in a screaming match. She might have matched Heather's Bloody Mary with her white wine. With the provocation she'd had in the last five minutes, she might even have taken Heather out, in spite of the fact that off-duty bar fights are bad for a peace officer's career. But Gina was in unfamiliar territory, physically and emotionally. She had overcome her doubts about the male of the species to come see this guy, this seemingly nice guy, play jazz in an art gallery. For her trouble, she got a drink tossed down her front by a freaked-out girlfriend.

"Gina, I'm so sorry," whispered Vishnu. "I, um, is there..."

But Gina, tough little Gina Kowalski, just said, "That's OK." She handed Vishnu his towel. "That's OK," she repeated. "I think I better go." She began toward the door.

"Gina, wait! Don't go!" Vishnu called, but his feet took a few seconds to get into gear and go after her.

Tony was slow off the mark as well. Pushing through the crowd toward the door, he yelled, "Don't go out that door, Gina!"

Thirty Nine

An observant person standing outside Honque about three minutes after nine o'clock would have noted a silver Acura cruising past at a stately pace. As it happened, there wasn't an observant person standing outside anywhere nearby. There was one person paying attention to the street from inside the gallery, and he noted the passing of the silver car without any obvious sign of recognition.

For their parts, the occupants of the Acura took note of the 'Cuda, the relative placement of the gallery windows, and the two vacant parking spots about a hundred and fifty feet behind it. The Acura pulled around the block and parked. The two occupants sat for eight minutes. At eleven minutes past nine, the passenger, Tony's contact, said, "Looks like a go," slipped out of the passenger side door, and began walking up the street. The driver restarted the engine, which purred very quietly.

The thief strolled past the 'Cuda without looking at it, and standing away from the gallery window, glanced inside. Two women, one tall and the other short, were squaring off. The tall one threw a drink down the short one's shirt, commanding the rapt attention of everyone in the gallery. This might do as well as music.

Walking back to the driver's door of the 'Cuda, the thief pulled out a slim-jim and deftly unlocked it. Just at that moment, the gallery door swung open and the woman wearing the drink came out, followed by a man.

"Please, Gina! Just wait a minute," he said loudly. The woman turned back to face him. They were about forty feet away from the 'Cuda, and absorbed in their own affairs, but the diversion had ended, and there was no telling what would happen next. The thief began to walk back towards the Acura, staying in the street past a couple of cars and then cutting over onto the sidewalk. The woman and the man had begun to walk down the block in the same direction, about seventy-five feet behind.

"Vishnu, just let me go home." The woman's voice was controlled but firm.

"Not until we've talked. Come on, Gina, give me a chance. Just give me sixty seconds!"

The thief reached the Acura, opened the passenger door, and quickly got inside, head down to avoid eye contact with the people on the sidewalk. As she shut the door, her partner pointed through the windshield to the 'Cuda. "Check this out. We got competition!"

Forty

Sonny walked down the street on the side opposite the bar where the music had been playing. His left hand was curled around the .32 in his jacket pocket, his right hand cradling his keys. Streetlights were just starting to flicker on. The sidewalks were empty except for a guy standing outside the bar.

Sonny stopped in a shadow. The guy outside the bar was looking through a window into the bar, then he turned and walked over to the 'Cuda. As he did so, light from one of the streetlamps illuminated his face and upper body, showing Sonny that he was, in fact, a she.

As Sonny watched, the woman shimmed the driver's door. Sonny gripped the handle of his .32 and took a step forward. Just then, two more people, a woman and a man came out of the bar and began walking down the sidewalk toward Sonny's car. They stopped to yell at each other, and the woman who was jacking the car left it and began to walk quickly down the street away from them. After a moment, the woman and the man continued on, walking past the 'Cuda.

Sonny made his move. Trotting down the sidewalk until he was just across the street from his car, he sprinted across to it and leaped in. The sound of the big engine blared against the surrounding brick walls. He jammed the gearshift into first and floored it, careening into the street and sideswiping the car parked in the space ahead, knocking it partway up on the sidewalk.

A heavy-set, muscular, middle-aged man had come running out of the bar, just as Sonny had started the motor. Sonny traded fleeting looks with him as he blasted up the empty street, made a wild skidding right turn off into the otherwise peaceful summer evening.

Forty One

Tony's worst fear, as he muscled his way to the door, was that he would find Gina in physical combat with his thief. He suspected that neither Gina nor the Voice was armed, but he wasn't sure in either case. Ready for mortal combat to protect his beloved niece, he burst outside to find the nearby area quiet and devoid of people. The Voice was conspicuously absent. Vishnu and Gina were having a heated conversation down the block. As Tony started moving towards them, the 'Cuda roared to life and leaped forward, shoving a smaller car partly onto the sidewalk.

Vishnu and Gina ran up the block. Vishnu yelled, "Stop him!" as though Tony could grab the door handle and apprehend the car like an errant child. The three of them stood there as the 'Cuda skidded around the corner and out of sight.

Behind them a silver Acura made a quiet U-turn and rolled southeast into the night.

Vishnu looked at Tony suspiciously. "Did you do this?"

"I swear, kid, I had nothin' to do with that guy."

Pastor Bob emerged from the gallery and stood by the doorway, about ten feet away from the rest of the group.

Gina was already on her cell, reporting the incident. Finishing her call, she fixed a look on Tony. "Tony. What do you know about this?"

Tony said nothing, looking chagrined.

"Tony!"

Tony found his voice. "Honestly, Gina, I don't know that guy."

"That's a bullshit answer, Tony. What aren't you telling me?"

Vishnu stared at Gina. "Gina! You know this guy?"

It was Gina's turn to look chagrined. "He's my uncle," she admitted.

"Then you knew it was him that sold me the car when we met on Friday night?" Gina nodded. "He tried to buy it back this afternoon. He wanted to screw me so he could resell it!" Vishnu glared at Gina. "Are you in on this, too?"

"No, Vishnu, I don't – Tony," she stared at her uncle, "just what in the hell is he talking about?"

Vishnu answered for him. "He came to my place this afternoon wanting to buy the 'Cuda back. He offered me a Firebird and five grand in trade. And since I wouldn't sell it to him, he came here to steal it, or hired someone to steal it! And he came here to make sure the job was done. And for all I know you lured me down the street to help him."

Gina looked at him, hurt in her eyes. "Is that what you think?"

"No. Oh shit, I, I didn't mean that. But Gina, what the hell is going on?"

They both looked at Tony, who was staring at his feet

"Tony," said Gina. "You need to tell us what's going on.

Tony was saved by Alex 3, who poked his head out the door and gestured to Vishnu. "Get in here! I need to talk to you!"

"Uh, yeah, I'll be right in," said Vishnu. He looked at Gina and Tony.

Pastor Bob spoke for the first time since stepping outside the gallery. "I have an idea. This all sounds rather complicated. The police will need to talk to Vishnu about his car, and he may need to finish playing his music. After all that, why don't we go to a nice quiet café, have something to wet our whistles, and maybe a bite to eat, and see if we can sort it out. I think the Seiner's Inn is open all night."

Tony, leaping at the chance for divine intervention, agreed. "That's a real nice idea, Father."

"Father?" exclaimed Gina. "You know him?" She looked at Tony, gesturing to Pastor Bob.

"Gina, I'd like you to meet Father Bob, excuse me, Pastor Bob. Randall, right? An old friend of my new friend Vishnu. Bob, this is my niece, Gina Kowalski."

"Hello," Gina said to Pastor Bob. "So you met Tony…?"

"Just this afternoon, when I was at Vishnu's shop," answered Tony for Bob, eager to establish for Gina his relationship, however brief, with a man of the cloth.

Gina looked at Pastor Bob to confirm this.

"So it would seem," he smiled.

Gina looked back to Tony. He opened his mouth to speak, but no sound came out. He was staring past Gina down the block. His eyebrows wilted into semicircles of defeat. "Aw, fuck," he moaned. The group followed his eyes to a pair of women who had just rounded the corner. One was a shorter, older version of Gina; the other was tall and lanky, her height accentuated by a pile of honey-blond tresses. "Aw, fuck," repeated Tony. "Just what I fuckin' need. Mother Teresa and Annie Fuckin' Oakley. Is this the wages of sin, Father?"

"Depends on the sin, I suppose. I'm guessing you know them?"

"Mom!" exclaimed Gina. "What in the – ? How did you – ?"

"Hello, dear," said Remi. "Hello Tony. What a nice surprise. You remember Bev, don't you, Tony?"

"How could I forget?" Tony tried to smile at Bev, managing only a sickly grimace.

"Charmed, I'm sure." Bev smirked back at him.

Remi turned to Pastor Bob. "Hello. I'm Remi Kowalski, Gina's mother. It appears you've already met her and my brother Tony. This is my friend, Beverly Hall."

"Bob Randall. Pleased to meet you both."

"Pastor Bob is the pastor at Saint, uh, Thompsen's Lutheran Church," said Tony to Remi.

"Since when are you a Lutheran, Tony?" asked Bev. "Last I heard you were a lapsed Catholic." She looked him up and down. "Lookin' kinda heavy on the lapse, big boy."

"Well, now, Bev, I – "

"Tony's not a formal member of St. Thorfinn's, Beverly" said Pastor Bob. "Not yet, anyway. We're still working on that, aren't we, Tony."

"Lordy, guard your candlesticks," said Bev.

Remi turned to Vishnu. "And you would be – ?"

"Vishnu," said Tony, Gina, and Vishnu simultaneously. "Tensleep," added Vishnu.

"Vishnu," repeated Remi. "So glad to meet you." She smiled warmly at Vishnu and gave a quick look of approval to Gina. Gina rolled her eyes.

An awkward silence fell, and Pastor Bob stepped in once again to give aid, of a sort. "Remi, Bev, a rather unusual chain of events has taken place. Someone spilled a drink on Gina's blouse, and then Vishnu's car was stolen a few minutes ago. He needs to talk to the police, and he's still in the middle of his musical performance. To top it off, there seems to be some history among Tony, Gina, and Vishnu that they wanted to talk over. But after all is said and done we thought we'd go over to the Seiner's Inn and discuss things. Would you care to join us there?"

"History?" said Remi. "I love history. I'd be fascinated to hear some history. Wouldn't you, Bev?"

"Oh, I just love history too, hon, you know I do. It's my favorite pastime. That and gelding draft horses." She smiled sweetly at Tony.

"Unless one of you minds," added Remi, looking in turn at Vishnu, Gina, and Tony. "We wouldn't want to pry into things we shouldn't know about."

"OK by me," said Vishnu.

"Uh, yeah, fine, Mom," said Gina.

Tony shrugged.

"Good," said Pastor Bob. "It's settled then."

Alex 3 popped his head out the door again. "Are you coming back in, or what?" he demanded, looking at Vishnu.

"Shall we?" said Pastor Bob, and the group filed in after him. Gina stepped up beside Tony and gripped his elbow. "This better be really good," she hissed into his ear.

"Trust me," said Tony. "It'll exceed all your expectations."

Forty Two

Inside the gallery, someone had cleaned up Heather's critique, and the crowd stood about in small groups making erudite gallery chat. The truly chic among them applauded quietly as Vishnu and Gina entered.

Hans was holding court with the redheaded woman and several other females, while some male escorts hung at the fringes of the group, affecting insouciance and sending text messages. Seeing Vishnu and Skippy enter, Hans gracefully extracted himself and made his way over to the gang.

Heather sat in a folding chair in the corner, her head between her knees. One of her newfound admirers was standing next to her, looking concerned, his left hand resting solicitously on her shoulder.

Alex 3 crouched next to her, talking a blue streak. "...possibilities for objective correlation are endless. Consider the elements. You've got the piece itself. Then there's the lighting, which we know has a strong affect on the viewer's psychophysical state. Then there are the surrounding pieces. You know, what relationships exist among them? And as we saw tonight we have the use of music or other sound effects. There's the food itself. There could be simple color contrasts, like the way you used the carrots to set off the blue of the bedpan. Beyond that, we've got the possibility of an abstract nexus, or more than one. For example, shrimp, interjected onto a piece with a marine theme. I think you'd have to swallow them whole for visibility. Can you do that? You did it with the lemon wedge, so I'd think you could do shrimp. I imagine the trickiest thing would be emetic timing, but I'm sure there are substances that would provide a more controlled result than alcohol. Oh, I'm *so* excited! Think about it, will you? I want you to be one of my star performers. I've never seen such stage presence! Here's my card. I'll call you. This could be big! Really big!"

Alex 3 tucked a business card between the fingers of Heather's left hand. She moaned incoherently in response. Alex 3 turned to the man standing with Heather. "Are you her agent? Splendid, splendid. Do give me a call!" Alex 3 pumped the man's hand vigorously, handed him a card, and moved over to Vishnu and the crew.

"My car just got stolen," began Vishnu, before Alex 3 could launch into his spiel. "I saw it happen. The cops are coming. I'm not sure how long I'll have to talk to them. If you want, we can finish the set after I'm done with that."

"Stolen? How marvelous! Who could ask for more? This is the most amazing night I've ever had in my career! In my life! But you're done for the night. With full pay, of course. But absolutely no more music! No, we can't have any distraction from the seminal work done here tonight. People are talking – can't you hear it? Some of these people here are from the art press. This will be big, and we were here when it started. I mean, vomit performance is old hat, as far as that goes, but this is much more! It's like being there at Ginsberg's first slam, before people knew what he was doing! You know what I mean?" Vishnu and company either didn't know or couldn't think of anything to add. "We'll need a band," Alex 3 jabbered on. "A versatile band. Not every night, of course. The essence will be surprise. Each performance, the audience would have to guess. Who are the performers? Is the music a primary element, secondary, or conceptually orthogonal? Will the band members have spoken word parts, like you did tonight, or not? Will it be one of you who vomits? They won't know until, as they say, the fat lady sings, but up until that point, they won't even know who the fat lady is! By the way, can any of you sing? No matter. I suppose one could say that vomit performance is just punk. But real hardcore punk is so old now that it can be done as retro! I don't think I'll sleep for days! There's so much to do! I'll call you!" Alex 3 shook hands effusively with each of them, handed each a card, and hurried off to his office.

Bev looked at Remi. "Did he say vomit?"

"That's what I heard," said Remi. She looked at Gina with concern. "That's not vomit on your shirt, is it, dear?"

"No, Mom. Just someone's drink."

"My *ex*-girlfriend," said Vishnu. "She's not used to drinking, and kind of lost control. Gina, I'm really sorry about that."

Gina shrugged. "We can talk about it later."

Vishnu looked at Skippy and Hans. "You heard Alex. I guess we're done for the night. Skippy, can you fit my bass and amp in your car?"

"I would be delighted to provide the means of motion. Especially to a house of all-night breakfasts."

"Why don't Bev and I go on over to the cafe?" said Remi to Pastor Bob. "We'll get a table and wait for you all. That will give Vishnu a chance to talk to the police. Vishnu, are you alright, dear? This must be stressful for you. Having your car stolen and everything."

"Oh, thanks, Mrs. Kowalski, I'm fine."

"Call me Remi. Shall we go, Bev?"

"Sounds good," said Bev. She grinned at Tony. "See you there, big boy. Don't get lost on the way or nothin'."

Vishnu motioned Gina aside. "Can I get a ride with you? Just over to the Seiner's Inn? That is, if you're going." He hesitated. "I said some things that, well, I shouldn't have accused you of stealing my car. I never thought you did. I was just really mad. I'm sorry."

"I accept your apology. And yes, I'll give you a ride. Tony has some explaining to do, and I want to make sure he does it. As does my mother. I'm extremely interested to hear her explain how she arrived here."

"I was wondering that myself."

"And *you* have some explaining to do. I want to know who this Heather character is. You can fill me in while we go by your place so I can clean up. And you can loan me a shirt. This one's kind of sticky."

"Deal. And Gina, I just want you to know. The gigs aren't usually like this."

"I should hope not."

Forty Three

Vishnu, Tony, Gina, Remi, Skippy, Bev, and Pastor Bob sat at a big round table in the back of the Seiner's Inn. Hans had begged off as they'd departed from Honque, barreling off with the redheaded woman on his old BSA like Odin and a Valkyrie princess heading for a nightcap in Valhalla.

Remi, Gina, Pastor Bob, and Vishnu had cups of coffee sitting in front of them. Vishnu also had a piece of blackberry pie smothered in vanilla ice cream.

Skippy had a mug of licorice tea and a waffle supporting a large mound of whipped cream and strawberries. ("I always eat waffles when someone else is cooking them," he told Gina. "Professional courtesy.")

Bev had a bottle of beer and big pile of onion rings slathered with barbecue sauce.

Tony had a bottle of beer, a T-bone steak, and mashed potatoes with gravy. He really wanted the double whiskey soda he'd promised himself earlier in the evening, but, even more, he wanted his wits about him.

"So," said Pastor Bob, "why don't we all just tell our parts of the story, and see where we come out?" He looked around at his companions.

Vishnu indicated agreement.

Gina nodded, her expression a mix of hopeful trust because Bob was a pastor and resignation because Tony was her uncle and she was a cop.

Remi smiled her inscrutable smile. She looked over at Bev, who was grinning like she'd scored first-row tickets at the Bullriding Finals in Las Vegas.

Tony wore a look of mild good cheer and helpfulness, following his soldier's instincts to stick it out to the end no matter how bleak things looked.

Vishnu started the tale. "My car died Thursday. Friday morning, I bought a car – the 'Cuda – from Tony." He looked at Gina. "Tony's your uncle?"

Gina nodded.

"And when you rousted me on Friday you knew this, after I told you where I bought it?"

Gina nodded.

"And when you pulled me over you thought I was the previous owner, this drug dealer?"

Gina nodded.

"And you told me on Saturday to get rid of the car because of that guy?"

Gina nodded.

"And *you*," Vishnu turned to Tony, "knew about this guy when you sold me the car on Friday."

It was Tony's turn to nod, avoiding the eyes of Gina and Remi.

"And you tried to buy it back from me this afternoon."

Tony nodded.

"So if, as you claim, you weren't just trying to buy it back to resell it, what were you up to?"

"I was worried about Gina!" Tony squirmed in his chair. "I knew you two was an item. I wanted to protect her."

"*What*?" exclaimed Gina, leaning forward. "Let me get this straight. You knew we were an *item?* And exactly how and when did you come up with that?"

"When you told me on Saturday," Tony replied.

"I what?"

"You came to the lot Saturday afternoon. You was worried about him."

"I didn't say anything about being interested in him," said Gina. "I was concerned about you! I wasn't even planning on seeing him again."

Tony gave her a skeptical glance. "You came by the lot about what time? About four o'clock? Five o'clock?"

Gina thought. "Yeah, about then."

Tony turned to Vishnu. "Did you see Gina on Saturday?"

"Yeah. She came by my shop."

"And about what time was that?"

"Uh, I'd say about seven in the evening."

"And what happened then?"

"Nothing much. She came over. We had coffee and talked. We went for a walk. She went home."

"Nothing else?"

"No. At least not like you're thinking."

"That's not how it happened!" objected Gina. She started to say more, then appeared to think the better of it.

"I rest my case," said Tony, smiling and resting his palms on the table as though Vishnu's statement had cleared him of all charges. "And while we're on the topic, might I call my beloved sister to the stand? Did you, or did you not, Beloved Sister, instruct Gina to go to Vishnu's on Saturday night?"

"Instruct her? Me?" Remi placed a modest hand on her breastbone. "Tony, she's a grown woman. I hardly think I could instruct her on such things." She smiled at Vishnu. "She's a strong-willed woman, as you may have found out already."

Gina looked at her mother, then at her uncle. She opened her mouth then closed it again, shaking her head. Finally she looked at Vishnu. "You see what it's like?" she said. "I present to you the Romano clan. Anything you say can and will be used against you. You have the right to remain silent, but if you do, my mother and uncle will fill in the blanks for you." She glared at Tony. "It's beyond me how you could come up with me saying Vishnu and I were an item."

Tony sighed. “Gina,” he said. “Listen to me. You’re my niece. My *nipote speciale*. You think you need to say everything out loud for me to know what’s going on with you? And anyway, you was the one who went out with him Saturday night.”

“Went for a walk,” said Gina.

“Went for a walk, just like you said.”

Vishnu cut in. “Actually, Tony, something else did happen on Saturday night.” He waited until all eyes were on him. “The cops came and picked up some drugs and guns that were in the trunk of my car. And then today you come by my shop wanting to buy it back. And now you say you were trying to protect Gina. From what? From me?”

“Not from you. Sheesh. From the guy who used to own it. Some putz named Sonny. I heard a rumor he was lookin’ for it. I didn’t want it around Gina.”

“So you lied to me this afternoon when you said you didn’t know anything about the drugs. And when I wouldn’t sell my car back to you, you didn’t give up, did you?”

Tony was silent.

Gina looked hard at Tony. “I want the truth now. All of it.”

Tony looked at Pastor Bob, who nodded. “Let’s hear it, Tony.”

“No, I didn’t give up,” said Tony. “After you wouldn’t sell the ’Cuda back to me, I arranged to have it stolen. It was supposed to go down during the gig, while you was playing. But it didn’t happen!” Tony looked around the table. “My contact didn’t snag it.”

“Let me get this straight,” said Vishnu. “You hired a thief to steal my car, but someone else stole it instead?”

Gina slapped the table. “The Acura!”

“Huh?” Vishnu looked at her, baffled.

“The Acura. The silver Acura. Parked down the street from us. There was a woman standing next to the ’Cuda when we came out of the gallery. She walked ahead of us and got into the Acura. She was the thief you hired!” Gina looked at Tony with a triumphant smile, and Tony nodded.

“I don’t remember any of that,” said Vishnu, shaking his head.

“I’m a cop, remember?”

“Then who stole my car?” asked Vishnu. He looked at Gina, then at Tony.

“I don’t know!” said Tony. “I swear I don’t know. I saw the guy as he drove away, and I have an idea it was Sonny, but I’ve never met him. That’s the truth. And if it was Sonny I swear I didn’t have nothin’ to do with it. Like Gina said, you guys spooked my thief. And before she could get another crack at your car, it was nabbed by this other guy.”

“So you conspired to commit a felony,” said Gina to Tony.

“Only to protect you!”

“And what was your plan after stealing it?”

“Sell it. Chop it. Get rid of it. I don’t know. I hadn’t made the plans for that yet. Just get it away from you.”

Gina’s response was cut short by a ring on her cell. She pulled it from her purse. “This is Gina.”

Tony glared at Vishnu. “None of this woulda happened if you hadn’t been so goddamn stubborn! Excuse me, Father.”

“Excused,” said Pastor Bob, with a smile. The tale revealed by Tony so far had exceeded even his seasoned expectations. Through the years, a lot of people had wanted to confess things to him, and he always let them, even though the Lutheran faith didn’t hold by confession. Tony’s tale was definitely in the top ranks for sheer originality.

“For cryin’ out loud!” Tony yelled at Vishnu. “I was offerin’ you a Firebird, practically mint condition, for two grand! Why the hell wouldn’t you take my offer?”

“Yeah,” said Gina.

“Because it was too good of a deal! I thought you were just trying to rip me off! Anyone would have thought that!”

“You’re not kidding,” said Gina.

“Besides,” continued Vishnu, almost apologetically, “I love that car. It’s fast. It’s hot. It’s—”

Forty Four

Sonny flew south on Aurora with no clear plan. He flew south out of instinct, like an addled homing pigeon. He roundly cursed Tiny and his henchmen for ripping off his tape deck. He unleashed a foul rant at the cops, who he knew must be looking for him. He impugned the virility of Fish, who had tainted his driver's seat merely by sitting in it. All in all, he was in rarified high spirits, which couldn't be touched by the minor detail that he had just committed a felony in front of several witnesses, or that he was in deep shit with The Man, or that he might be in yet deeper shit if the drugs weren't in the trunk. Sonny had his baby back, and that was all that mattered to him as he flew down the Alaskan Way Viaduct.

But Sonny, whacked and giddy as he was, was not so whacked that he didn't know he had to face a certain reality, and soon. He pulled off near the First Avenue Bridge, and parked behind a warehouse. He got out, walked around to the trunk, and stood stock-still in the deepening shadows, listening. The moment of truth had come. "Fuck it," he said to the shadows and the ever-present audience in his mind. "It just doesn't matter. It...just...doesn't...matter."

He opened the trunk. It was dark inside, but he saw immediately that someone had removed the decoy trash he had accumulated. He yanked the spare out and tossed it on the ground behind himself. The bag wasn't there. Maybe he hadn't put it in the trunk. He dashed to the driver's door, which still hung open, and dove headfirst inside, groping around wildly under the seats, on the back seat floor. Nothing. He launched himself back to the trunk, pulling out every last scrap of debris, feeling around with his hands as though there might be a secret compartment containing an old gym bag. Nothing there but unindentifiable moldering detritus. Certainly nothing wrapped in plastic, or reassuringly chrome-plated.

A wave of nausea overcame Sonny. He doubled over the empty trunk and retched up the remains of the Ham-N-Angus Rebel Rouser. Shaking, he gripped the rim of the trunk to keep his face out of the puddle. And as he hung there, snot and vomit running out his mouth and nose, he whimpered, feeling for the first time in many years how very alone he was. The Man was after him. The cops were after him. Tiny and his boys would fuck him up on sight. He had nobody, nobody in the world who would be glad to see him if he turned up on the doorstep.

And as he hung on the trunk rim, face suspended above a puddle of his own puke, he began to distinguish a rising and falling tone that was different from the general ringing in his ears. He wasn't so alone after all.

Hurling himself upright, he cracked the back of his head on the open trunk lid. "God *dammit!*" he yelled. But this new assault threw a fresh supply of adrenaline into his bloodstream, and with it he clamped down on the sorrow and fear and replaced them with his familiar rage. "Fuck 'em! Fucking *fuck* 'em!" he hissed, slamming the trunk shut. He leaped into the driver's seat and roared out of the parking lot.

Sonny made his way to the West Seattle Bridge, crossed the Duwamish Waterway, and took the exit to Delridge Way. Although he'd grown up only several miles away, he'd rarely been to West Seattle before, and his poached mind produced the thought that, because of this, the cops wouldn't expect him to go there.

He rolled along through the twilight, and perhaps because it was better than being alone, an all-star cast of people he'd known in his wretched, twisted, fucked-up life wandered through his mind. They came on stage alone and in groups. He cursed them all.

A slender man with a receding hairline and a cigarette dangling from his mouth, wearing a denim jacket and dirty jeans, stood in the shadows. Sonny had only met him in a few bent photographs, and his face wasn't clearly visible to Sonny. "Fuck you, old man," he cursed his father. "Fuck you and every one who looks like you. Lousy motherfucking ratshit bastard."

A teenage boy with pig-like eyes and a striped shirt that didn't quite meet his pants leered at Sonny and pointed to the coalchute of the abandoned house on the corner. "If I ever see you again I'm going to fuck you over so bad," Sonny hissed.

Sonny took a left onto Fauntleroy Way, winding southwest to the Vashon Island ferry dock. "Goddamn bitch never gave a fuck anyway fucking cunt!" A whining tone had entered his voice and tears began to stream down his face. A hard-used woman, looking older than her forty-five years, sat on a cracked orange plastic couch in front of a black-and-white TV. She turned slowly to face Sonny over her morning vodka, and just as slowly turned away from him, as a smiling man on the grainy screen gestured towards a refrigerator.

"Fucking bitches, I *hate* you!" His voice broke as all of the so-called girlfriends he'd ever had stood in a shadowy group, smiling derisively at him, arms folded. "I hate your fucking *guts!*" he said, as he took a yellow light crossing Alaska Street, blind to the police cruiser rolling up the intersection on his right.

"All units, Car 77 in pursuit of suspected stolen red Plymouth, south on Fauntleroy at Alaska." Officer Dave Melton flipped on the siren and lights, while Officer Joe Camacho hit the gas and pulled onto Fauntleroy behind Sonny.

The red-and-blues flooded Sonny's rear view mirror and the siren filled his ears. He jammed the gearshift down into second and floored it. The rear tires screeched and the car fishtailed away from Joe and Dave. Within seconds, the two cars were hurtling down Fauntleroy at about ninety miles an hour.

"Fucking fuckers not gonna get me fuck *you!*" Sonny pulled into the oncoming traffic lane to pass a van, swerving in front of it to avoid a head-on collision with a Metro bus.

"Car 77 still in pursuit, just passing Juneau. This guy is a real nut."

"Car 77, this is car 89 approaching Fauntleroy on California. Will try to intercept."

"Car 93 with car 89."

But Sonny beat cars 89 and 93 to California Avenue, flashing through the intersection just before they arrived. The cruisers performed inventive maneuvers to miss each other before following Sonny's trail.

Sonny made the big left-hand bend north of Lincoln Park at and put the 'Cuda in fourth down the hill past the park. Had a radar gun been on the scene, it would have clocked the 'Cuda at one hundred and fourteen.

"77, this is 41, 23, 33, and 39, approaching Vashon Ferry dock northbound on Fauntleroy."

"41, this is 77. We're just passing Lincoln Park. This asshole must be doing a hundred and ten. Can you intercept north of the ferry dock?"

"77, this is 41. Negative. Will barricade south of the dock entrance." And the four northbound cruisers skidded into a barrier formation on Fauntleroy Way.

"Goddamn motherfucking shit fuck!" screamed Sonny. He double-clutched into second gear, jammed on the brakes, twisted the wheel violently to the right, and threw it back into third gear. The lone ticket vendor at the dock entrance looked up to see a big red car take aim on her little wooden shack, then correct its course ever so slightly, flying by her elbow and grazing the corner of her booth with a woody crunch. Her dinner rose in her throat as she looked over her shoulder to see the car come out of its wild skid pointing straight towards the end of the dock.

And as the 'Cuda straightened out, Sonny saw that he was at the end of the road. Flanked by fences on both sides, outnumbered and outgunned from behind, and a ribbon of rapidly shrinking pavement before him, his path led straight into the fading remnants of a sunset reflected off the inky waters of the Sound.

"Shit fucking goddamn—" Thirty-two years of pain, hate, and abuse taken and given filled his head as he redlined the engine.

"—rat-piss ass-bite fuck shit—" He jammed the gearshift into fourth and stomped on the gas. The 'Cuda bellowed like a wounded beast.

"—fucking goddamn not gonna fucking get me goddamn fucking FUUUUUUUUUUUUUUUUUUUUUUUUUUUUCK!"

"Jesus," muttered Dave Melton. "Joe, I think he's…" Dave let the sentence hang as he, Joe, four other cops, six ferry system employees, and eighteen paying customers watched in disbelief as Sonny rammed the barriers at the end of the dock. The signal arm exploded in a shower of wood fragments; the chain between the pipe bollards snapped like a string.

The 'Cuda left the dock at just over a hundred and ten miles and hour, descending in a parabola towards the water, engine screaming, front end dipping. The tide was low, and the water was about twenty feet below the end of the dock. To those watching it seemed to take forever, but in reality it only took a little over a second for the car to hit the water a hundred and fifty feet from the dock. The big car stood on its nose for another twenty feet then flipped on its roof. Those close enough to the end of the dock saw the frigid water pouring in through the open windows, and then an expanding circle of bubbles on the surface, as Puget Sound claimed Sonny, and the 'Cuda, for her own.

Forty Five

"Dead," said Gina, dropping her cell back into her purse. The group stared at her like dogs watching a card trick. "Your car, that is," she said to Vishnu. "That was Hank." Gina looked around the table. "He was covering my shift for me tonight. The thief was – big surprise – Sonny himself." She ignored Tony's look of vindication. "He got as far as the Vashon ferry dock, seven cruisers on his tail. Hank says he drove straight off the end of the dock, full speed. His only problem was, there wasn't a boat there to meet him. He just put it straight into the Sound."

"On purpose?" asked Skippy.

"It's not clear whether it was an accident or just bad judgement," said Gina. "With Sonny, it's probably hard to tell the difference."

"Good Lord!" exclaimed Pastor Bob. "Is he dead?"

"Amazingly, no." Gina looked professionally unimpressed by the story. "Somehow he made it to the surface. A private boat witnessed the whole thing and went over to the bubbles. They even had the sense to kill their engine so they didn't cut off his head with the prop. Sonny comes up practically underneath them, all banged up, about two-thirds drowned and half hypothermic, but alive. They took him back to the dock and turned him over to the police. It's a miracle."

"Yes," repeated Pastor Bob. "A miracle. Where is he now?"

"Harborview, I'd guess. Probably under guard."

"Can he have visitors?" asked Pastor Bob.

Gina looked at him curiously. "Not really. I mean, there would have to be a reason."

"Not even a professional visit from a man of the cloth? Even if accompanied by one of Seattle's Finest?"

"Well, I guess. I mean if—"

"Gina," interjected Pastor Bob, "would you do me the favor, sometime in the next couple of days?"

"I could probably see my way to that. Given the circumstances." She shot Tony a look. "But Pastor, don't be fooled into thinking he's going to have some kind of conversion just because you show up. This guy's got the major bad attitude."

"Precisely why I want to see him. And any conversions he might have wouldn't be because of me, in any event. I'm just curious. And I've probably seen worse. Up in Alaska I used to do some counseling work with the state police. One guy I remember shot up half of his village with a machine gun and cut the legs off the bodies with a chain saw to feed to his sled dogs. Now *there* was a hard case. Maybe Sonny just needs a little art therapy."

Vishnu snorted, spitting some pie filling onto his plate. Gina and Tony looked at him. "Private joke," he mumbled through his napkin.

"There's still one part I want explained," said Gina, pointing at her mother. "Just how in the hell did you two end up at the show? And don't give me any crap about how I gave you the address. You know damn well that's not true."

Bev looked at Remi, who gave the laugh a mother gives when her child has said something endearingly humorous. "No, you certainly didn't," said Remi. "I suppose you could say motherly intuition had something to do with it. But you did give me a lot of leads. When you called me on Saturday night, you told me Vishnu's name, and that he lived on Canal Street, and that he owned a bike shop."

"I told you all that?"

"Yes, dear, you did. And you told me you were worried about him. For the same reason that Tony was worried about you. It's OK to be concerned about people, honey. And yes, if the truth be known, I suppose I did suggest that you might visit him. And then today, out of the blue, you called to ask if your father and I were happy."

"I still don't get it," said Gina.

"I suspect that this is where the motherly intuition came in?" asked Pastor Bob.

"Exactly, Bob! After Gina called me, it came to me somehow that maybe she was going to see Vishnu tonight." Gina stared at her, dumbfounded. "Don't ask me how it works!" said Remi. "It just does. When I called the station, they said you weren't on duty tonight. The rest was more mundane. Probably just like your job, dear. Simple detective work. I looked in the phone book, and there was Vishnu's shop. Bev and I drove down there to see what we could see. We probably would have been stymied had it not been for Vishnu's delightful neighbor. The sculptor. Eldon."

Bev waved her last onion ring in the air. "Eldon Harper! I went to high school with him, if you can believe it. He was supposed to become a bigshot lawyer. Looks like he got stuck at a Grateful Dead concert."

"Eldon?" asked Vishnu. "Information patent lawyer. Microsoft millionaire. Got in on the ground floor with all the stock options, and retired just before the dot-com bubble popped. Sorry," he said to Remi. "I interrupted."

"That's all right, dear. This evening is just full of surprises, isn't it Bev? But Eldon showed us the poster, right outside your shop, and we thought we'd come."

"Well, that ain't exactly it," said Bev to Gina. "We thought we'd come see if you were there. Just take a peek through the window. I figured if you saw your mother and I pokin' around you'd plug us. We didn't figure y'all would be standin' around outside waitin' for us."

"We didn't want to embarrass you, honey," explained Remi. "But you piqued my curiosity with your phone calls. And Vishnu sounded so interesting! And when Eldon told us he was in a band, well, how could a mother resist?" She raised her hand to cut off Gina's answer. "Now, I know, some might think I was meddling. Well, maybe so. But Bob, if our intentions are good, is it so wrong to meddle a tiny bit in the lives of our loved ones?"

Bob smiled broadly. "I'm definitely the wrong person to ask. A core part of my job is meddling. I'm what you might call a strategic meddler. And always with the best of intentions."

"There, you see," said Remi to Gina. "And look what came of it! All of us gathered together, getting to know one another, having a nice meal and enjoying ourselves." She picked up her coffee cup and beamed around the table.

Tony, who had been absently shoveling food remnants around on his plate, abruptly rubbed his hands together. "Well, I guess that about clears things up, don't it?"

Vishnu nodded, then shook his head. "Wait a minute. What about my car? How will I get it back?"

"The police salvage folks are taking care of that since it's a stolen vehicle, but it could take a while. That water's pretty deep." replied Gina. "But I don't think that car's going to run again." She looked at Tony.

Tony pondered a moment. "Don't sound good," he admitted. "Impact damage from hittin' the water, and whatever the cops will do to it while they're haulin' it out, and salt water, which means you'll never get rid of corrosion problems. Of course, I did tell you this afternoon that, if you wanted, Vito would check the car over, that we'd fix any problems for free. You didn't actually turn me down. You just said you'd call me tomorrow. Which is today. That sounds like a lot of trouble, under the circumstances. Now, if you want, the offer on the Firebird still stands. The 'Cuda in trade for it plus two grand. But given the extra time and trouble, how about I just refund your seven grand and give you the Firebird free and clear." He looked at Gina.

She returned a cool gaze. "There's still the outstanding issue of conspiracy to steal a car, and—"

"Without any evidence," Pastor Bob cut in. "All we have is hearsay. No Miranda warning. No offer of legal representation. Testimony collected without following proper police procedures. Not really up to your usual spit-and-polish standards, Officer Kowalski. I could just as easily say I hired a thief who didn't steal Vishnu's car. All of this would be awfully hard to hold up in court. No admissible evidence, and no crime. Or rather, a crime, but one in which the perpetrator was caught red-handed. Maybe I should say blue-lipped."

Tony jumped in. "And as I was sayin' earlier, Vishnu, I got a wide selection of vehicles. It don't have to be the Pontiac. Got some trucks you might be interested in. Good for haulin' merchandise." He nodded at the wisdom of this suggestion. "Come on by. I'll take care of you."

Vishnu forked the last shard of pie on his plate, sopped it in some melted ice cream, munched it thoughtfully. Then he nodded. "Tomorrow, if it works for you." He looked at Gina. "I guess I'll have to come down the station and sign some papers or something?"

"Major paperwork. Having a car stolen is bad enough. Having a stolen car retrieved from underwater is more. Getting it out of impound is more yet."

"How about this," said Tony to Vishnu. "You bring the title over to the lot first thing, and we'll set you up with some wheels, and then we can transfer ownership of the Plymouth back to me. That way you don't have to deal with impound fees."

"You got a deal," said Vishnu. "Might as well get this taken care of. I'll see you about 9:30. But listen." He pointed his finger at Tony's face. "No monkey business."

Tony looked at Vishnu in mock hurt. "Monkey business? Since when was I able to put any monkey business over on Vishnu Tensleep? Last time someone tried that, I heard they was the one come out lookin' like a monkey. Besides, like Remi says, ain't this been fun? Everyone sittin' around, havin' a bite and gettin' to know know each other?" He looked at Remi and Gina, who were wearing identical looks of long-suffering. "What? Did I say somethin'?" He speared the last bite of steak into his mouth and chewed with noisy satisfaction.

"Tony," said Pastor Bob, "I'd like to talk further. Just you and me." He turned to Gina. "To allay any lingering concerns you might have about your uncle," he said. "Call it pastoral counseling, if you will."

"Maybe you could throw in some of that art therapy," said Tony.

"Don't joke," said Pastor Bob, "unless you're ready to find out what you're joking about."

Forty Six

Vishnu and Gina stood outside the Seiner's Inn, enjoying the relative quiet after the crowd's departure. "All in all, I enjoyed myself tonight," said Gina.

"You have unusual tastes."

"I mean it. Most of it anyway. I didn't appreciate being dressed down by your ex-girlfriend in front of a crowd, or getting a tomato juice bath."

"I'm sorry about that."

"No need for apologies. But let's get something straight. She's your ex, right?"

"Yeah. Well." Vishnu hesitated. "Just for the record, officially speaking, we only broke up yesterday. I mean Sunday. But it started to come apart months ago. And you saw the remains of the tomato she threw at me. She's definitely an *ex*-girlfriend."

"Good. She seems to have a thing for tomatoes. Just for the record, I really wanted to punch her lights out."

"I can sympathize."

"I could, you know."

"I have no doubt. I'm glad you didn't."

"Me too."

They stood for a moment. "You know what?" Vishnu asked.

"What?"

"I was really upset about having my car stolen, but when I heard what happened to it, that Sonny drove it off the dock, and hearing that it's basically totaled, something just snapped. I didn't really care anymore." He shook his head in amusement. "It was like I had Aladdin's magic carpet for a long weekend, and got to take it for a wild ride, but then Aladdin came back and got it. You know what I mean?"

"Yeah, I think so," Gina nodded. "The 'Cuda didn't really seem like you, anyway."

"So what seems like me?"

"Certainly not the 'Cuda. I know I have biases about that particular car. For you, I'd see something a bit more practical. But fun."

"Like a small pickup with sport wheels, four wheel drive, and a matching canopy?"

"Yeah," Gina laughed. "Something like that."

"That was what Hans told me to get Thursday night, the day before I went to Tony's lot. But I don't even remember whether Tony had any trucks. First thing, he's trying to sell me a Mazda, then Vito arrived in the 'Cuda, and that was all she wrote. I never had a chance with Vito and Tony. No offense, but you've got to admit, they're a formidable pair."

"No offense taken." Gina paused. "Tony's not so bad, you know. He can be a great guy, once you get to know him."

Vishnu wasn't quite sure what to say to this. He finally settled on, "It's pretty obvious he'd do anything for you."

"I know."

"You really think he hired someone to steal my car?"

"I'm sure he did," Gina said. She held her hands over her face. "Jesus, that's so embarrassing. I'm really sorry about that. Heather's little outburst pales in comparison."

"Now you're the one who's apologizing when you don't need to. But he must really love you. To go that far, just on the chance that you might be in danger."

"Well, he did have a hand in starting the whole mess. Him and Vito and their shady dealings." Gina shook her head. "One of these days...I don't know. I just hope I'm on vacation when their number comes up."

"You'd take Tony in, wouldn't you, if it came to it."

"Damn straight. He knows it, too. I'd go visit him in the pen every week, and write him a letter on Sundays, and keep his picture on my dresser. But if I had to do it, I'd do it." Gina looked off down the street. "I mean, he's family, and I love him, but he makes his choices. You gotta draw the line somewhere, you know?"

"I'm impressed."

"That I'd bust him, or that I'd bust him and then visit him every week?"

"Both, I guess. Tough love."

"I don't know." Gina shrugged. "It's just how I need to do it." She thought a moment. "And then there's my mom. Jesus, sometimes she—"

"I really like your mom," said Vishnu

"You do?"

"Sure. She's fun, and smart, and—"

"Overbearing, and meddling, and scheming, and—"

"Sweet, and caring," finished Vishnu. "She's a mother. What's not to love?" A few moments passed.

"So what would you be doing on vacation?" asked Vishnu.

"On vacation?"

"You said you hoped you were on vacation if it hits the fan with Tony. Forget about vacation. Just tell me some more about what you do when you're not Officer Kowalski."

"You mean apart from going to weirdo art galleries to listen to jazz, meeting up with the bass player's shitfaced ex-girlfriend and coming about an inch from giving her a major ass kicking?"

Vishnu laughed. "Aside from that."

Gina considered the question. "Well. This time of year, running, a little rollerblading. In the winter, I like to ski. Downhill." She grinned at him. "I like the speed."

"I'm shocked to hear that." He looked at Gina's Fiat with interest.

"And shooting."

"Shooting?"

"Target shooting. With my handguns."

"Not while you ski, I hope. But that sounds fun."

"You think so?" Gina looked at Vishnu in surprise. "I kind of got the impression you didn't like guns."

"I don't like finding bags of them in cars I buy. And I've only shot them a few times. But it was a kick. A lot like shooting pool." He gave Gina a sideways look. "You should know right now, Officer Kowalski, I've been known to sink the occasional eight ball. My youth wasn't entirely well-spent."

"Now I'm shocked. I figured you for an altar boy."

"Gone bad. Maybe I could strip one down sometime."

"Say again?"

"One of your guns. Take it apart to see how it works."

"Oh, really?" Gina gave Vishnu her half-smile. "I can arrange that. I can show how a Sig Sauer P229 is put together, and then we can go to the shooting range. How about Thursday?"

"What time?"

"I'm working graveyard this week. How about I come over to your shop about two in the afternoon. That'd give us time to play with the Sig, go to the range, and get some dinner. I'd have you home before curfew."

"That sounds great," said Vishnu. "But Gina, there's, uh...there's something I want to say." He sighed and looked at the ground. "I just think...I mean..."

"Vishnu, if you're going to give me some maudlin speech about not knowing what you want, or just wanting to be friends, or wanting to go slow, don't drag it out. If you don't want to go out, just tell me. But we're talking about a simple date. Handguns and dinner. I know it doesn't get more romantic than that, but that's all it is. Do you want to go, or not?"

"Yes. I do. Definitely."

"OK then. Was there something else you wanted to say?"

And Vishnu was all set to say something like "I just think we should just keep our eyes open" or "I just don't want either of us to get hurt" or some other irrelevant nonsense, but Gina had made it obvious that she didn't want to hear any tripe like that. And anyway, a man isn't offered a date of handguns and dinner every day. For some, it really doesn't get more romantic than that. So instead of saying something stupid, Vishnu just said, "No."

"Good. Now, how about I give you a ride home."

"That would be great." They walked to her car. "Gina?"

She turned to face him. "What?" Her voice was even, but her eyes showed that she was bracing for the possibility that he was going to take one last crack at blowing it.

"Can I drive?" He grinned and pointed to her car. "I've never driven a Fiat Spider."

Gina looked him in the eyes, frank as a clock. She grabbed him gently by the shoulders and kissed him, a sweet, pragmatic, Gina Ivelia Kowalski kiss, right on the mouth. Then leaned back. "Yes," she replied, handed him the keys, and walked to the passenger door.

"Is it OK if we make a quick stop on the way?" he asked.

"For what?"

"I'm out of milk."

About the Author

Bill Leif lives in the Ballard neighborhood of Seattle, has Scandinavian bona fides, is a cyclist, and worked in a bike shop while in college. Bill has also worked as a geologist and engineer, plays music appealing to a discriminating crowd (his friends), and enjoys riding his motorcycle around the highways of the Northwest.

Made in USA - Crawfordsville, IN
14336_9781470098995
10.29.2020 1026